BATGIRL™

POSSESSION

By Jade Adia

Based on characters created by Bob Kane with Bill Finger.

Random House New York

Published in the United States by Random House Children's Books, a division of
Penguin Random House LLC, 1745 Broadway, New York, NY 10019, and in Canada
by Penguin Random House Canada Limited, Toronto.

Random House and the colophon are registered trademarks
of Penguin Random House LLC.

ISBN 978-0-593-80814-6 (trade) — ISBN 978-0-593-80816-0 (ebook)

Printed in the United States of America

1st Printing

For Jah and Yasir
—*J. A.*

LATER

"**B**atgirl," it says, voice like gravel, low and harsh. My name in its mouth sounds like an insult, or perhaps a curse.

In the dark, the black smoke rises, coats my face. An acrid smell fills the air, my nostrils, my lungs. It feels like drowning but worse. So much worse.

"Why are you doing this?" I gasp. But all it does is laugh at me. It laughs and laughs and laughs, though the way its voice cracks sounds more like choking. *I may know this human's face, but I am not talking to a human anymore. I don't know who or what I am talking to anymore.*

My breath hitches again. But this time, it's with fear. I swallow it down.

"What do you want from me?" I ask.

I try to sound brave. I fail.

In answer, it grins at me, eyes wild, teeth bared, and hisses, *"Thisss,"* before rushing straight for my throat to show me.

EARLIER

There is a sudden, breathless silence after the shot rings out. A second later, the warm gun clatters to the ground, followed by the thump of its wielder's body against the linoleum floor. He tried to shoot me, but he missed. Luckily, I didn't. He growls, then curses at the top of his lungs, gripping his kneecap—where a Batarang is now lodged deep in the joint.

This is how it begins: Gotham City on the cusp of fall, a robbery, an uneven fight. Three versus one. I can hear the sirens in the distance, but I don't pay them much attention. I'll already have this handled by the time they arrive.

"It'd be very cool if you let everyone here go, please," I say, drawing the attackers' attention to myself and away from the dozen early-morning shoppers cowering in the corner of the grocery store. The three men holding up the place all look alike, like a father and two sons, or maybe an uncle and his nephews. A wholesome family crime outing.

The young one with the beard and the gun had been emptying the cash register before I ran in. The other is cowering in the corner looking useless, gaping at me like a fish, while the elder tightens a rope around a crying child's wrists. In Gotham, it's never enough to only rob a store these days. Criminals have started kidnapping bystanders too in hopes of securing a ransom. Dream big, like they say.

We're in Gotham Heights, the gentrified neighborhood near my new school, which is where I'm *supposed* to be right now, but I got a call about these guys. Or, well, technically, my father got a call about these guys. He's the police commissioner. And . . . I may or may not have tapped into his phone and set up a system to automatically route his police alerts to my own phone. He doesn't know I did this. Or that I'm Batgirl. Or that I'm late to school.

It's safe to say there's a lot that people in my life don't know about me.

"Well, I'll be—the new Bat kid really is Black," the bearded one lying on the floor whispers.

I roll my eyes. I get this a lot. "Yeah, yeah. Surprise. You can complain about it online later. Now can we just put the weapons down, please?"

The weaponless older man pauses, considering my suggestion while reaching for a twenty-seven-dollar jar of duck bone broth. He rolls it around in his hand lazily. He laughs, says, "No, thanks." Then he hurls the heavy jar straight at my head.

I slip sideways and lower myself into a grounding, steadying stance.

This is the part where the instincts kick in. It's a form of disembodiment. My body moves, my brain anticipates. My competitive nature surges forward, fueled by pure adrenaline. It always happens so fast. Even with my strong memory, it's difficult to remember the details of a fight after the fact. I cling to the big picture—did it go well or not so well—but my brain smooths over the rest. Maybe it's a coping mechanism to keep me from replaying every moment of every fight again and again. Who knows.

The man on the floor tears the spiked edge of the Batarang from his knee, tosses it aside, then dives for the discarded gun. I kick it out of reach, so he pivots, cocks his fist back, and aims for my stomach. I block the punch and land a swift kick to his side. He lunges for my head and my fist collides with his solar plexus. I hear a loud *crack*.

The leader growls low in his throat as he picks me up from behind in a crushing bear hug. I thrash and thrash, but I can't break free from his grip. I hate being overpowered, even for a second. It happens occasionally—I'm sixteen and often fighting adults twice my age and three times my body mass, for god's sake. But I'm good at fighting. And, more important, I am smart. I can escape most holds. All I have to do is—

"Aww, don't worry. You tried your best, sweetheart," he coos into my ear. I can feel his muggy smoker's breath on the back of my neck. My vision goes red.

Well, then. I know one surefire way to get free.

I take a deep breath and swing my head back, shattering the man's nose. He screams bloody murder and drops me. With a low swinging kick, I knock his feet out from under him. One perp down, two to go.

I take two steps before something like a baseball bat slams my ankle.

Pain consumes every thought, blackening the edges of my vision. Did I hear a crack, or was that just the sound of the door slamming as a bystander escapes? I can't tell. Not over the loud cackling laughter of the bearded creep as he winds up to strike again.

I will not lose today. The words become my mantra, repeating in my head as I block out the pain and punch him in the jaw. The blow lands hard enough that he drops his weapon. I snatch the weighted baton from the floor and limp behind the counter. I throw the stick hard. It ricochets off the wall, hitting him in the temple. He falls to the floor, out like a light.

Two down, one left.

But where'd the last guy go?

I crouch behind the cash register to catch my breath. I was on the cross-country team freshman and sophomore years before I transferred schools, but dang. Vigilante cardio is forever humbling.

From the corner of my eye, one of the hostages catches my attention. When we lock gazes, she freezes. She's young—maybe college-aged—with pretty brown eyes that stare at me, terrified, as if I'm about to pounce on her next. Why is she nervous? I know my black suit looks intimidating, but I never want the people I'm saving to be afraid of me. Maybe she—

Oh.

When she shifts her arm, a tomato rolls out from underneath her coat, along with several carrots. Her face turns bright red. Suddenly, I understand.

Here's the thing. When I put on this cowl, I pick my battles wisely. For example:

- **Things I Care About as Batgirl**

- Stopping and preventing violent crime
- Protecting Gotham City from terrorism
- Infiltrating drug rings, human-trafficking net-
  works, illegal arms deals, and whatever the mas-
  sively messed-up mobsters and regular freaks of
  Gotham cook up to sink this city into the ground

- **Things I Absolutely Do Not Care About
  as Batgirl**

- Jaywalking
- Fare enforcement on public transportation after
  the mayor just raised the prices, again, for the
  fourth time this year
- Petty theft

I prefer to mind my business and take care of the
actual crime unfolding in Gotham. If she gets caught
one day, she gets caught. But you're not gonna see Batgirl
punching someone out for stealing food.

The girl's eyes widen with guilt, but before she can
murmur an excuse, I cut her off. "Did you see where the
last guy went? The skinny one who's been hiding the
whole time?" Her mouth falls open with surprise for a
split second before she points to the third aisle from the
right. "Thanks," I huff.

I drag myself to my knees and rise carefully, keeping

my weight off my rapidly swelling ankle. It hurts like hell, but I don't think it's broken. It can't be broken. I'm starting as a new student at Gotham Academy today and, to be honest, I'm terrified. Gotham Academy is . . . stressful. Messy. Cutthroat. Batgirl is my only form of stress relief. The last thing I need is to begin the year on medical leave from patrol. Or to let an injury leave me vulnerable at the end of a fight.

I will not lose today.

My pulse skyrockets from pain at my first step, but I force myself to keep moving. I take one last rest against the produce display and toss the girl a souvenir. She catches it, her jaw dropping as she rubs her thumb over the extra tomato. "Don't let Batman catch you," I say before moving to take down the final assailant on aisle three.

I smile.

I will not lose today.

There is a faded bat-symbol sticker on the wall across the street from the deli. Beneath the sticker, someone wrote *Batfamily 4ever* in silver marker. Someone else crossed the words out and instead wrote *Eat the rich.* Beside this, someone scribbled *IDK if Batgirl is rich,* to which someone replied *BATGIRL SUCKS LOL.*

How creative.

The names and innuendos should annoy me, but it's not like I haven't heard it all before. In fact, I've heard much worse. I have a lot of nicknames. Just this week, I've been called the Bat Chick and Bat Brat. Then, of course, there's the preferred pick of the internet incels, the one that rhymes with "rat witch." And those are just the ones for when I'm suited up. At my school, I have nicknames too. A lot of people call me PCD, which stands for Police Commissioner's Daughter. It's meant as an insult by the kids who think that because my dad is the head guy at Gotham City Police Department, I must worship cops, which is insane because this city is screwed and the police department is a mess, and if I believed in the police so much, then why would I spend my nights risking my life, running around trying to protect this place anyway? But they don't know that I'm Batgirl, obviously. So when the cool kids shoot icy glances my way and cough "narc" under their breath when I pass, I let it slip. Double lives, secret identities, etc. The less glamorous perks of being Gotham's newest vigilante.

I turn the corner and don't look back. I walk faster than necessary—mostly because I'm glad to be back to my usual brisk pace.

My ankle was fractured at the grocery store fight, and I was stuck in a boot for the six weeks. Until today. I celebrated being able to see my toes again with a quick patrol before coming out tonight.

My phone vibrates with a notification.

Alysia: hey quick question wherethehellareu?!

Alysia Yeoh, my best friend, is five feet two inches of pure fire. Loves museums and cooking. Hates when I show up to everything late. She has a painting in the student art show at our school tonight. At my old public school, a student art show would've been a normal, boring event. But because Gotham Academy is over-the-top, the event tonight is over-the-top too. There's been drama surrounding the art showcase all month. *A lot* of drama. *Controversy* might be more accurate.

I type quickly.

Barbara: be there soon

Alysia: fyi u were right. those idiots are protesting the art show. the vibe is . . . tense

Barbara: dont they have anything better to do?

Alysia: being jerks is their "better" thing to do

I speed up. Graffitied walls give way to pristine, tree-lined streets until I arrive at the intricate wrought iron gate of Gotham Academy. I look up at the ivy-covered walls, the majestic brick steps, the school crest waving on a banner in the wind. A heavy sigh crawls from my chest.

It's been a hard adjustment transferring here as a junior.

Gotham Academy is even weirder than all the rumors say it is. The school itself is one of the oldest buildings in Gotham City. Gothic architecture, long corridors, and stained glass windows give the school an old, stately feeling. It's pretty, I guess, if you're into that kind of thing. But what really draws the most powerful families in the city to this place is its deep pockets. Gotham Academy is a private high school, but it has more money in its endowment than the entire five-year budget for every single public school in the city combined. People call Gotham Academy *elite*, but what they mean is *expensive*. I guess it's both.

The classes are rigorous. The teachers are attentive. The class sizes are small. I am lucky to be here.

The learning environment is cutthroat. The student body is riddled with scandal. The parents and senior faculty are constantly arguing over whether offering scholarships to kids like me and Alysia "furthers the mission of fostering an elite educational experience" for Gotham City's one percent or "mars the school reputation." I am constantly being reminded that I am lucky to be here.

Six weeks in and the pressure to prove that I belong

is already exhausting. But what other choice do I have?

"Finally!" Alysia shouts seconds after I step onto school grounds. "Oh my god, wait, look at you! Sans boot!" Alysia smirks as she pulls me into a side hug. She's wearing black jeans and a thin green T-shirt. Her chin-length black hair falls in layered wisps around the mischievous smirk she wears on her face.

"You have hat hair, yet you're not wearing a hat," she observes, eyeing me carefully.

She didn't know that I stashed my bike nearby, changed into my regular street clothes, and removed the black makeup I use to obscure my eyes beneath my mask. All part of my regular postfight routine. Except I forgot to fix my hair. Oops.

"I . . . tried on a beanie at home. Took it off last-minute," I say, fluffing out the hair that's been smushed under my cowl all evening. Beneath the cowl, I wear a copper-colored wig too, just to throw people off. It's probably overkill, but the last thing I need is someone figuring out my identity before I've even gotten the hang of the whole vigilante thing.

"Good," Alysia says approvingly. "Don't you dare try to hide all those curls."

I met Alysia on the first day of sixth grade. She lives down the street from me, so we both went to the same public middle school before she transferred to Gotham Academy. During that first-day assembly at our old school when we were eleven, she had been called out for an alleged dress-code violation. This was before the school instituted its long-overdue policy about students' rights to wear clothing that expresses their gender identity. The principal was going in on her, spewing some transphobic gender norms crap, and it was horrible, but Alysia wasn't having it. She looked Principal Winans straight in the eye and told him to kiss off. It was incredible. Easily the coolest thing I had ever seen. I couldn't believe that when she sat back down, she chose a spot next to me. Even more incredible was that when I whispered a joke under my breath, she laughed.

Now, five years later, a slightly taller but no less daring Alysia interlaces her arm with mine, dragging me up the grand driveway that leads to the entrance of the Gotham Academy. She's pretty much my only friend here. There's no way in hell I would've made it even this far without her.

"Guess who called the hotline again tonight," Alysia says. I tense up at her words and keep my eyes locked on the walkway ahead of us, avoiding eye contact at all costs. Alysia has been volunteering at 88-88, a new mental-health crisis lifeline that offers 24/7 counseling. They also have case managers to send to emergency scenes. It's pretty cool, which is why—

"Batgirl called in!" Alysia shouts excitedly.

Yup. I did. I called for the first time on the day I

broke my ankle. There were three guys at that grocery store when it happened, but when I finally found the last member of the group, he was crouched at the end of an aisle, holding his knees to his chest. Throughout the entire robbery, the guy didn't hit me, didn't threaten anyone, didn't even help his family with their scheme at all. I approached him slowly, but he didn't seem to notice me. He just sat there, frozen, mumbling to himself. When I asked him if he was okay, he said he "can't do this anymore." When I asked what that meant, he pointed at his head, then squeezed his eyes shut and kept rubbing his fists into his temples. He clearly . . . needed help. More help than GCPD would give him. I left the other two zip-tied for the cops to arrest, but this last guy? Giving Alysia's hotline a shot felt like the right thing to do.

I wasn't even planning to call the hotline again anytime soon, but earlier on patrol, there was a hysterical witness who wouldn't stop freaking out, and I was late enough already trying to get here tonight.

"I'm so pissed I wasn't the one to pick up Batgirl's call," Alysia grumbles. "I wonder what made her try us out."

"Who knows. Gotham's a mess. Anyway—"

"Wait, shhh." Alysia taps my forearm and points discreetly up ahead. Her face slips into a stone wall of pure hatred. "Told you they'd be here."

Lurking beside the entrance to the art show, lo and

behold, six student protesters hold hand-drawn signs. Alysia's grip on me tightens as we pass.

I hold my breath. Maybe if we avoid eye contact with them, this won't be so bad?

"BOOOOOOOOOO." One of the guys wearing a salmon-colored polo uses his hands as a microphone.

Nope. Never mind.

The other protesters all laugh and hoot along with him. Alysia spins on her heels, hissing at them like a snake.

The leader's name is Kyle. He's in my history class— infamous for playing the devil's advocate whenever we talk about basic human rights, but I didn't expect him to take it this far. "Are you seriously . . . booing people? For coming tonight?"

Tonight's art showcase is the first of its kind at Gotham Academy. It's a Diversity Art Showcase for students of color and LGBTQ+ students to share their work. Gotham City's not particularly conservative, so I was honestly surprised when several students and parents complained about the showcase. They claimed it's unfair to have an event that only some students can participate in, whining that it's an unequal use of school resources. Mind you, this is coming from a school that has both a ski club *and* a polo team, both of which require participants to have their own snow gear and horses—

so they don't have an issue with *some* school activities being exclusive, as long as they're exclusive to wealthy families. It all feels pretty performative to me. Luckily, though, the Concerned Conservative Corner is a campus minority. For the most part, everyone else is fine with the showcase. Still, it's been a weird time to be on campus—as a new kid, a Black kid, and a scholarship kid.

One of Kyle's minions cackles and leans back, shouting, "Free speech!"

"Great. Very productive, intelligent dialogue," I mumble.

Alysia glares daggers at them before tugging me inside.

"You okay?" I ask her once we're safe in the cafeteria. The space has been transformed into a series of booths showcasing student visual art, while the auditorium across the hall is being used for the dancers, theater kids, and performance artists. Alysia's painting hangs right near the entrance. It's a landscape of Hong Lim Park in Singapore with the remnants of a rally littering the lawn. It's beautiful.

"I eat dumbasses like Kyle for breakfast—you know I can handle a little heat, GBG," she says, leaning beside her painting.

GBG. One more nickname. It stands for Gordon-Barbara-Gordon, which is how I very awkwardly introduced myself to Alysia when we first met while suffering from a brief moment of social anxiety that apparently left me believing I was in a James Bond movie or something. Luckily, Alysia's the only person who calls me that. I don't mind it coming from her.

"Kyle and his minions are just trying to distract us," Alysia says before taking a long sip from a can of coconut water—the kind from the bodega with the cartoon logo and the chunks of coconut flesh floating in it.

"Distract us from what?"

"I don't know. From, like, making art, taking care of business—anything. They want to bait us into this stupid argument about whether we deserve to be here. And while we're losing sleep over trying to prove ourselves, they'll just keep on studying, doing their thing. It's all a big game. Distract us so that we fall behind. We can't let them—"

"Way to make another self-righteous painting, Alysia. You're from Singapore. *We get it*."

"Eat it and die, Kyle!" she shouts back. He falters as she enthusiastically flips him off with both hands. A teacher stares at us disapprovingly.

"Jesus, Alysia." I laugh.

"Never said I'd be the bigger person." She shrugs innocently. "Hey, if we want seats for the performance, we should go now. It's filling up."

Ah. The performance—aka the epicenter of all the

campus controversy. Apparently, a senior named Austin debuted an experimental project for the Diversity Art Showcase during an art class last week and ... it didn't go great. People freaked out and told their parents, who then told the headmaster, and then suddenly we're all receiving a schoolwide email from the administration about "tradition and core values," then a counter-email from the art department arguing against the censorship of student art, and it's become a whole thing. The showcase is already contentious enough, but Austin's performance is the cherry on top of it all. Hence, the line out the door.

"So it's a magic show?" I ask Alysia when we join the crowd of classmates waiting to get in.

"It's immersive horror theater," Alysia says.

"Sooo, a magic show with better branding?"

"It's art, GBG. Have an open mind," Alysia says, nudging my shoulder.

I recognize both the people handing out flyers up front. The girl is Lily Convey, the beautiful, elusive, constantly vaping daughter of Gotham City's most famous model. Beside her is a guy from my English class, Nico Baluyot. He's tall with short, messy hair dyed a shade of pale bubblegum pink. The faintest hint of brown roots peeks out between messy spikes that stick out in all directions. He wears two small silver hoops, stacked closely together, in his left ear. He never volunteers to participate in class, but I can tell he always does the reading because his book is always annotated with pen markings and black page-marker tabs. We've never spoken before.

When we reach the front of the line, Alysia smiles at Nico and Lily and asks, "On a scale of one to ten, how likely is it that Headmaster Hammer will shut it down midperformance?"

The corner of Nico's mouth quirks up in an almost-smile. "Ten." He passes us a flyer. In stark contrast to the pastel softness of his hair, tonight he's wearing all black. Black sneakers, black cargo pants, black T-shirt, black puffer vest. The nails on both middle fingers are also painted black. I can't help but stare a little too long while I try to think of something to say. Something to contribute to the conversation. But suddenly we're being rushed inside by the people in line behind us. The moment passes. Why is it so much easier for me to talk with my mask on than without it in my normal life? Maybe I need to add Icebreakers to my weekly training schedule.

Inside, the auditorium is too dark to see much, but the music is pounding. Heavy industrial speakers sit on the floor, music blasting at a volume that makes my chest vibrate. Most of the teachers who volunteered to support tonight's event have chosen to stick around the cafeteria with the fine art rather than journey into the performance-art space. Too loud. Too dark. Too much trouble. But a few curious ones—the art department, the English teachers, and some of the younger science staff—huddle together in the back row, whispering behind their hands.

I always prefer to sit near the emergency exit in a big crowd, but the only three seats available are right in the front, dead center. I try not to let Alysia notice my discomfort as we take two of them.

Soon Nico sits behind a folding table turned into a makeshift DJ booth in the far-right corner of the stage. Lily leans against his shoulder with the familiarity and comfort of a longtime friend, or maybe something more. Not like that's any of my business.

"They're siblings, you know," Alysia says.

"Nico and Lily?"

"What? No. Obviously not." She gestures at them, sitting cozily on stage. "Nico and Austin. That's why he's doing the music for the show."

They don't look anything alike. I figured they were just friends. "Nico's a musician?" I ask.

"Yeah. You didn't know?"

"I literally have never spoken to him before—how would I have known about his music?"

"You ever hear that song 'Make It Stop'?"

As soon as Alysia hums the chorus, it clicks into place. "Oh my god, yes."

"That was his song."

"Wow." That song was everywhere last summer. I never heard the rest of the album, though.

"Yeah. He's super talented. Makes kind of dark, synthy industrial music. Last year, out of nowhere, he released that album *Spiral,* which he made by himself. It's not really my vibe, but everyone went wild for it. Like, it went super viral. It was kind of like a musical memoir. There were tons of articles about him, calling him, like, the future of electronic music. Several record companies tried to sign him. He rejected all of them, though."

"Why?"

"No idea. But the crazy thing is—" Ms. Parker, the head art teacher, steps up to the microphone on stage, getting our attention with a sharp burst of feedback. "Tell you later," Alysia whispers.

The teacher adjusts her glasses, then grins widely out at the packed auditorium. "Welcome to the Autumn Diversity Art Showcase, Performance Art Edition!" Rowdy applause fills the room. "I'm excited to introduce a very talented, unique student of mine. Austin Baluyot is a senior. They have been leading the charge of creating space for more experimental, daring art on campus. We'd like to thank the PTA for graciously agreeing to reconsider their previous stance on banning this performance, and—"

Everyone boos. Ms. Parker tries to look diplomatic

but is clearly loving that their dig landed. No matter what school you go to, art teachers are always pro drama. "Anyway! Gotham Academy is proud to support new voices in the arts, representing diverse perspectives in our city." More cheers, more claps. But notably, a couple of loud snorts too. Did Kyle and his crew decide to come inside after all? Ms. Parker notices and shifts to a much more serious tone, regaining control over the crowd. "Austin would like to warn you all that this performance is interactive and contains elements of horror. If at any point you need a break, feel free to leave the room or find me or another faculty member for support. And with that, I'll pass the stage to Austin."

The lights shut off. We yelp in surprise. Alysia's fingers dig into my arm. But just as quickly as darkness descended, it is lifted. Austin is standing center stage beneath a lone spotlight wearing a long black leather trench coat and platform stompers with chains on the sides. They grin out at the crowd mischievously.

Pretty good opening trick. Maybe this will be interesting after all.

Austin steps forward, their gait slow and steady. "Recently, I've been feeling like I'm fumbling around in the dark. My arms are outstretched in an unfamiliar room and I'm trying to find anything—a light switch, an exit, a wall to lean on, a chair to rest in. But no matter how much I move, I can't see anything. I can't feel any-thing. I can't find the light."

They snap their fingers, but the sound echoes in the room. They must be mic'd up.

One moment, I am fine. Everything is normal. But then I feel a shift.

Something . . . strange falls over the room. Something that we can't see, but we can all feel.

My heart beats faster, frantically banging in my chest. My breath follows suit, becoming shallower with each inhale. Slowly, the air around us distorts. This is not the air of a healthy place. Not of somewhere humans should be. No. It is sinister and decaying. Claustropho-bic and heavy. Burdened. It is an air that does not want us here. We'd be happy to comply, but we all seem to be spellbound. Stuck in place. Held. Afraid. I want to cry out, but I can't breathe. And just when I think I can't stand it anymore . . .

It stops.

The fear lifts, vanishing with the swiftness of an interrupted dream.

Around the room, everyone is breathless for a moment, then two, before unleashing an explosion of applause.

"How are they doing that?" I ask Alysia, still trying to catch my breath. I don't know what the hell just hap-pened, but I don't think I like it.

"Who knows," Alysia says, forcing out a relieved laugh. "Cool though, right?"

Cool wouldn't be my description of choice.

"Now that we're all warmed up, let's have some fun," Austin says, smiling with all the charm of a seasoned performer. "For my first trick, I'd like to welcome up a volunteer."

Austin pulls a thin metal wand-like rod out of their back pocket and looks out . . . into the first row.

Wait. No.

No. No. No.

I want to yank on my hood and turtle into my sweatshirt, but it's too late. Austin points their stupid wand between my eyes.

"You ready, New Girl?"

CHAPTER 2

I've never liked the spotlight. That's probably why I choose to run around in dark colors, a cape, and a cowl rather than a neon-pink suit or a bat-print leotard. So, naturally, shadow-lurker that I am, when several phone cameras whip toward me now, I wish for a sinkhole to open in the floor and swallow me whole. Artificial lighting warms my face as everyone stare at me expectantly. I swallow. Clench and unclench my fists.

"Come up to the stage?" Austin asks.

Is this a trap? I check every exit, scan the ceiling. I look over both shoulders, surveying the room. Are there any potential threats? Any hiding places where someone could assassinate me from the stage? It's not like anybody here knows who I am, but still. It's Gotham City, baby. Everything feels like a trap.

I mumble a polite *no thank you,* to which Alysia immediately boos and betrays me even further by initiating a slow clap. "Bar-ba-ra. Bar-ba-ra. Bar-ba-ra." Within seconds, everyone in the auditorium joins in. Why must the rhythm of my name be so amenable to juvenile chants?

I have two options: I can either give in to the peer pressure or I can be stubborn and lose a few points with Alysia and my new classmates. Social math is intense, but the best choice is clear. My seat creaks as I stand. Alysia cheers. Whoop-de-doo.

I drag my feet up onto the stage, plastering a fake smile onto my face. Austin stands beside me, waving their creepy metal wand.

"Now, let me ask you: Are you afraid of the dark?"

I think for a moment before replying. "The dark represents the unknown. It's logical to fear it to a certain extent."

Muffled laughter. Austin leans against my shoulder and whispers, "Just say no. Play along a bit."

I shrink a little. "Sorry."

It's the truth, though. The dark is where we hide our anxieties. Of course I'm afraid of it. But being afraid of something doesn't mean that you don't respect it. I admire the dark and all the feelings that it brings up in us. It's that combination of fear and admiration that helps me move effectively and safely when patrolling at night as Batgirl.

"Don't apologize. Nothing wrong with honesty," Austin says. "But I guess that means you'll have to face your fears, then, huh?" Austin motions their hand toward the center of the stage. "Close your eyes."

No backing out now. I take a deep breath in, then do as I'm told. Soft fabric touches my face. I flinch.

"It's just a blindfold," Austin says casually. They must see the obvious nerves on my face because they lean forward and whisper so only I can hear, "It'll be okay. Trust me."

I swallow the lump forming in my throat and let Austin tie the bandanna. When they finish, I feel unsteady. Vulnerable. I don't like it. But it's only a game, right? A show. I'm here to make friends. Be part of the school community, or whatever. This is all just a bit. calm my breathing and interlace my fingers behind my back.

I count backward from ten, waiting for another cue from Austin to react in whatever way helps make this moment pass as quickly as possible. I only make it to six before I feel an itch deep within my brain—pesky and irritating, like a scratchy tag at the collar of my shirt. I shiver. The jittery feeling morphs into the sensation of ice water dripping down the back of my neck. I swipe at my skin, ignoring the laughter that I hear from the crowd. My hand comes back dry, but I can feel it—this strange, heavy chill creeping down my spine.

"Austin?" My voice is shaky. More laughter. I can feel the glow of cell phone cameras recording on the other side of the blindfold. I'm all for student free speech, but maybe the PTA was right about shutting this one down?

"How do you feel?" Austin asks in their performer voice.

I squeeze my hands together to stop them from shaking. "I feel . . ."

Too much.

The fear settles in slowly, then all at once.

The heavy bass of the music feels like it's permeating my skin, each beat burrowing itself deep inside me. An errant thought passes through my mind, that I hope the beats don't multiply and consume my body. My muscles tense as the prickling sensation quickly spreads to my shoulders, my chest. A ripple of goose bumps rises on my arms. My knees buckle and suddenly I'm on my hands and knees, fingernails scraping at the stage floor. Beneath my hands, the floor rumbles.

I rip off my blindfold. But everything is still dark. Did someone turn off the lights? I blink once, twice.

Three times. And then it hits me: The lights aren't off. There is simply no light at all.

I can hear the people around me, but I can't see them. I can smell the pine-scented cleaner used to mop the wooden floors, but now there's no floor. No ceiling either. I am surrounded by a blanket of shapeless pitch black. I reach out, but I can't feel anything. Panic swells in my chest. With each beat of my heart, a cruel feeling glows brighter. A pulsing pit of darkness opens up somewhere around me ... No. Somewhere ... *inside me*? Yes. That's it. The darkness is swelling from inside me now. With each passing second, I feel my body losing form. I unzip my mouth to beg Austin to stop this, but the darkness has already reached my mouth. When I try to speak, there are no lips to move. I have no access to words. I am melting into nothing.

Before the big bang, there was darkness. I guess that's where I am returning to now. I take one more breath with the sudden, violent awareness that this might be my last. The terror more final than drowning seizes my lungs, I wince, and—

"Time!"

The blindfold is pulled off. But this time it's real. The world rushes back in.

I'm back in the auditorium under the oppressive brightness of the stage lights. Everyone's clapping, but my heart is beating so fast that I can't hear them.

"You're okay. It's over," Austin says casually with a laugh, like everything's totally normal. For a split second, I want to punch them in the mouth.

I touch my face, relieved that it's still here. "What the hell was that?"

"That was you, facing your fears," Austin says, smirking. "How was it?"

"Terrible." I'm still struggling to catch my breath. "How does this count as art?"

"Art makes people think. Question their day-to-day lives."

Okay, yeah, sure. This is exactly why I'm not an artist, because the only thing that I'm questioning is how soon I can go home.

"How do you feel now?" Austin rests a warm hand on my shoulder.

I'm honestly seconds away from telling them off, asking what kind of twisted stunt they're running here, or at the very least storming out of the room. But the terror fades as a new feeling drifts in. A feeling that's sort of . . . pleasant. Bubbly. Like the fizz in sparkling water or the steady hum of my motorcycle beneath me.

"I feel . . . good?" As the words come out of my mouth, they shock me. But it's the truth. I feel *good*.

Everyone breaks out clapping again. "That's the feeling of having faced your fears and come out on the other side." Austin grins at me again, widely this time. "Pretty cool, right?"

"Yeah, actually." I smile a little too, despite my best efforts not to.

Austin lets go of me and I rush to my seat again beside Alysia.

"That was *wild*," Alysia says. "Oh my god, you should've seen yourself."

My hands are still shaking. "Believe me, I'm glad that I didn't."

From the corner, Nico turns up the music and the vibe of the show becomes electric. With a mischievous grin, Austin holds their arms open to the room. "Now, who's next?"

Everyone whips out their phones to record as Austin ties the black blindfold on and then helps volunteers face their fears, one by one. The more people who go, the rowdier the room gets, the crazier the antics. And as the participants leave the stage feeling that strange adrenaline high, it makes everyone else want to try it more and more.

Monica from my PE class wails as she swipes invisible spiders off her body.

Mr. Rogers, the eleventh-grade history teacher,

jumps around, screaming about a fire. He even starts sweating, like it's actually hot in here.

Austin calls Harper, a girl from my calculus class, up to the stage next. Alysia scoffs in response, crosses her arms.

"Do you not like Harper or something?" I ask.

"Before you transferred, Harper and I used to hang out all the time. But then she started dating, and all of a sudden..." I raise an eyebrow at Alysia. "Never mind. She's annoying, that's all."

"Well, you have me now, right?"

Alysia leans her cheek on my shoulder. "I have you."

Up on the stage, Harper looks nervous, but an excited grin peeks through her dimpled cheeks.

"So, tell me," Austin begins, circling Harper like a shark. "Are you brave?"

Harper nods.

"How brave?" Austin asks.

Harper smiles. "Braver than you."

At this, everyone jeers. Austin looks beyond pleased that Harper's playing the game. "All right, then. I need you to lie down on the floor right here." Austin pulls out a blanket and spreads it on the floor. "This final trick is something a little different."

At this, we all *Oooooo*.

"And hold this for me, will you? For good luck?" Austin passes the metal "wand" to Harper, who grabs it as she settles down onto the blanket, then waves it around above her head like a wizard.

"Do I have to do anything?" Harper asks, getting comfortable.

"Nothing but be your beautiful self," Austin says, voice like honey.

"Aye, easy, Austin! She has a boyfriend," Nico shouts from offstage, laughing.

Austin holds up their hands in faux innocence while Harper tries to hide her face behind her palms in embarrassment, but it's clear she's smiling underneath.

"We're gonna bring it full circle now. Back to the beginning. Back to the dark." Austin stretches out their arms, hovering their palms at Harper's sides. A slow-moving fog of smoke appears to flow from Austin's hands, then circle Harper's body like a storm cloud. Then, inch by inch, Harper begins to rise off the floor.

I don't know how Austin's doing this, but I'm officially impressed. It's sort of beautiful, the way the shadows circle Harper's body. She rises higher and higher, drifting upward from Austin's ankles to their knees to their shoulders until Harper is floating above our heads. Everyone takes out their phones to record when Harper's face touches the ceiling, her body seemingly held up by nothing more than dark swirling air. The crowd goes wild. I'm clapping along with them. I've never seen something so strange, so controlled.

The lights cut out and we're drenched in darkness once again. There's only cheering and laughter this time. Except the lights never turn back on.

I squint at Austin's shadowy outline as they lean down to check their phone. "Sorry, y'all. Someone must've hit the lights. But now—"

Harper makes a gurgling noise that pulls all the attention back to her. It sounded like a burp. We're all prepared to laugh. Until Harper starts writhing in pain.

Alysia tenses by my side. "... Harper?"

Harper makes another choking noise that crescendos into a high-pitched whimper.

"That's enough. Let her down, Austin," Ms. Parker says, tiptoeing up to the side of the stage. But Austin doesn't move.

Austin says nothing. Austin does nothing. Without the lights, it's hard to see clearly, but I don't think Austin even blinks.

"Are you okay, Harper?" Alysia rises from her seat, worry creasing her brows.

"She needs to get down," I tell Austin, standing too.

Harper makes another noise, much louder and much worse. It's a pained, strangled noise that cuts through the room like a dagger. Over at the DJ booth, Nico and Lily stand as well, clearly panicked. Something is wrong. Terribly wrong.

This isn't funny anymore. I've seen enough. I rush forward onto the darkened stage, trying to figure out how to get Harper down from the ceiling.

Alysia snaps her fingers in front of Austin's face, trying to get them to drop the act. "Something's wrong with Austin's eyes," she whispers, fear edging into her voice.

The dark shadows have Harper levitating too far out of reach. Even with my arms stretched above my head, she's too high up. I jump, trying to snag the fabric of her shirt. Behind me, the crowd murmurs, amused. They think this is part of the show. Nico and Ms. Parker leap for Harper's hand too, but none of us can reach.

The shadows around Harper shift. Slate-gray smoke darkens to pitch-black. The gentle mist surges into a violent swarm, hurtling straight into Harper's unhinged jaw like bees.

What do I do? What do I do? What do I do? Dread and hysteria war in my chest as my brain races to find a solution. My gaze collides with Nico's as a disturbing awareness passes between us that if we don't act fast—

Nico whirls away to climb the stage curtains to get to Harper, but the fabric rips. As Nico stumbles to the floor, the curtains tear from the ceiling and I look up just in time to see . . . Am I really seeing this? Or is this another one of Austin's nightmares? I wipe my eyes, but no.

This is real. As Harper's high-pitched scream pierces the room, wet spray paint drips on the wall behind the stage in a familiar symbol: a bat.

Clear as day.

Is anyone else seeing this?

Austin's next movements are first too quick, then too slow. They move like a glitch—unnerving and unpredictable. Above my head, Harper's trembling fist clenches Austin's wand, so tightly that her knuckles turn white. A tiny earthquake rips through her body before she plummets to the floor.

As Harper falls, her arms flinging, the metal wand in her fist clenched in a death grip. Austin snaps out of their daze and rushes to try to catch Harper before she hits the floor. But they're too late. We all are.

Harper's skull hits the floor with a violent, wet thud. Austin collapses beneath her body weight, their bodies now a jumble. The smell of blood explodes in the air like a scented aerosol spray just as Austin's wand pierces him like a knife.

Bile rises in my throat.

CHAPTER 3

Bone-chilling silence hangs in the air for somewhere between four seconds and forever. It's as though we're all suspended in time for one terrible moment, our collective reaction buffering before exploding into a burst of pure, unfiltered horror.

A communal scream rips through the room as a stampede storms the exit. But while the others run, my instincts kick in. I rush to Harper to check her pulse. When I don't feel it, I begin CPR. I try to focus on counting the chest compressions, but I can still hear clips of conversation as the crowd flees.

"Was that a *bat*-symbol?"

"Did he do this?"

"Of course Batman didn't do it. We watched Austin kill her. Austin did it."

"Yeah, Austin did it."

"That was so sick!"

"Is Batman on his way?"

"Are the cops on their way?"

"I dropped my phone."

"Forget your phone, keep moving."

"Get out of my way. I'm gonna bar—"

Blood pools around Harper's head like a halo. Austin's hair spills forward, their face angled down at the dark liquid spreading over their own shirt where they've been impaled, as if checking to see if this is real, if this is really happening. Lily wraps her arms around her body, face frozen, while Nico gapes at his sibling. Alysia's holding Harper's limp hand, crying.

Part of me feels like crying too. If this was back in the Before Times—before I started wearing the mask, before I had seen too much—I probably would've cried too. I used to be a crybaby when I was little. Always so sensitive. Turns out that tears are one of the first things you learn to control as a vigilante. I've gotten good at locking away my emotions, holding them at bay until I'm alone, then pushing them down even further until I forget where I hid them in the first place. Is it healthy? Probably not. But is it useful? Absolutely.

Nico wraps Austin in a tight hug and whispers, "Austin, what did you do?"

Austin's shoulders shake as they sob into their brother's arms. "I don't know. I don't know. Everything was fine, and then—"

There are sirens in the distance. Ms. Parker called the ambulance and is now running around the room, searching for a med kit.

By now, mostly everyone has cleared out. A few visibly horrified people have stayed and are quietly debating among themselves about whether they should talk to the police when they arrive, and if it'd help or hurt the situation. They cast worried glances at Austin between hushed whispers. They watch me, my hands bloodied, pounding as hard as I can into Harper's chest.

Austin overhears them and sobs even louder. "I promise this isn't my fault. I swear to god. I have no idea what happened. This is all fake. I promise this is all fake."

"Fake?" Alysia asks. She looks back down at Harper in disbelief for a moment, perhaps wondering if this is all just another nightmare. That maybe this is still part of the performance piece too, and that at any moment now, Harper will wake up. For a split second, Alysia looks so hopeful. I wish this were all fake too.

Beneath my palms, Harper's heart is still. Everyone

watches me as I slowly sit up straight. My right hand is sore and slick with blood. I swallow, my voice thick in my throat before I will myself to face them.

"She's dead."

"I need two officers riding in the ambulance with the suspect—the kid in black. Do *not* let them out of your sight," my dad says, barking orders to the frenzy of officers racing in and out of the school building. Outside, it's cold. The gray sky drowns the scene in a sinister blanket of mist.

I call my dad's name, but he can't hear me over all the chaos. Police officers are taking terrified students' statements while paramedics race up the school stairs, stretchers hitched on their shoulders. As one young officer runs by, Dad grabs his shoulder. "Call the parents. When the kid wakes up, read them their Miranda rights. Have handcuffs ready and send me an update from the hospital."

"Handcuffs?" For Austin? While they're hospitalized?

"Barbara." Dad finally spots me and folds me into a protective hug. He's wearing his usual work attire—white button-up, black tie, his favorite long brown jacket with his badge over his heart. The warmth of his body and the familiar smell of his clothes make me realize that I've been shaking this whole time. "Thank god," he murmurs into my hair, squeezing even tighter.

"What's going to happen to Austin?" I ask, my voice coming up all broken and tired.

"I need you to go home. Now," he says. I can see the light of the sirens reflected in his thick square glasses. His bushy mustache tilts downward in the way that I instantly recognize means business.

"I can stay. I can help. I saw the whole thing. I—"

"I love you. I'm glad you're safe. But go home. *Now*."

"But, Dad—"

I can feel the burning eyes of my classmates on us as my dad runs off toward the other police officers, effectively dismissing me. Behind me, I hear someone whisper, "Damn." My cheeks burn. I want to push more, but what can I do?

Alysia's parents rushed to campus as soon as they heard the news. We all ride the subway together, then they walk me home before steering a shell-shocked Alysia back to their own apartment.

When I step inside my living room, the silence is oppressive. It's only me and my dad these days, so I'm used to the quiet, but tonight feels different. My dirty dishes from breakfast this morning are still in the sink, my dad's running shoes lie haphazardly across the floor.

The last thing that I want is to be alone right now, yet here I am. Alone. I know my dad loves me and I know he has to work, but I can't help but sometimes feel ... I don't know. I never know how to feel every time I walk into this lonely, empty apartment.

I plop onto the couch and call my mentor, Batman himself: Bruce Wayne. It rings only one time before he picks up.

"What happened?" His voice is urgent and gravelly through the phone.

Normally, Bruce does have (slightly) better phone manners, but he's undercover right now, and I'm only supposed to call in case of emergency.

"A Gotham Academy student was killed at the art showcase tonight. It was this horror magic thing and something went wrong."

He grunts. "Doesn't anyone do normal talent show stuff anymore?"

"Bruce."

"Were you there?"

"Yes."

He hesitates. "Are you okay?"

"I'm ... fine." I wait a moment to see if he's going to press further. I can hear him trying to suppress a worried sigh. He's gotten a lot better over time at the whole checking-in part of being a mentor. But I can also hear people in the background wherever he is. There's not much he can say, since he's not alone. I take a shaky inhale, the stress of the night eating at me. Bruce listens to my breath and says nothing. He holds space for my sadness in the quiet, subtle way that only he knows how. I gather myself and keep talking. "There was a bat-symbol. Freshly painted on the wall right behind where it happened."

"I'll look into it as soon as possible. Wait for my word before proceeding."

"Okay."

More silence.

"I have to go," he says, a hint of regret in his voice. "Stay in tonight, please."

"Okay."

And that's it. He hangs up, and I'm back alone.

I retreat to the shower to let my brain try to make sense of what the hell happened tonight. The good thing about having an eidetic memory is that I can always remember all the details. The bad part about an eidetic memory is that I can always remember *all* the details. The sound of communal screaming, the smell of blood pooling on the stage, the surge of bile crawling up my throat as I watched an innocent girl fall to her death right in front of my eyes. I didn't know Harper well, but she seemed nice. She didn't deserve to die. She didn't deserve to have an audience watch as it happened. Where's the dignity in that? I turn the water up to near-boiling, hoping that the scalding of the water is enough to distract my mind.

It doesn't work.

What do you do after you watch a classmate die and then get banished from the crime scene by your cop dad while the kids who call you a narc behind your back *because* of said cop dad stare at you like somehow the messy fallout of the crisis is your fault?

Stress eating feels like an appropriate response.

I wander into the kitchen and pull out the family-size bag of tortilla chips. We just got them yesterday, but it looks like Dad has already torn through half. I pour some onto a plate, sprinkle it with pre-shredded cheese, and stick it in the microwave. I devour the nachos, then scavenge for more snacks. I make it through a box of cookies before another high-definition memory of the night resurfaces that threatens to make me throw it all back up.

Okay. New plan.

I pull my laptop out. I've been working on a coding project to improve the comm system that I use for missions. Normally, I get lost in this for hours at a time. Dad usually has to remind me to sleep once I'm locked in. Except today, I type for only maybe ten minutes before my mind wanders back to Harper. The way she hung in the air, the sound she made when—

I shudder.

Nope. Not working.

I shut the laptop harder than necessary.

Eating isn't helping and neither is coding, so that leaves me with only one other reliable hobby-distraction. I open an app on my phone that I built with an interactive map of Gotham City. The screen immediately zeroes in on a tiny red dot, moving quickly downtown. I know he said not to, but—

I change into my suit, put on my cowl, and go.

CHAPTER 4

From the rooftop of the old hotel, Gotham City is an endless spread of skyscrapers. Gentle fog swipes my face as it moves across the skyline, the moon illuminating the rounded arches of buildings, awnings, and rumbling traffic down below. The subtle beauty of Gotham City after dark feels like a betrayal on nights like this when the violence is so front-and-center. On a different day, maybe I'd stick around up here and let the thrumming life of the city lull me into a state that feels something like comfort. But I'm not here for the view tonight.

Carefully, I pull a Batarang from my yellow Utility Belt and launch it down toward my target. The blade strikes perfectly, landing in a small crack in the pavement. The curved blade nearly grazes the calf of the boy crouched behind a delivery van. He jumps backward in momentary shock before glaring down at the weapon. I can practically hear him sigh as he looks up, scanning the tops of the surrounding buildings. When he finally meets my gaze, he crosses his arms and frowns. "Ow," he says pointedly, before shooting a grappling hook at the railing of a nearby billboard and joining me on the rooftop.

"Don't be so dramatic. I didn't even cut you," I say. I catch a glimpse of him under the moonlight. Dark hair, pale skin. A smirk. A mask.

"Where did you hide it this time?" Robin asks.

"Hide what?"

"The tracking device."

"What tracking device?" I ask, playing innocent.

"Oh my god."

"I have no idea what you're talking about."

"Please stop building technology to stalk me."

"If it bothers you so much, then you should get better at detecting it, shouldn't you?"

He crosses his arms and sighs again. He's wearing his usual suit, a dark red chest plate and black pants. The cape is black on the exterior, gold on the inside. He looks down at his calf and tries to frown, but I know him well enough to detect the thinly veiled smile beneath it.

"Was it necessary to attempt to stab me?"

"I didn't *attempt* to stab you," I say. "If I wanted to stab you, you'd be stabbed."

At this, he allows a hint of a smile to slip from the corner of his mouth. "True." He kicks some rubble beneath his foot. "You must really worry about me, huh? Think about me all the time?"

"Okay, I change my mind: maybe I will stab you."

"Ah, yes. Just like old times," he says, holding a hand over his heart.

When we first met, Robin and I didn't necessarily get along. At all.

He couldn't stand how I had forced my way into his and Batman's little Bat world. I'll admit that my initial path to taking up the mask wasn't conventional. It may or may not have involved working on my own for several months, trying to convince Batman to train me. Then repeatedly breaking into the Batcave for weeks despite Bruce's incessant pleas to leave him alone and increasingly drastic security measures until Alfred started letting me in through the front door. Robin personally tried to stun me for trespassing on at least five occasions, and at least twice more even after Batman finally agreed to mentor me, but you know: you gotta do what you gotta do sometimes.

After getting over our initial beef, I realized that

I actually like working with Dick Grayson. I would never admit this to his face, lest his ego get any bigger than it already is—and it's plenty big—but he's hyper-competent. He tends to leap before he looks, but not because he's reckless. He takes risks because he has this massive wealth of experience that makes it easy for him to strike with confidence. And then there's the way he moves. God, I'm so jealous of how he moves. Watching Bruce fight is incredible—it's all power and domination. But watching Dick throw hands? It's mesmerizing. Before Bruce took him in after Dick's parents died, Dick grew up as a trapeze artist. He hasn't set foot in a circus in years, but there's still a fluidity to his movement—the way he can flip and tumble and bend through the air— that's engrossing. A performer to his core, and the confidence of someone born on a tightrope. Plus, in this past year, his muscles have filled out and he's grown at least two inches, which makes him even stronger and his agility more impressive, though I'm trying very hard not to notice these things. Noticing how he's growing more and more into himself can be . . . distracting.

I'd rather die than say any of that to his face, though.

"Hey." The even tone of his voice brings me back into the moment. "You look a little . . . I don't know. Less *you* than usual."

"Less me?"

"Not less. A little down, though?" Robin tilts his

head, eyes still fixed on me, as if he's trying to read a book in a language that he hasn't studied in a while. "What's wrong?"

"Something happened earlier," I say quietly. A hint of my distress slips out even though I'm trying to hold it in.

"Are you okay?"

"You know the Diversity Art Showcase at school?" Dick goes to Gotham Academy too; he's a sophomore and I'm a junior. He had told me beforehand that he wouldn't be there tonight. He's been busy patrolling most evenings, since Bruce is out of town.

"Look at you!" he says. "Getting outside. Attending school functions." I glare at him. He shrinks. "Sorry. Continue."

"During Austin's show, someone died. Harper. She's a junior."

Robin takes a sharp inhale.

"Yeah." This time it's my turn to take a deep breath. My skin crawls as I remember the scene. "It was this weird shadow trick. I don't know how they did it. It looked so real, but Austin swears that it was fake. Then, right before the girl died, th-there was a bat-symbol."

Robin's eyebrows shoot up his forehead, high above his mask. "You tell Bruce?"

"Of course. He said to hang back, wait for him to look into it." I kick a pebble beneath my boot. "He also told me to stay in tonight. So don't snitch that I'm here."

I'm expecting a snarky reply threatening to tell Batman anyway, but Dick just gives me a small, sort of sad smile. "Never," he says.

We hear some metal doors clanking in a nearby warehouse. It's a little late for the blue-collar types to be working, even in a city like ours. Without a word, Robin takes off at a jog and leaps over the ledge onto the neighboring building. I follow him as he dashes for the nearest fire escape winding up an even taller building. We climb. A layer of heavy, dense fog looms low in the sky around us, typical for autumn in Gotham City. The night—and the threat of a storm that it holds—feels like it's listening to us as we sneak up the scaffolding. Robin dashes up the first set of makeshift ladders, but as soon as we reach the first landing, I rush forward, overtaking him to climb in front. I shoulder-check him, stick my tongue out. He rolls his eyes. It doesn't matter who climbs up the building first, but one does not pass up an opportunity to annoy Robin. It's comforting to let myself slip into our usual dynamic, even for a fleeting moment.

"So, after it happened, did your dad come to the scene?" he asks.

"Yeah, but . . ." I don't want to tell him about the whole *narc* thing. He's probably heard the nickname, but it's still embarrassing. Plus, Robin and I don't tend to talk about personal stuff much. He knows who I am and who my father is (though it should be noted that he only found out *after* I found out *his* secret identity all on my own, and I only decided to reveal my own identity to him as a strategic offering of peace so he could stop resenting me so much), but, yeah. We don't talk about our relationships with our dads. Or, well, *my* dad for me, his guardian for him. Even though Bruce adopted him more than seven years ago, I don't think I've ever heard Dick call Bruce Wayne "Dad" before. Even the thought of him trying it out is kind of hilarious. Bruce "Batman" Wayne is *not* exactly the dad type, even though I think there's more heart under the cape and cowl than he lets on.

Robin and I reach the top of the towering building just in time to hear a gunshot. He runs a hand over his Utility Belt, double-checking his supply as always before peering over the edge. His expression slips into a firm mask of unbroken focus. Despite the jokes and the laughs and the winks, there's a quiet intensity to Dick. "We'll finish talking later?"

I nod tersely before sliding open a window below us. Once inside, Robin pulls out his phone to check the mission notes once more. "I actually, uh, saw you today. Earlier, right before school," he says, flipping through building blueprints.

I step closer to the open window on the opposite end of the room, glancing out at our targets below. Nine men, each one armed. A white van and an all-black pickup truck full of explosives. Shouldn't be too bad. "Why didn't you come say hi?" I ask.

Robin runs one green-gloved hand through his hair impatiently. "I didn't know if you would've wanted me to."

There are many things that I find interesting about Robin, but none more than the moments when his shyness peeks through his regularly confident vibe. "Of course you could say hi. People have seen us together in normal life. They know we're both in the school lab a lot, so it's not suspicious." I roll out my shoulders to loosen up before the fight. "Plus, we're friends. Friends are allowed to say hi to friends."

Robin twists his face in the same way that he always does when I call him my friend, which is stupid because we're definitely friends, whether he likes it or not. When we first met, he was still in his loner, traumatized mini-Batman phase, but now he's super social at school. I like to think that I played a small role in that shift. For a second, he chews his bottom lip in a way that makes me think that he has more to say, but instead he just shrugs and stares down at the crime operation below.

"I think these guys work for Scarecrow," Robin notes, changing topics. I don't feel frustrated by his evasiveness anymore. I'm used to it. "The trunk of the van is full of gas tanks. Potentially fear gas."

"Fear gas?" I flinch, needing a moment to process. Fear gas is the highly illegal substance sold by Scare-

crow. One time, Scarecrow hit me with such a high dose of his infamous toxin that I hallucinated my worst nightmare: being murdered in a fight without having ever told my dad about my secret identity, then watching helplessly from the grave as everyone I love turned against each other during the fallout. It was disturbing, to say the least. The only other time I felt anything even half as twisted as that was during ...

"Austin's performance," I mumble.

"What?"

"At the art showcase, something was weird about Austin's show. It wasn't nearly as bad as the time we fought Scarecrow—the school show was super mild compared to that—but I don't know. It was similar. But also very different. I wonder if there's maybe a connection here."

"Add it to the case notes while you're waiting to hear from Bruce."

"Right." I have orders. I'm supposed to wait for Bruce. Right. One step at a time.

Robin passes me the binoculars so I can take a look. I focus my eyes on the scene. "Hey. I think I recognize two of those guys."

"From where?"

"They tried to pull a hostage stunt at a grocery store a few weeks ago. Except there were three of them that time, not two." The third guy, the one I called 88-88 on, isn't here. I wonder where he is. Out of trouble, I hope. And how'd his old partners get out of jail, anyway?

"Let me see," Robin says, holding out a hand for the binoculars. I pass them back to him.

"That one is the one who hit my ankle." I point at a bearded man.

"You want dibs on taking him down?"

"Definitely." I adjust my gloves. "Ready?"

I pull a small black sphere from my Utility Belt. It's a smoke bomb, compliments of our good ol' mentor. When I first started fighting crime, I didn't have any of this stuff. No gadgets, no tech, nothing. Now I have resources. Not a ton, but enough. It's one of the perks of coercing The Batman himself into being your sensei. It makes fighting a lot safer. But there's also a trade-off. So long as I'm using Batman's resources, I'm expected to follow his rules. Sometimes, I think I want to go about this whole vigilante thing solo, but other times, it's nice to work in a team. I get frustrated, though, because Batman and Robin sometimes have their own ideas on how I should move as Batgirl. Plus, they don't always get what it's like for me. We may all share the same goal of keeping Gotham City safe, but we're vastly different people, doing this work under vastly different circumstances.

Bruce is this mega-billionaire rich guy who is kind once you get to know him but moves through the world with this hard shell of aloofness. He's able to go on so many crazy missions because he doesn't have much of a family or life here outside of Dick, Alfred, and now me. He's not tied down by financial issues or social obligations. Dick didn't grow up rich, but he certainly has no need for money now that Bruce has adopted him. What Dick has in common with Bruce—and what I admire about them both—is that they've managed to turn the trauma of their respective childhoods into a powerful force to help people. But this is also what sets me apart from them. I don't have a tragic backstory that brought me to this work. My parents weren't murdered. I wasn't tortured. I chose this mask willingly. I've grown up in a working-class neighborhood with a single dad, and after watching one too many systems around me fail, I decided to take matters into my own hands. They don't know what it's like for me to be out here as a girl, as a person of color, as someone without money to fall back on if things go wrong. We don't always have the same priorities. I respect them both, but I don't know. It's complicated. It's hard not to think about these things whenever I reach into this fancy Utility Belt.

I hold the smoke bomb above my head before I feel Robin hesitate before jumping.

Robin *never* hesitates.

"What?" I ask when he keeps looking at me.

He swallows, then adjusts his mask. "This morning you were wearing a green sweater. You don't wear green a lot." I jerk slightly in shock. His skin blooms red, cheeks flushing brighter than I've ever seen. "It looked nice."

What the—

Before I can say anything, he jumps out the window, falling with an aura of calm like it's the only thing he was ever meant to do. Right before he plummets out of view, I catch the faintest glimpse of a smirk. *Smooth.*

I shake my head, listening to the metal of Robin's retractable staff crash against the hood of the truck, before leaping out into the dark.

The fight is quick. The guy who fractured my ankle last time tries to stab me in the thigh with a cut-rate army surplus knife, but the material on my uniform is thick enough that the tip barely cuts my skin before I roll back, kicking him under the chin so hard that it's difficult to tell which is louder: his cracking jawbone or shattering teeth. Normally, I don't take pleasure in the violence, but I can't say I'm sorry to see him slump to the ground.

Robin takes a brutal punch to the face, but he takes the hit like a champ, then uses his staff to take out the dude's kneecaps. Soon enough, Robin has three of the guys tied up, I have the other four—including the father and son from the grocery store—in zip-ties, and it's all over.

I motion toward the two piles of men and smile. "I won."

Robin furrows his brow and counts the guys we caught, but before he can complain, another two men burst out from behind the parked van to try to ambush us. Dick takes them down easily with a flip and a few swift swings of his staff. It happens so fast that I don't even have time to help.

"What was that again? About you winning?" He pretends to wipe the sweat from his forehead with a smug grin.

I cross my arms as I watch him drag the final two guys to his zip-tie corner. "You and your stupid acrobat reflexes. Not fair."

"Whatever, loser." He snorts and crosses his eyes behind his mask, smacking my middle finger away when I lift it.

We laugh, and when we finally settle down, he gives me that look again. The one where I can feel the heat of his gaze hiding behind the lenses of his mask from the way he inhales slowly, letting his head tilt in my direction as he bites back a smile. He's been giving me this look a lot recently. It makes my breath feel fizzy. It's confusing.

We snap back to reality at the sound of sirens. I flee the scene with Robin, racing him back to his bike, which is stashed on the top floor of an abandoned open-air parking lot. As the adrenaline wears off, I find myself thinking about Harper . . . and Austin. I'm not ready to be alone again yet.

I linger beside Robin, leaning against a concrete pillar as I watch him pull out his helmet. A terrible bruise is already forming on his cheek. I reach forward, almost wanting to touch it, but I'm sure that will make it worse, so I let my hand drop and settle for resting my palm on his knuckle instead. "Ice this, okay?"

"Aww. You're worried about my face?"

"Shut up," I say, trying to pull my hand from his, but he catches it before I can move. "You have a secret identity to protect."

"I will. And so do you," he says with a soft smile. He uses his thumb to draw a tiny circle on the back of my hand before letting go. He walks over to the side of his motorcycle, but drops his keys. I swipe them from the ground before he can. For a split second, I crank my arm and pretend I'm going to throw them over his head and make him run for it. He laughs softly, clutching his side. "C'mon, dude. Please. Not today. I'm exhausted."

"Fine." I toss him his keys. "Only because you look like crap."

"Thank you." He swings a leg over his bike. I start to walk away, but I turn when I hear him call my name.

"Yeah?" I reply.

"I know you've been wearing the mask for a while

now, but earlier tonight at school . . ." His voice lowers a bit. "Was that the first time you saw someone die?"

An image of Harper's body flashes across my mind and I wince at the memory. I blink rapidly a few times and try to calm my breathing. I hear something like a sad sigh come from Robin.

Bruce, Dick, and I all follow the same core rule: no killing. I couldn't do this work if we did. So, yeah, I've never seen someone die before. Never in person, not as Barbara Gordon or even as Batgirl. Maybe if I wasn't there as myself, but if I was there as Batgirl, I could've prevented the tragedy, or at least—

Strong, lean arms wrap gently around my back and pull me in close. The hard Kevlar weave of Robin's suit is cold against my cheek, but as he rests his chin on top of my head, I can feel the warmth coming from the exposed skin of his neck, his steady breath above.

Alarms go off in my mind. This is new territory. We do *not* hug. It takes my brain a few moments to even process what is happening. When he speaks, I can feel the subtle vibration of his voice through his suit. "I'm sorry you had to see that."

Death is not an easy subject for Dick. The first people he saw die were his mother and father, right in front of him. He must be thinking of them, yet he's still trying to comfort me.

I don't know if it's because of the adrenaline

comedown or the relief of being able to talk about this with someone, but I squeeze him back a little tighter. And when I do, a tiny intrusive thought springs forward. One that wonders what it would feel like to wrap my arms around his neck and—

He pulls away. I feel the ghost of his hand on my back. He walks back to his bike and nudges the kickstand. "Text me when you get home."

I swallow all the things I've left unsaid.

CHAPTER 5

The school sent out an email last night explaining that there had been a tragedy on campus and social media filled in the rest of the details—who was there, who tried to help, who thinks that Austin is going to jail for life. I slip past the wrought iron gate onto campus, ignoring the dozens of heads that swivel my way. Word must've spread that I was the one who tried to give Harper CPR ... and failed. While there won't be any formal classes today, we're all still "highly encouraged" to come to campus for an emergency assembly and grief counseling.

From the moment I arrived, I've been looking for Alysia. We texted a bit after I got home from patrol last night, but a text can only do so much. This morning, my Number One Priority is clear: I need to give my best friend a hug.

I can't stop counting. It's eight-thirty a.m., and twenty-four hours ago, Harper and Austin were both walking through these same hallways. Less than twelve hours later, one is dead and the other is facing criminal charges. A life ended, a life ruined. How fast things can change.

We're shuttled into the massive auditorium, but I still don't see Alysia anywhere. I pull out my phone.

Barbara: hey where are u?

Alysia: talking to the grief lady. be there in 5

I grab us two seats in the back, then text Bruce while I'm at it. He promised he'd keep me informed, but I still haven't heard from him.

Barbara: Any updates?

He responds immediately, before I can even switch apps.

B: No.

Cool. Super helpful. Thanks, Batman.

When I look up, a lot of my classmates are crying.

Others wear expressions of lingering terror on their faces. Everyone's pretty quiet. We're not allowed to keep our phones on at school, but I swear I see a few kids staring blankly at their phones' dark screens anyway, as if just holding the device is a comfort. I guess people all react differently when a tragedy like this happens. And yet, I feel weirdly . . . detached.

I've always worried that my mind is a bit too analytical, too capable of compartmentalizing facts and suppressing emotions in favor of mental organization. This ability has only increased since training with Batman. In a lot of ways, I'm getting stronger, but in other ways, do I even know what I might be losing?

"GBG!"

I shake my head clear when I finally spot Alysia shoving her way down the aisle. She yanks me into a fierce hug as soon as we're within reach of one another. I pat her shoulder, feeling the stiff fabric beneath my palm. We wear uniforms here. White shirts, navy blue shorts, skirts, or pants. Matching blazers and red ties. Most people wear the uniform as is, the stuffy costume, but the art kids like Austin and the rich kids like Lily always embellish it. Still, no matter how much leeway we get with the uniform, after a nightmare like yesterday, I think we'd all rather be in sweats.

"How are you feeling?" I ask.

"Horrible," she says. "You?"

I'm about to respond, but I'm distracted by the sudden feeling of someone glaring at me. I scan the room until I lock eyes with Nico.

Nervousness swirls in my stomach. "Is Austin going to be okay?" I ask.

"I think so. I heard the wand lacerated their spleen, so the doctors had to perform surgery. They're stable now, at least. But because of what happened to Harper, they handcuffed Austin to the hospital bed last night. Apparently, your dad . . . he, uh, gave the order."

Well, that explains the glaring from Nico. I frown. Standard police procedure, for sure, but still. I'm not beating the narc allegations with this. As if on cue, I hear a mumbled "PCD" from somewhere to my right.

It's moments like this that drive me crazy, make me want to forget about the whole secret-identity thing and scream, *You people don't even know who I am! You have no idea what I do or what I stand for!*

"Everyone needs to take their feelings out on somebody," Alysia says, giving me a sympathetic look. "Don't let it get to you."

Easier said than done.

"Attention, students!" The hum of chatter slowly dies down as our head of school, Alexa Anderson, strides to the front of the room escorted by Headmaster Hammer. The head of school is wearing an oversized beige sweater over tailored slacks, her face stern as a Secretary of State. Kyle and the other self-proclaimed New Right "truth-tellers" who were protesting the showcase take up the last empty seats in the row behind me.

"As you all are aware," Ms. Anderson begins, "our community has suffered a tremendous tragedy. Last night, at the Autumn Diversity Art Showcase—"

"Of course, it was at the *diversity* showcase that someone got murdered," Kyle jeers behind me. Several people around us whip around to gawk at him. I knew Kyle was awful, but this? C'mon.

The girl next to him whacks him on the back of his head, hard. He winces. I want to cheer. Not all heroes wear capes.

"Ow!" Kyle whines, rubbing his head. "Everyone was thinking it."

"Nobody was thinking that," I say, shooting him a sneer.

He narrows his eyes at me. "I'm sorry, who even are you again?"

I roll my eyes and turn back around in my seat.

"Ignore him," Alysia mumbles. "Distraction, remember?"

I try my best to focus on Ms. Anderson's speech, but I can't hear her over the grinding of my teeth. This whole Austin-Harper situation is so messed up, it didn't even occur to me that anyone would stoop so low as to connect what happened to campus politics. A tragedy could happen at any time, anywhere. It's not the fault of the event organizers. If the power-hungry anti-diversity faction of the PTA tries to use this as an excuse to block any future programming because—

"I couldn't sleep at all last night," Alysia whispers into my ear.

It's her voice that makes me realize how fast my heart is pounding. I take a deep breath, try to calm down.

"I couldn't stop seeing it happen over and over," Alysia continues. "Guess it's convenient that I have my internship today."

Right. She's working the 88-88 crisis line today. Being around a bunch of mental-health experts after last night does seem like a fortunate coincidence.

"You can always call me, you know. If you can't sleep," I offer.

"I would, if you'd actually pick up your phone." She's joking, but there's some real hurt in her voice. I can't always respond when I'm out as Batgirl. I know it makes her think that I'm blowing her off. I wish I could let her know that it's not that simple. But I'm not ready for that conversation. I might not ever be.

Across the room, Nico's hair catches my attention. He's wearing headphones now, his forehead resting against the chair in front of him. Half the room is staring at him instead of at Ms. Anderson. I'm sure he's noticed, but he's doing a good job at acting like he doesn't care.

"Do you think what Austin did last night was real?" Alysia asks.

I tilt my head. "I think it was real in the sense that Austin had a complicated trick planned but lost control of it somehow."

A girl in front of us spins around to shush us. Alysia makes a face at her and keeps whispering. "Yeah, but now there are rumors going around that Austin is, I don't know, a witch or something? Like, maybe they have powers?"

"I don't think so. And if they wanted to hurt someone, then they wouldn't have done it in front of a crowd." Plus, I've seen a fair number of villains and they don't usually try to save their victims and immediately cry after.

Alysia taps her chin. "Well, then how'd they do the whole levitation thing?"

"*SHHH.*" The girl in front of us is absolutely over us. I give her an apologetic half grin while Alysia rolls her eyes.

"Bathroom?" Alysia suggests.

We scoot out of our seats, asking the teacher by the door for permission to step out. Once we're alone in the hallway, Alysia stretches her hands above her head.

"Austin probably used some combination of lights and smoke machines. Or—" I shut up when Nico and

Lily appear in the hallway. They walk right past us.

"Nico!" I call.

The look he shoots me is icy. Lily stands by his side, quietly observing.

"How is Austin doing?" I ask.

He glances at me for a moment, brows furrowed, then keeps walking, not bothering to dignify me with an answer. Lily frowns at Nico, then gives me a sympathetic shrug. I'm about to try again, but a teacher is eyeing us suspiciously, so Alysia and I duck into the restroom. I groan when the door shuts. "I know Austin said they didn't do it, but they're literally the only suspect. Harper *died*. Nico can't be *that* mad at my dad. What did he think was going to happen? They were going to see the body of a child from a wealthy family and walk away without making an arrest?" I lean against a bathroom stall, the cold metal chilling the back of my head. "Sorry, I shouldn't be complaining. It's not about me."

"I know. I get it." Alysia jumps to sit on the perch near the window. "Let's talk about something less depressing, yeah?" If I'm good at suppressing my emotions, then Alysia's great at shifting hers. She scrolls on her phone. "We can watch the new video of that Black Canary concert from the other night, the trailer for *Red Thunder*, or . . . OH my GOD."

"What? *What?*"

"Woooow. You hate to see it." Alysia shakes her head

at her phone. "That boy was single-handedly keeping the bi in my bisexuality alive."

"Who are you talking about?"

"Robin is officially off the market."

I drop my backpack. "WHAT?"

"He's been spotted with a new girlfriend. It makes sense, though. Predictable, but a reasonable choice."

My blood boils. I snatch the phone.

No.

"Since when do you have a thing for Robin? I thought you said he was an overhyped show-off who— and I quote—'isn't even that hot.'"

It takes everything I have to hold back a scream when I stare at Alysia's phone, watching Robin saunter off his motorcycle and pull a girl into his arms. Pull *Batgirl* into his arms.

The video is grainy, taken at a distance the other night when I walked Robin back to his bike. From the angle the video was taken, we look . . . comfortable. Sure, it's a long hug, but not *that* long. Seems like a giant leap to go from seeing two people hug to thinking they're dating. But then again, whoever posted the video edited it so that there's some sappy Top Forty love song playing in the background and Robin's moving in slow motion, like some romance character. But it's the caption that makes me want to die: **Robin and his girlfriend! Cute!**

"Robin dating the Girl Batman is a little too on the

nose for me. Boring. He seems like the type who'd go for models anyway, with all that body he's got goin' on," Alysia says casually, leaning over my shoulder to replay the video.

Embarrassment. That's my first reaction. The absolute torturous embarrassment of being caught looking like I was practically melting into some guy's arms.

Next comes frustration. Sure, it'd be awkward if we were caught and we were dating, but HELLO. We are *not even dating*.

I've never even had a boyfriend before, and now apparently the entire internet thinks that I'm dating my work wife. Or I guess not *me* but Batgirl. They think Batgirl—the cooler, more confident, more interesting alter-ego version of me—is dating my friend.

After the frustration comes the fury, compliments of the comments section:

> No wonder she wanted to be a vigilante
>
> Batman's probably so pissed his sidekicks are dating lol
>
> Batgirl's not Batman's sidekick, she's Robin's. Batman recruited her as a present for Robin anyway. A sidekick for a sidekick. Makes sense that she's also his sidechick lmao

I want to scream.

First off, I'm not Batman's sidekick, and I never

have been. Sure, he inspired my suit and name, but I've always done my own thing. I made my own mask and found the strength to put it on. I got myself started, routing tips from my dad's phone to mine. Batman has taken me in as a mentee, but I don't work for him. And I especially don't work for Robin.

"I must admit that I feel very vindicated that he's dating a woman of color," Alysia says. "The internet's gonna freak out trying to figure out who she is now. She looks Black, maybe Latinx . . . hard to tell from the videos. Brown skin and red hair should be a dead giveaway, though."

Wig, I think. Red wig. It used to feel like overkill, but maybe it's time for me to up my identity protection efforts even more. This would hardly be an issue if I were white. How much distance can I forge between myself and my alter ego before all this extra weight starts to really eat at me?

"Anyway," Alysia says. "I guess I'd fight crime too if it meant I got to spend time with him."

Great. Fantastic. Wonderful.

All of the brutal work I've put in, just for everyone to reduce it to some elaborate ploy to get the attention of some dude in tight pants?

I shove Alysia's phone back into her hand.

I hate it here.

CHAPTER 6

After school and after my dad heads to the precinct for work, I go out on patrol by myself. I'm restless from still not hearing back from Batman about Austin. I'm also maybe sort of potentially avoiding Dick Grayson.

It ends up being a long night. Two armed robberies and a busted drug deal. Exhaustion seeps in during my walk back to my bike, but when I turn the corner, there's a police car parked haphazardly across the sidewalk. I bolt to attention.

Swear to god, if there is *another* emergency happening in this city right now, I might lose it. I know it's Gotham, but even this feels excessive.

I'm about to scan the scene, but luckily, I spot the officers. They're in line to grab coffee across the street.

"Not again," a voice mumbles behind me. I step aside and see a young guy, probably around my age, in a wheelchair. He stares at the police car obstructing the sidewalk and groans.

"Do you want me to ask the officers to move their car?" I ask.

The guy sees my face—or my mask, I guess—and jumps. "Holy— You're—"

"Yeah," I cut him off. "I can get them, if you want. They're over there." I point at the coffee shop. The guy's eyes zero in on the officers, then narrow.

"They do this all the time," he says bitterly. "It's hard enough getting around Gotham City in a wheelchair without cops leaving their cars like this whenever they're too lazy to find real parking." I don't know what to say, so I just stand there awkwardly. "Don't call them," the guy decides after a moment. There's a backpack hanging on the handlebars of his wheelchair. He spins it around, unzips it, then pulls out a spray can.

"What are you— *Oh.*" I cover my mouth to stifle my laugh as the guy begins to spray-paint a giant F on the side of the car.

He looks back at me over his shoulder with a smirk. "Can you keep a secret?"

Another thing on the Batgirl Do Not Care List: minor

property damage in light of ADA-violating behavior.

"You didn't see me here," I reply. It's not exactly the work of Picasso, but N.W.A would approve of the sentiment. I shake my head, smirking. One thing about born-and-raised Gothamites? They're punk as hell. No one can say otherwise.

Just then, the cops come out of the coffee shop, yelling as soon as they see us. Out of pure instinct, I throw a smoke bomb. The guy whips his wheelchair around in the other direction and we book it. We make it down a one-way side street, laughing our asses off before the cops even think to actually chase us on foot.

"We're not going to forget this, Batgirl," one of the officers shouts.

"Yeah, we're telling Commissioner Gordon!" the other screams. "Then you'll see how funny defacing public property is!"

We stifle our laughter before parting ways. The incident gives me a little bit of hope. At least I've gotten to do one thing this week that isn't totally terrible.

The next night, though, there's no avoiding Robin. I spend the first twenty minutes of the stakeout compulsively checking my phone, seeing if Bruce has gotten back to me yet with any information about the Austin situation.

Still no news. I know he's undercover, but damn. A little urgency would be nice.

I spend the next twenty minutes wondering if Dick has seen all the stuff trending online. He's acting normal and hasn't mentioned it, but how could he not see it? I know Alfred runs regular searches on all of us to make sure our identities aren't leaked, so . . .

Ugh. A mortified chill shivers down my spine. I forgot that *Alfred* has probably seen this. And he probably thinks it's true. He's too sentimental for his own good.

"You okay?" From the way Robin says it, I can tell when I finally look up that this is the second or third time he's asked.

"Yup." I lock in on the task at hand, dismantling the computer systems for a warehouse holding a stash of illegal weapons. A routine mission. We're sitting on a rooftop overlooking the docks by the river. "Security systems are down. I replaced the footage. We're good to go."

"How'd you get around their firewall?" he asks.

"By being smarter than the person who initially coded the firewall."

"Whoa, someone's cocky today."

"I'm actually legitimately very good at my job," I say, a little too defensively. Robin raises an eyebrow at me. I sigh. "Sorry."

"Don't take it back," he says. "You should own up to stuff more. You're too modest."

"Not really."

"If I was a literal computer genius with a photographic memory, I'd brag about it much more than you tend to do."

He's trying to be nice, but I'm not in the mood. "Whatever. You ready?"

His smile deflates a little, but he nods.

Once the weapons dealers are tied up good and tight and the cops are on their way, Robin walks me to the nearest safe house, where I stashed my motorcycle. I think our conversation feels more forced than usual, but I can't tell if that's real or I'm just on edge. He's in the middle of telling me some story about this one time he tricked Kid Flash into running through a random prom, when my phone rings. "It's Bruce," I announce. Robin motions for me to take the call.

"Hello?" I say into the receiver.

"The girl who was killed at the art show—I'm not sure what happened, but it seems like a low threat. Hang back and I'll handle it when I get back."

My mouth falls open. I was expecting a full debrief. Not instructions to . . . ignore it.

"But what about the bat-symbol?" I ask.

"Disturbed people leave bat-symbols for me all the time," Bruce says.

"I already have a lead, though. Robin and I busted some guys transporting fear gas the other day. I don't know for sure, but I'm thinking that maybe it was used during the show? Maybe if I could talk to the police, they could share what evidence they found too and I can at least help them out by—"

"The police aren't really . . . thrilled with Batgirl right now."

I flinch. "Why not?"

Bruce is silent for a moment before I hear him take a deep breath. "There's a video circulating online."

A video . . . ?

Oh. My. God.

Batman saw the "Robin's girlfriend" video? GCPD has seen it too? *My father* has seen it?

Okay. You know what? Actually, it's fine. This is fine. Change of plans. I'm just going to hang up, crawl into a hole, and die of embarrassment.

My eyes shoot over to Robin, who clocks the sheer terror in my expression and raises an eyebrow. I turn my back to him.

"Batgirl?"

Right. Bruce is still on the phone. I clear my throat. "It wasn't what it looked like," I say, quietly.

"Well, to me, it looked like you very clearly watched someone deface a cop car, laughed, and then helped the culprit get away."

Wait. What?

"I'm sorry, but wh-what are you talking about?" I stutter.

"Yesterday. There was a red-light camera that caught an exchange between you and—"

"OH." Thank *god*.

"What did you think I was talking about?" Bruce asks.

"Nothing!" I force out a laugh. This time, I deliberately do *not* look at Robin.

"GCPD is angry. They're seeing this as a sign of disrespect that you didn't interfere on their behalf," Bruce says.

I roll my eyes. Cops are mad someone called them out on their crap. What's new? "Bruce, you know that's bullsh—"

"I know. Also, language." On the other line, Bruce sighs. "I got a call from GCPD, personally asking me to tell Batgirl to lie low until I'm back in town to . . ."

Hot anger boils up in my chest. "To what? To *supervise* me?"

Bruce knows the deal. Our relationship is that of mentor-mentee—he helps train me, gives me advice and access to his tech. But at the end of the day, I do not work for him. Apparently, my police commissioner dad thinks I do, and has taken it upon himself to call the Bat and ask him to keep the girl in line. If GCPD had something to say to Batgirl, then they should have contacted *Bat-girl*. But I guess they don't see me as capable of handling myself. No surprise. I wonder if it's because I'm young. Except not really, because I have a distinct memory of GCPD contacting Robin through Batman last year when they had some questions for *him* about a case he was involved in where an officer was injured. Looks like they're happy to extend the courtesy of direct communication to Robin and engage with him as an equal, but not me. So GCPD's disregard for me isn't about me being young. That leaves two other theories, because I'm a girl or because I'm Black.

"You didn't do anything wrong," Bruce says. "But the last thing I want is you walking into some investigation without GCPD as backup while I'm out of town. Do you know how many times GCPD officers have tried to kill me when I've pissed them off?"

"But—"

"It's too risky. You're still learning. This is a murder case. Not a robbery or a nonviolent crime. A girl your age, from your school, was *killed*. Trust me, okay? Whoever's trying to get to me might have something up their sleeve. I'll handle it when I'm back."

"Fine."

He ends the call without a goodbye.

"What'd he say?" Dick asks.

"He's being all protective and weird." I clench and unclench my fists twice.

"Sorry. He's been extra intense since he's been undercover. Don't take it personally."

But how can I not take it personally? Couldn't he have a little more faith that I can handle this on my own?

"Yeah, well . . . ," Dick says awkwardly, trying to change the stale mood hanging in the air. If anyone knows what it's like to be on the receiving end of the Batman's orders, it's him. "I was wondering if you, uh, wanted to hang out?"

I freeze. "Hang out?"

"Yeah, like, outside all of this. As . . . normal." He tries to sound nonchalant, but I can hear the poorly concealed anxiety in his voice.

So he *has* seen the stuff online. I narrow my gaze. He holds his hands up. "I'm not asking because of the rumors. I was going to ask you anyway. I've been thinking about it for weeks, swear to god. Ask Alfred. He did a practice run with me."

He asked Alfred for advice?

His eyes are hidden behind his mask, but I can see the hopeful smile on his lips. It's unexpected. Cute.

But also overwhelming.

Bruce and Dick are the only people on the planet who know the biggest secret of my life—who I am and what I do when I sneak out at night. Sometimes I worry that whatever . . . feelings . . . I have about Robin is me conflating our friendship and intimacy for something else. But then sometimes we'll be going over inventory and he'll make a joke. Or I'll tell him about my frustration with my dad and his job, and he'll listen. Or he'll bring a highly specific selection of snacks to a stakeout that he meticulously gathered based on random snippets I've dropped about what I like to eat, even though he doesn't like half of the same foods as me. And I'll see him around outside of school, his face buried in a book, and suddenly my breathing isn't so steady and I'm not so sure that I'm conflating anything at all. But even so, none of that has anything to do with the reality of our situation, which is that we work together. And I'm trying to make a name for myself by keeping this city safe—not by dating social media's favorite parasocial crush.

I press my fingers to my temples. "All of the captions just said Robin's girlfriend this, Robin's girlfriend that. None of them even called me by my name. It was like I didn't even have a name."

"People are stupid."

"I'm being serious."

"I am too. Yeah, the stuff people are posting is . . . awkward. And I don't like that they're not calling you by your name either. But—"

"But *what*?"

He seems to want to say something. He parts his lips, sucks in a quiet breath, but is unable to get the actual words to come out.

I sigh. "Look, Robin. I don't want the internet to ship us. I don't want strangers dictating my relationships. Just because they expect us to be together doesn't mean that we have to be together."

He smiles softly. "We don't *have* to be together, but . . ."

We're friends. He's hot. Of course I'm aware that he's hot. And I like spending time with him. And he's fun and funny and doesn't get weird about having real conversations. Dick Grayson is a catch. But is it that crazy to want some separation in my life? I can't think about him in that way. There are feelings there, sure. I won't deny that. But that's all a fantasy. I can't let things get real. Our partnership is more sacred than a crush.

"I don't want anything to change between us," I say, but then a streak of moonlight slips through a break in the clouds, momentarily painting his features in a light so soft that it makes my heart stutter. *He's gorgeous.* I quickly push the idle observation aside. "We, uh, have a job that's bigger than us both. It—if there was an *it*— would only get in the way."

"Best-case scenario: it works out." He takes a tiny, uncertain step closer. For some reason, I let him. "And it doesn't get in the way."

That soft, magnetic smile of his floats back and I feel myself drifting toward him. I blink and suddenly we're right back where we were the other day—standing face to face, close enough to touch.

My reservations unravel when his hand reaches out to draw a low, steady line from my elbow to my hand. The touch is light but I feel it everywhere.

". . . And worst-case scenario?" I whisper. His lips curve into a smile at the slight falter in my voice.

His chest is rising and falling rapidly now. He's so close that I can feel it brushing against mine with each breath. I'm hyperaware of the distance between our bodies—and the lack of it.

"Well. Worst-case scenario . . ." He shakes his head, chuckling softly. "The internet calls you Robin's *ex*-girlfriend?"

His words hit like a punch to the stomach. A scream curdles inside me. Blood rushes in my ears. "Why would you even say that?"

His expression goes slack. "Wait, Babs," he says, but I don't wait. I have no desire to hear another word from him. He holds out his hand, but I whirl out of reach. The look on his face morphs from regret to panic. "Babs!"

My emotions are a roiling storm. Uncontrolled. A pot of boiling water, finally bubbling over. I dash for the nearest emergency exit, setting off blaring alarms in the process, but I don't care. Robin follows me. "I'm sorry. That was a joke. It wasn't funny. I'm—"

"Leave me alone." I slam the door behind me as I stomp up a narrow set of stairs, clenching my fists until I reach street level.

I pace back and forth over the cracked concrete, my breath unsteady. Anger and embarrassment war inside me. I want to explode or break something.

Or both.

I'm used to others constantly trying to define me not by who I am, but by my relationship to the men in my life. I've been Commissioner Gordon's daughter. Batman's mentee. Never Barbara, never Batgirl.

I never took this personally. I choose to give people the benefit of the doubt. My relationships are important to me, and it's nobody's fault that both my father and mentor are famous public figures in their own way. Plus, I understand the benefit of being underestimated. People never see me as a threat until my hand is wrapped around their throat. But there's something about the dismissiveness of "Robin's girlfriend" that pisses me off. This is different. This is beyond me.

I'm so tired of being understanding.

I care about my dad, Bruce, and Dick. They're without a doubt the three closest people to me in my entire life. And I know that they care about me too. But why can't any of them see how important it is for me to exist independent of them? Why is it that I'm always alone in screaming out my own name?

Frustration breaks in my chest. I kick over a trash can. Except that doesn't help because now there's litter all over the sidewalk, which makes me imagine all the trash finding a way into the gutter and joining with that massive island of plastic polluting the ocean and killing all the innocent fish or mixing with the rest of the trash that chokes Gotham City every day. I curse under my breath as I pick the can back up and return the stained fast-food bags and plastic bottles to their receptacle. I'm holding my breath, trying not to gag as I toss a dirty diaper back in the can, when my phone vibrates with a text.

Alysia: Looks like Nico's pretty desperate. Poor guy.

She sent a link too. I open it and find myself confronted with a video of Nico's face, staring at me through the screen with that almost glare of his—a slight furrow between his brows and a dark expression in his eyes. His pink hair, damp and sticking out in all directions, looks even messier than usual.

"This is a message for Batgirl." Nico's voice is a low rumble, tinged with emotion. The sound of it stirs something in me for a moment, so much that I pause the video to recenter myself. What is with me tonight? I'm probably just emotional from my fight with Dick, I guess. That's all. I brush away the weird feeling sparked by Nico's voice and click Play, watching his stormy eyes bore into the camera.

"Two nights ago, my sibling Austin was arrested for a crime that they didn't commit. There were a lot of witnesses, but what they're claiming that Austin did is impossible. I know for a fact that Austin is innocent. They . . . Austin doesn't have the ability to do what the police have accused them of, and even if they did, they don't have the heart. Our home life is"—Nico stares off camera—"complicated. But GCPD won't investigate— they think it's a done deal. There haven't been any Bat-man sightings in Gotham City for over a month. Please. Look at the data. The police aren't good at investigating crimes like this, concerning people like us. But you are. If you're willing to help, please contact me. I don't have any other options."

Bruce asked me to hang back. I should close the video, but then Nico holds up a T-shirt. It's black, purple, and yellow. It's the bat-symbol, but . . . *my* bat-symbol. My suit colors.

"This is Austin's."

Next, Nico holds up a sweatshirt. It's purple with *Batgirl bites back* written on the back.

"This is Austin's too."

Then a black beanie with *BATGIRL 4EVER* stitched in yellow.

"Austin doesn't trust the detectives. They don't trust the government. They don't trust the private companies. They don't trust the corporations. But they trust *you.*"

I glimpse my own conflicted reflection in the glass surface of my phone.

"Please. Will you help us?"

CHAPTER 7

If Austin believes in Batgirl, then Batgirl can step up to believe in Austin. Or at least hear them out, despite the evidence against them. Bruce will be pissed when he finds out that I'm taking on the case despite his warning, but so what? It's not like he's never broken a rule before. Batman lives by his own code. If anything, he should be impressed that I've been taking notes on his esteemed methods.

I make a list of initial suspects, starting with everyone I remember being at the Diversity Art Showcase that night. I have a good—like, *really* good—eidetic memory, so I'm able to populate most of the list on my own. I cross-check my memory with the event flyer. I'll have to double-check the list later, once I get my hands on school security footage, but it's a long list. Practically half the sophomore, junior, and senior classes were there. This is going to take a while.

I run background checks on Austin and Nico, then move on to Lily. All three are mentioned in various school newsletters about the art program—Nico's music, Lily's mixed-media collages, and Austin's performance art and sculpture. Beyond that, though, most of their digital footprint comes from their own social media accounts. No secret burner accounts, ranting manifestos, or previous arrests. All clean. Easy enough.

When I continue to run an online search down the list of my other classmates, though, I hesitate. Should I be prying into my classmates' lives like this? Being Batgirl kind of necessitates it, I guess, but what does that have do to me as Barbara? Maybe Bruce had a point about my proximity to the case.

I roll my neck and shoulders. No time to stress out about this now. If I go down this ethical wormhole, I'll never make any progress. I need to do what I do best: take a deep breath, then compartmentalize.

As I make my way through background checks on the first half of the attendance list, nothing particularly surprising comes up. I find a couple of buried scandals— a couple of underage-drinking charges, some leaked photos that I wish I hadn't seen—but nothing that makes me believe any of these people had it in for Harper or Austin.

When no red flags jump out there, I pivot to the next logical task—the one that I've been dreading. I swallow down the lump forming in my throat and click Play on a dark, grainy video.

Every part of me wants to look away, but I force myself to watch every single recording of the incident that I can find online. I don't know what twisted urge made people want to post the video in the first place, but several did. By now, all the videos have been flagged and removed for violating content rules about graphic violence, but I run a time machine program to recover the lost videos from the social media server. The first time I rewatch Harper's fall, I want to throw up. By the fifth video, the nausea has settled into a vague discomfort, and by the fifteenth watch, I've managed to push away my own visceral reaction in order to focus on the fine details hidden in each angle: facial expressions, body language, shadows, whispers.

For the most part, everyone looks like they genuinely think it's all part of the act for a while, but as soon as Harper hits the floor, everyone's face slips into undeniable terror. It seems like nobody saw it coming. Then again, I go to school with a lot of very talented people. Gotham Academy's drama department is top-tier. Who knows who could be acting?

Rewatching the footage, there's another aspect of Austin's performance that's bothering me: my fear gas theory. The toxin is back on the streets, so is that what Austin used during their show? It didn't feel anywhere near as strong as when I got hit with the stuff from the Scarecrow himself, but it seems plausible. If so, why? And how'd they get their hands on it in the first place? My brain races with a dozen more questions that can't be answered from just sitting alone at my computer.

Time to arrange a meeting with my first suspect.

"It's actually you," Nico says in awe, his eyes dancing as they trace over me. We're standing in the alley where I told him to meet me.

"You thought I'd be an imposter?" I ask.

Nico exchanges a look with Lily beside him, shrugs. "Maybe."

I blink twice, my eyes still adjusting to my mask. I'm wearing a different one than usual. If I'm going to be investigating a case involving my classmates, my every-day mask won't cut it—it's great (and breathable), but it shows my eyes. This stealth one obscures my face better. The eye cutouts utilize an old trick of two-way mirrors. I can see out clearly, but no one can see in.

"Then why'd you come?" I ask.

"Like I said. I'm desperate." Nico takes a step closer and holds out his hand. He gives me a small, shy smile. "It's nice to meet you, Batgirl." Despite my best efforts, I kind of like the way he says *Nice to meet you, Batgirl.* Like he means it.

"I'm Nico," he says as I shake his hand. "This is Lily." Lily gives me a polite wave.

"I told you to come alone." I had used an app I built to send him an encrypted, self-destructing message with very clear instructions. The fewer people involved, the better. But apparently, the boy doesn't follow directions. We're off to a wonderful start.

"Someone framed my sibling for murder and killed one of my classmates. You think I'd show up to a random location alone?"

Valid point. The three of us hover in awkward silence. I'm nervous. I shouldn't be, but I am. I've never worked a case with people I actually know before.

I clear my throat. "Did you kill that girl?" I ask Nico abruptly. It's strategic to try to catch people off guard. You'd be surprised by how many idiots straight-up admit to a crime when taken by surprise. Plus, half the time when stuff like this happens to people like Austin, it's usually a brother or husband or ex-lover behind the crime. Just ask any true-crime podcaster.

Nico's eyebrows fly up his forehead, and I study his reaction. His lips part slightly in genuine confusion and he steps backward reflexively.

When confronted, a lot of men tend to get aggressive, combative, or overly defensive. They clench their fists, widen their stance, or lean forward. Nico, however, does the opposite. He shrinks slightly and looks hurt by my accusation.

"Wh-what? No. Of course not," he says at last. "I have—had—nothing against Harper, and I'd never do anything to hurt Austin."

Nothing in his face indicates that he's lying. At least, not yet.

"I love Austin more than . . . more than anyone in the world," he adds quietly. The way he says it makes something warm in my chest. People don't really talk about their siblings like that, so sincerely. Except Nico, I guess. But that's not important. I need to stay focused.

I snap to Lily and make my voice sound as matter-of-fact as possible. "So then you killed her?"

Lily's reaction is the same. Pure shock. "No, I would never," she says. "Austin's my best friend. We've been in the art program together since freshman year—we've helped each other on every project. Even on this one for the diversity showcase, when I couldn't participate myself. And I've known Harper since kindergarten."

A subtle mist makes her sad eyes glitter. "Nico and I weren't even near them when everything went wrong."

"Yeah, but you were in the room," I point out. We don't know *how* Harper was killed yet, so there could be a whole host of things that happened. Someone could have rigged Austin's trick and automated the sabotage to unfold remotely.

"We didn't do it," Nico says firmly. "Did you agree to meet us only to question us?"

"I can't help if I don't have facts." I try to ignore the disappointed, frustrated look in his eyes. It shouldn't matter to me whether Nico likes Batgirl or not—this is an investigation, not a social call—but I can still feel the tiniest pull in the corner of my mind, urging me to tone down the intensity. "Can you show me how Austin's performance was supposed to go?"

"Yeah. Austin practiced with us a lot," Lily says.

"They kept their materials at home," Nico adds. "I live nearby. We can show you there."

We turn in the direction where I already know he lives. I looked up his address before coming, of course. The three of us walk to his apartment building in painful silence.

"My, uh, little cousin has a Batgirl picture as her screen saver," Lily says to me after the first block.

I blink twice. "Really?"

"Yeah. She's a big fan." Lily smiles, a little shy. "Is that weird?"

"No, no. It's not weird, it's just . . ." I don't do this for attention. I avoid the cameras for a reason and have even sabotaged reporters' photos before. The video of me and Robin is the first image leak in months. But Lily's trying to be nice, so I smile and repeat, "It's not weird."

"People are so fascinated by you, you know. Bringing so much diversity to—"

"Lily." Nico says her name, a tight warning.

She shakes her head, embarrassed. "Crap. Sorry. I just meant—" She sighs. "Sorry. I'm just really excited to meet you. So, uh, what's Robin like? You . . . know him well, right?" She tries to keep her voice casual, but I can detect the hint of excitement in her question. She's clearly asking for two reasons: (1) she's seen the rumors, and (2) she has a crush herself. I get hit with several conflicting emotions at once: annoyance that she's into Robin, annoyance that I'm annoyed that she's into Robin, and confusion. I thought she and Nico were dating? Are they not?

"Lily, chill," Nico says gently before shooting me an apologetic look. At least somebody realizes how awkward all that stuff online must be for me.

Nico's apartment building is on a very dark street. Like, *dark* dark. It's so poorly lit that I'm immediately irritated on behalf of the residents. Every year, the Gotham City government promises to install more streetlights. Every year, they never actually do it. I've watched this debate play out in the local news too many times to count. Budget limitations, competing priorities, bureaucracy, blah blah. The wealthy neighborhood of Burnley is surprisingly well-lit, but that's because its residents banded together to pay for their own streetlights. I can't decide if I'm happy for them or depressed knowing that something as basic as safety lighting has been privatized and turned into yet another commodity exclusively for the rich in this city. I wonder what Nico thinks of all this. In another world, if I weren't here with him right now for work, maybe I'd ask.

Once we arrive at the door to Nico's unit, I rush inside at the sound of footsteps before anyone can see me. Nico and Lily follow me in, but before we shut the door, we overhear a snippet of the world's worst attempt at whispering.

"I called it, you know," Nico's neighbor says to a woman walking with her as they carry heavy bags of groceries to their unit across the hall. "They go to that fancy school, but there's only two places kids like that end up: juvie or Arkham."

"With parents like that . . . ," the other says.

Damn. I try to offer Nico a sympathetic glance, but

he's staring at the floor, shoulders hitched as he deliberately avoids my eyes. The corner of his face is twisted with undeniable embarrassment. Who the hell do those neighbors think they are? And how cowardly for grown-ass adults to talk crap like that, and about literal teenagers, no less? I slam the door shut, loudly, so the jerks across the hall can hear.

Lily jumps at the bang while Nico stares at me, equally startled. His thick eyebrows shoot all the way up his forehead, nearly merging with his pink hair. When his gaze finally collides with mine, he's wearing a sharp, focused expression that I can't quite decipher. Nobody says anything for a few moments. What is there to say?

Eventually, it's Nico who breaks the silence. "Sorry it's kind of a mess in here. Our parents have been staying at the hospital ever since, well. You know." He coughs into the nook of his elbow. "I've been coming back and forth, though. Not enough room for all of us to sleep in Austin's hospital room."

Inside is a mess, but it's also cozy. Family photos line the walls, with wooden knickknacks covering nearly every surface. Even though I've only ever seen Nico and Austin wear all black outside of the school uniform, the walls in their home are a bright, cheery yellow. A keyboard rests on a folding table in the center of the living room beneath a painting of what looks like a Southeast

Asian landscape. Several mini-keyboard-looking-things full of confusing, light-up buttons cover every inch of the makeshift desk beside it.

"What are these?" I ask.

"Synths. Drum machines," he says. "I make music. My dad taught me."

Right. I remember what Alysia told me a few days ago about his brief stint of viral fame and how he instantly rejected it.

"Family of artists," I observe.

Nico must find this amusing because he chuckles to himself. "Yeah. Guess so."

When our eyes meet again, there's a softness there. I look away. We're getting off track. I clear my throat. "Okay, so, uh, at the showcase, Austin—" No, that's not good. I can't sound too familiar with the case. I start again. "You said in your video that you know Austin is innocent because the whole trick was a fake. Show me how they did it."

Nico and Lily exchange a nervous glance. "If we show you how Austin did the performance, you're not going to ... turn on us, right?"

My mind automatically zooms to the worst-case scenario and I eye the exit. Is this a trap?

"No, sorry, we don't mean, like, anything that bad," Lily says, holding her hands up. "It's just ... Well. Austin's trick required, uh ..."

"Fear gas?" I guess.

Nico and Lily exchange an anxious look, visibly shaken.

I was right. Definitely not a good sign for Austin.

"How'd you know?" Nico asks.

"I have prior experience in the matter." I fight back a shiver. "How'd Austin even get their hands on that?"

"They were working on a graffiti mural in the tunnels beneath the city with some other art kids and they found it lying around. I swear they didn't do anything shady to get it."

"Where's the mural?"

"At the tunnel entrance beneath the pier. Right below the biker bar."

He seems like he's telling the truth, but I'll corroborate this story later. Batman has surveillance cameras hidden in a few key locations around the city. The pier is one of them. Nevertheless, *how* Austin got hold of the stuff is only half the story—I need to understand why they chose to use it.

"Austin drugged a crowd of people and called it art? Am I understanding everything?" I say.

Lily's brows knit. "Austin only used a tiny dose. Completely safe. You can ask anyone who was there—there were no lasting effects."

I mean, I was there and Lily's right—whatever dose

Austin administered lasted less than twenty seconds. Still.

"Austin's not a bad person," Lily says passionately. "They probably shouldn't have used this stuff, but they were trying to make art. Do something different. They weren't trying to hurt anyone."

"Fine." I'll make up my mind about how I feel about this later. "So they used the fear gas for the illusions, but then how did they make everyone see the same stuff at the same time? The power of suggestion?" I guess. I've seen something similar before—hallucination work, illusions. Nothing groundbreaking.

"Yup," Nico says. "Austin had been studying communal dreams for a while. It was all in the setup."

"And how'd Harper levitate?"

"That's the weird part. Harper was supposed to levitate, but only a foot or so off the ground—not all the way up to the ceiling. It was supposed to be an optical illusion. A mix of hidden wires and stage design. There's no way fear gas alone could've done that." Nico leans over a cardboard box and tosses me a plastic bag full of wires. "These are the backup ones. The police took the real ones from the auditorium as evidence. But I swear they're the same."

I will confirm this later, the next time I stop by Dad's office. "Great. Let's try it, then."

Disgust wells up on Nico's face. "It's a little . . . too soon for that. Isn't it?"

Lily raises her hand. "I'll do it."

Good. I like a girl who takes initiative.

When I get home, I can't open my laptop fast enough. My brain buzzes with the anticipation of beginning a new case. I'd be lying if I said the fact that I'm working against orders doesn't add at least a little to the excitement. Though I remind myself that this is a murder investigation and any thrill I get needs to be tempered with just how serious that is.

As I suspected, Austin's performance was all classic street magic, packaged into a glossy "concept art" form. Nothing beyond the easily explained. I don't see how any technical failure—or even a higher dose of fear gas—could've caused Harper to rise over twenty feet in the air, then freeze up before she fell.

While I verify Nico's claim about how Austin found the fear gas, I pull up Nico's album *Spiral*—the one Alysia told me about. There's something vulnerable about engaging with someone's art once you know them in real life. Or at least that's why I think I'm suddenly nervous to listen to Nico's music. A quick image of the way his oversized jacket hung off his thin frame back at his house earlier flashes in my mind. My face gets all hot. I don't know why I'm being weird. This is an investigation. "It's research," I whisper as I click Play.

The first song on the album is haunting. He says things in his songs that most people would be afraid to ever say out loud. He sings about loneliness, about frustration, about disillusionment, over musical tracks that burst in your brain like fireworks. There's a song that I assume is about Austin, written with warmth about their connection as siblings in a complicated home. It's all very honest. Shockingly sincere. When I take out my earbuds at the end of the half hour, I'm speechless.

Nico isn't just talented. He's a musical savant.

I mentally file this information away for future examination, then pull up my growing case file. Except something weird happens. I thought I had watched the last video of Harper's death before I left earlier, but a notification pops up. My dark-web-scanning software picked up on a new copy of the video. Someone posted it to another forum. And not just once, but several times. I click for more details and see that they were all uploaded by the same person.

Someone keeps reposting the video of Harper's death.

What type of person would repeatedly share a video of someone dying? And not just any video, but this one in particular?

I trace the video's IP address to Gotham University. The computer used to re-upload the footage of Harper's death is on the sixth floor of a dorm in student housing.

College apps are still a couple years away for me, but it might be a good time for a campus tour.

CHAPTER 8

I use a Batrope to grapple up the side of the dorm to an illuminated window. Two students live in the room where I traced the address. The first is a basketball player majoring in communications. The other is Andrew Vizzini. Twenty years old, college junior. Theology major with a minor in art history. Between the two roommates, I'm going to go out on a limb and guess that Andrew, the one who founded the overtly named Occult Occurrences club on campus when he was a freshman, is who I'm looking for.

Andrew's the only one home when I arrive. When I look through the glass, his skinny figure is curled up on a futon. In his official school ID photo taken a couple years ago, he has an easy, nice smile, a popular hair-cut, and bright eyes. Now his hair is long and shaggy, falling heavy over his eyes. He probably hasn't washed it—let alone cut it—since he arrived at college. Empty pizza boxes and takeout containers stack on the table in front of him. The walls are covered in black posters with strange symbols on them. A life-sized skeleton hangs from a hook in the corner beside a stack of leather and old velvet-bound books.

I pry open the window from the outside and climb in. The smell of stale bread and dirty laundry is so rank that I have to breathe through my mouth.

"Hi there," I say.

Andrew takes one look at me, then bolts. I tackle him before he can even touch the doorknob. He squirms beneath me, but I pin him to the ground. "I just have—" He throws an elbow back at my face. I dodge. "A few—" I let up enough to let him turn around so we can face one another. "Questions for—"

He spits right in my face. Classy.

"—you," I finish. My mask blocked the loogie from hitting my skin, but I still recoil when I use my sleeve to wipe it off. I can't wait to get this visit over with already.

"Why do you keep posting this video?" I ask. I pull out my phone and press Play on the footage of Austin and Harper. His expression slips from anger to amusement. He *likes* watching this video. I pause it before Harper falls to the floor. There's an obvious trace of disappointment on his face that I cut the video short.

"Wouldn't you like to know?" Heavy, unkept bangs hang over Andrew's eyes. He uses the back of his hand to part the curtain of hair and smirks.

"Do you have something to do with what happened that night?"

He laughs unnervingly. "Do *you* have something to do with what happened that night?"

I roll my eyes. "If you answer the question, I'll leave."

"*If you answer the question, I'll leave.*" He mimics my voice in this awful, high-pitched whine. God, I hope I don't sound like that. Do I sound like that?

"Are you sure you don't want to cooperate?" I square my shoulders. "I just need a few answers."

"Sounds like a personal problem." He shoots me an oily grin. "Are you sure you don't want to click Play and let us finish watching that beautiful video?"

Everything about this guy sends gross chills down my spine.

I take a deep breath, trying to summon every ounce of patience in my body. Clearly, this dude has some issues. He's trying to get under my skin, but if I stay calm—

Whoa.

Andrew slips out of my grip like a worm. Then,

suddenly, the metal end of a golf club is hurling toward my head. I duck as Andrew swings the club as hard as he can at my temple.

"There's no need to bring out the sporting equipment," I say.

"You're lucky I don't have a baseball bat," he says with a grin as he takes another swing, this time throwing his full weight behind it.

Okay, then. Never mind. My patience has officially evaporated.

I grab the club midswing and use it for leverage as I kick Andrew in the chest. He fumbles backward, knocking over the trash on his coffee table. I reach for his arms to secure him, but he rolls out of the way, grabbing a glass beer bottle on the table and slamming it into my shoulder. Sharp pain blossoms at the impact point.

The bottle shatters, leaving glass on the floor. The shards break into even smaller pieces when I step on them to knee Andrew in the back as he crawls away from me. He's reaching for another golf club from the driving set behind the couch, so I guess I have to switch interrogation tactics.

"Do you like adventure sports, Andrew?" I ask. He falters for a moment, considering my words, then yelps when I yank him toward me. It's easy enough now to swipe at his ankles and get him back onto the floor. I pull out a cord from my Utility Belt, wrap it around his ankles, then haul his skinny ass to the window.

"Let me go, bitch."

I smirk. "As you wish."

His eyebrows quirk at me in confusion before I push him out the window.

He screams the whole way down. The wire wrapped around his ankles is fixed to a steel rod secured to the window frame. I pull the line just as his head reaches the second floor of the building. Then I reverse the line and pull him back up like a yo-yo.

I lean out the window. "Ready to tell me about this video now?"

"You stupid—"

Looks like we have a thrill-seeker. I flick the switch and he falls once more, though this time I let him drop a little closer to the ground, hovering at window level of the first floor. An extra ride, just because he's been so well-behaved. When I wind him back up, he's clutching his heart. "How about now?" I ask.

"I didn't make that video," he says between pants. The blood is rushing to his head from hanging upside down, his face flushing a deep scarlet.

"I know you didn't make it. I asked why you keep sharing a video of a young girl dying on the internet?"

"It's for us."

"Who is 'us'?"

"The ones who believe." He smiles a little now, but the expression lacks any warmth. It's sinister. Smug. Unnerving.

"I'm going to need some more specifics than that, Andrew." I make a big show of raising my hand and hovering it close to the switch. His eyes widen.

"DFG. Demonic Forces of Gotham. We are a society that researches demonic activity in Gotham."

"You call turning innocent people's deaths into gross entertainment for you and your creepy friends 'research'?"

"The girl sounded so beautiful when she died. It's incredible to witness such raw, dark power like that, is it not?"

"*Is it not?*" I repeat in a dopey, nasally imitation. Who does he think he is, with this pseudo-Victorian accent? Edgar Allan Poe? "How do you know that the video isn't fake?"

"I've spent my whole life watching videos of every suspicious death on the internet, looking for clues. This is the first evidence I've seen in years that so clearly shows demonic activity."

Demonic activity? Seems like a big reach to me.

Andrew lets out a giddy, broken cackle. "Gotham City is in for a treat."

I'm done here. Andrew is clearly a creep, but a dedicated one. I don't buy the demon thing, but if he's been holding on to footage of crimes around Gotham City, maybe I can find something that might explain how someone could've sabotaged Austin's show. I'll look into his wannabe *X-Files* group later, but first there's one more person I need to visit tonight.

I release Andrew again. He falls all six stories fast, but I stop the line right before he hits the pavement. His shaggy hair brushes the wet concrete beneath him. I steadily cut the line, lowering him to the ground gently. I adjust my belt, preparing to leave.

"Wait!" Andrew yells. "My ID to swipe back into the dorms is still on the futon."

"Sounds like a personal problem," I say, backing away from the window and returning to the darkness of the night.

CHAPTER 9

Austin's mom blinks slowly as she watches the gentle rise and fall of Austin's chest in the cold hospital room. Austin's not asleep. They stare blankly at the ceiling, their face solemn. Together, the mother and child make for a quietly devastating sight. They look sad. And tired.

It makes feel me sad. And tired.

I don't want to interrupt, but I need to speak with Austin. Alone.

I hacked into the hospital security camera system to give myself cover so I could enter the building undetected through the northeast emergency exit. I looked up Austin's patient file before coming here tonight. The night of the accident, they were hurt even worse than I thought. Their spleen was torn so badly that the doctors had to remove the organ entirely. They're staying in the hospital for a few more days to monitor for any potential complications from the surgery. I know they need to rest, but I have questions that Austin needs to answer if I'm going to help.

I pull a tiny speaker from my Utility Belt and slide it beneath the door before ducking into the nearest closet. Leaning against a stack of clean hospital bed linens, I open my phone, raising the mic to my mouth. "Would the guardian of Mx. Austin Baluyot check in with the front desk, please. I repeat, would the guardian of Mx. Austin Baluyot please check in with the front desk."

I count the seconds until Austin's mom finally opens the door to the room, looks in both directions, then follows the arrow pointing to the front desk, per my fake announcement. I only have a few minutes. I rush into the room and shut the door behind me.

"Austin." My voice echoes strangely in the quiet, all-white room.

Austin doesn't respond at first. Doesn't even look my way. They just keep watching the ceiling. I say their name again, louder this time. They pivot their neck toward me, slowly at first. I clock the exact moment when they see me. Even from across the room, I can hear their sharp intake of breath.

"Can we talk?" I whisper.

Austin's eyes are bulging out of their head. "Bat-girl?" The blinking monitor beside their bed shows a rapid increase in their heartbeat.

I offer an awkward smile and take that as an invitation to come closer. They watch me, warily, with each step I take. It takes a lot of self-control to not stare at the police monitor anklet peeking out from under the covers at the bottom of the bed.

"I'm sorry you got hurt," I say as I crouch by the side of their bed.

Austin laughs. It looks like it hurts, though, because the chuckle is immediately followed by a tight grimace. "For a second, I thought you were here to get me for Harper."

"Your brother didn't tell you that he contacted me to help?" I ask.

"He did, but I thought he was lying to make me feel better." Warmth swirls in Austin's eyes at the mention of Nico. Their face softens a bit, muscles relaxing ever so slightly.

"I don't think you meant to hurt Harper," I say.

A faint smile flits across Austin's face. "Thank you."

"Can you tell me what happened, though, please?"

"I have no idea. One second, I'm doing this performance that I've practiced dozens of times before. The next, I wake up and Harper's falling from the ceiling, I'm about to be stabbed, and she's ..." Austin white-knuckles the blanket.

"Yeah." I place my hand on top of Austin's, hoping the touch is comforting. "Was there anything weird about the show in the moments before, though? Anything that felt off?"

"Not really," Austin says.

"Are you sure? Every single detail up to that moment went *exactly* as planned?" I press.

"Actually ..." Austin pauses, frowning and clutching the blanket tightly. "The lights went off when they weren't supposed to."

"When? At the beginning of the show?"

Austin shakes their head. "They were supposed to cut at the start to scare people, but they weren't supposed to go out again during the finale. When the lights cut out, I checked the lighting cues on my phone to make sure everything was okay. I was about to make a joke to the crowd, and then ... nothing. It's all a blank after that."

I remember that moment. I figured the second blackout was intentionally part of the show. So that's at least one clue, then: someone tampered with the lights.

I look over my shoulder to check that the door's still

closed. When I do, I notice an old T-shirt draped over a square on the wall. "What's with the decor?"

Austin follows my line of sight and frowns. "That's the mirror."

"Oh." I guess if I accidentally killed someone, I wouldn't want to look at myself either.

"It's not what you think," Austin says. "My mom covered it. She's real superstitious. She says that mirrors can lure our souls out of our bodies when we're sick."

I've heard of this practice before. Other cultures and religions do this as well after deaths and such. I'm not superstitious myself, but I'm not closed-minded. "Do you believe in that too?"

"No. She also blames misplacing her glasses on elves and thinks it's bad luck to point your finger at trees at night."

"Huh. Why trees?"

"They have spirits and souls, and I guess they're shy? I don't know."

"Interesting."

"She might be on to something with the mirrors, though. Ever since . . . the other day, whenever I try to look in the mirror, I feel sick."

I search for something comforting to say. "I know it was an accident, but the guilt—"

"No, it's not that," Austin interrupts. "Like, I feel, literally, physically sick. The thought of looking at my reflection is horrible. And the one time that I accidentally passed by the mirror before she covered it, I felt . . ."

I hear footsteps down the hall. "Felt how?"

Austin looks at me, chewing their bottom lip between their teeth. "Scared."

Scared?

I have a million more questions, but the footsteps are getting closer. I'm out of time. I rush for the window. It doesn't open all the way, but it cracks wide enough for me to slip out and brace a hook to belay down. I can feel Austin watching me with an excited smile as I prep my escape. It gives me a tiny spark of pride. I need to solve this case and clear Austin's name, but in the meantime, providing mild amusement while they're stuck in the hospital still feels significant. Maybe that's why, before I climb out, I pause and find myself saying, "I'll be back. I promise."

They smile again. I can see their lips beginning to form the beginning of a *Thank you,* but then the door pushes open. Austin turns to see who's coming and I disappear.

I'm about to lower down to the ground level, but something makes me hesitate. Ms. Baluyot's back, but there's a panicked edge to her voice.

"I don't know what I did wrong that let a monster sneak into our home," Austin's mom says, frustration laced into each syllable. I hesitate, pulling back up high enough to listen without being seen.

"*Mom.*" Austin's tone is sharp. Exasperated.

"Do you still feel its poison inside of you?" Ms. Baluyot presses.

"Please. I can't have this conversation again," Austin says, tapping their finger on the hospital bed's railing. "I feel fine now. There isn't a monster inside me."

"Then it had to have been a curse. Someone cast dark magic on you. We need to undo it."

Austin's shoulders tense. "This isn't some monster, witchcraft thing."

"Then what happened, huh?" Ms. Baluyot crosses her arms. "If you have all the answers, then tell the police. Explain it. How did you hurt that girl?"

Austin sighs. "I . . . I don't know, Ma."

"Well, until you can explain it otherwise, this is what I believe. I called your aunt and she knows a nice man who has experience with these things and can come by and—"

"I don't want some random man who Tia Ynes knows coming here!"

I've heard enough.

Monster. Curse. Dark magic.

Ms. Baluyot's words blend in my mind with Andrew's.

Demons. Witchcraft. Occult occurrences.

I've seen a lot of weird stuff in Gotham City, and nine out of ten times, strange happenings always come down to science, tech, or money. Crimes born of the material world. It's easy to blame monsters, but I believe that humans are often behind what's scary in our world. Still, before I drive home, I watch the video of Austin and Harper one more time. I take in the details: a murderous impulse, a sudden jerk back to reality, no memories. My training wants me to believe that there's a reasonable, logical explanation behind this. But what if there is none?

I have two theories. The first is that Austin is lying and they did know what was happening to them. But the problem with this is that I don't know *why* Austin would then kill a classmate in a room full of witnesses and get themself arrested. From all I can tell, Austin and Harper were friends. No bad blood, but also no supertight friendship that could indicate a relationship gone wrong.

So that leaves my second theory: Austin is telling the truth and they weren't in control of their actions on everything that happened that night.

As soon as I get home, I log in to the public library database and pull up every single book that mentions dark magic involving a loss of control for victims. If any of the sources mention Gotham City, I mark them twice for extra attention.

One word jumps out from every article I pull up: *possession.*

The Dictionary of the Occult describes possession as "the phenomenon in which demons take control of a person's body without their consent." The idea that humans can be "possessed" by the devil, demons, or spirits has been an enduring cultural myth for millennia, if not since the dawn of civilization. Although possession beliefs have been in relative decline over the past century, apparently 40 to 50 percent of the population still believes in demonic possession. If you had asked me last week if I were part of that 40 to 50 percent, I would've laughed and said hell no. But the more I read about the symptoms ... It's getting harder to not believe.

There's an old Arthur Conan Doyle quote that Alfred loves and often recites to us: "When you have eliminated the impossible, whatever remains, however improbable, must be the truth."

Harper's death wasn't a hoax. There's no scientific or technological or known medical explanation for what happened.

I think I understand Alfred's favorite quote now.

I remember Ms. Baluyot's talk about dark magic.

Andrew's log of demonic activity. My own feeling that something was deeply, disturbingly, spiritually wrong in the moments before Harper's death.

Maybe Austin was possessed. A big maybe. *Very* big.

But if that's the case, then what (or who) possessed Austin, and why?

CHAPTER 10

When I reach our meeting spot, Nico smiles at me. A bigger smile than I've ever seen from him before. I didn't even know the guy could smile, let alone smile at me.

"Austin told me you visited them," he says. "Thank you."

"Um." The sensation of being on the receiving end of one of his rare grins momentarily throws me off-balance.

I had asked him and Lily to meet me after sunset behind the abandoned apartment complex on Forty-Second Street. I hope Gotham City officials will one day stop futzing around and actually turn some of these vacant properties into affordable housing, but in the meantime, I admit that all the abandoned, dilapidated buildings are convenient for covert meetups. Tonight Nico is wearing black skate pants and a long-sleeved black shirt with a drawing of a hand reaching out of a grave printed in the center. His pink hair peeks out from beneath his black beanie. Lily hangs off his arm, eyeing me with her usual mix of wariness and amusement.

It's only when Lily clears her throat that I remember why I'm here. I fumble my phone out and hold it up. "Do you recognize any of this?" I ask, skipping the small talk. It's the website for Andrew's Demonic Forces of Gotham Society. The site's designed with a black background, white text, cheesy graphics. Occult symbols galore. Over-embellished, hard-to-read fonts. Extremely predictable.

Nico squints, leaning forward to tap his finger to scroll down the screen. "What is this?"

"It's a group in Gotham City that seems to be very interested in Austin. I'm wondering if you know whether Austin was interested in them too."

"Nah, no way." Nico shakes his head. "Austin's taste in art is kind of creepy, but it comes from a love of horror movies and pop culture. Not . . . whatever this is."

"One time at a sleepover, I tried to get Austin to play with a Ouija board and they literally ran out of the room and made me promise to get rid of it," Lily says. "I doubt they'd ever intentionally mess with people who are into that kind of thing."

Me and Austin both. When it comes to recreationally exploring anything occult, I stay far away. I tend to abide by the ancestral warning of "mind your business." You won't see me walking straight into some spookiness for fun.

"What do you think of all this?" Nico asks, his expression hard to read as his eyes meet mine.

"Well. I'm, uh, starting to consider the possibility that Austin may have been ... possessed?"

I'm not going to lie—I was expecting at least some reaction to my new theory. But all Nico and Lily do is stare back at me blankly and say, "That checks out."

I roll my eyes. How are they so chill with immediately accepting the fact that we might be dealing not with a regular murderer but a literal *demon*? Everyone watches too many movies. Doesn't anyone believe in science anymore?

"So then Austin is the host?" Nico asks.

"That's my current theory. Which means that ..." I try to find the most tactful way to express what's on my mind. "Maybe it is safer for them to be in the hospital for now ... where someone can keep an eye on them. Until we can figure out how to help them." If they aren't in control of their actions, then it's probably best that they're not currently at risk of accidentally hurting someone else. Or at least I don't *think* they're currently a risk. I guess I don't know for sure.

Nico frowns, so I try to explain more.

"I'm sure your family probably wants to bring Austin home immediately to recover, but—"

"Not really," Nico says. "If they're released from the hospital, they go straight into police custody. Murder charge and all."

"Oh." I can't believe I forgot about that part. After seeing Austin, it's so clear to me that they're innocent. Why can't the police see that too? But I guess the evidence they have is pretty . . . damning. Austin was the one performing the trick. Still. Don't they realize that their "evidence" doesn't make any sense?

"You're still going to help Austin, right? Even if they're, uh, consumed by the devil or something?" Nico asks.

"Of course," I say firmly.

Warmth returns to Nico's expression again. He offers another smile, but a smaller one this time.

"Hey, Nico, I'm getting us a taxi. We're late." Lily taps a watch on her wrist that looks brand-new. "We have a school event," she explains to me.

I already know this, though. There's a football game tonight at school. Gotham City is probably the most claustrophobic city in America, with every towering building practically smushed together, but Gotham

Academy is so wealthy that they've managed to snag the ultimate luxury: open space. The one and only nonprofessional football field in the city is owned by the school, a few blocks away from campus.

I'm meeting Alysia at the game tonight too. There's going to be a vigil at halftime for Harper, which should be nice. Obviously, Nico and Lily don't know that I know all this, though, so I offer a chill "Sounds fun."

Nico shifts uncomfortably. "We're right next to the Q line, Lily. We can take the train."

Lily wrinkles her nose. "You know I hate taking the train at night. It's not safe." She turns to me. "You'd know that, right, Batgirl?"

This is clearly an ongoing argument between the two of them, so I choose to stay out of it by murmuring a very eloquent "Hmm."

Lily turns her attention back to the busy street at the end of the alley. "I'll go hail a cab."

"Might be easier to use a rideshare app at this hour," I suggest.

Lily waves a hand lazily. "My phone is broken. Taxis are quicker anyway. I'll be right back."

As Lily walks back into the light of the main street, Nico lingers. He shoves his hands into his pockets, looks around vaguely. He seems anxious.

"You okay?" I ask.

"Lily's my best friend, so I know she doesn't mean

anything by it, but she always does this. She calls cars even though she knows I can't afford it."

"Oh."

"She can. Afford it, I mean. And she always offers to pay, but still." He shrugs awkwardly. "Sorry. I'm oversharing."

"No, it's okay. I get it. I'm also . . ." My mind does a quick calculation, wondering how much I can reveal. I choose my next words carefully. "I don't come from money either. It's awkward when friends don't recognize how not everyone has parents able to give them cash for cars and restaurants and stuff."

"Batman doesn't give you an allowance?"

I laugh loudly. "Why would he do that?"

"I don't know. I've heard the Batmobile is a tricked-out Aston Martin." Nico stretches his arms above his head. The hem of his sweatshirt rises with the gesture, revealing a thin flash of stomach.

"It absolutely is not," I say.

"Well, whatever he drives, his financial backers must have some serious money. I figured he probably gave you some cash every now and then."

I laugh at the idea of Bruce patting me on the shoulder and slipping me a twenty-dollar bill, like some corny uncle in an old movie. "It's not like that."

"How about a salary?"

"I don't do this for money."

"Then why do you do it?"

I'm about to chuckle again, but there's a sincerity to his expression that stops me. He watches me, earnestly waiting for an answer.

"Got one, Nico! Let's go."

We both look in the direction of Lily's voice as she waves up ahead, then back at each other. "So . . . I'll see you soon?" he says, a little nervous, a little hopeful.

He's acting different tonight. Less cagey. Maybe he's getting used to me. Or maybe my surprise visit to Austin changed his perception of me. Either way, I kind of like this more comfortable version of Nico.

This might be a problem.

CHAPTER 11

"**H**ow many people do you think are here for the half-time vigil versus here to see Ryan Alexander's ass in his football costume?"

"I don't think it's called a costume," I tell Alysia.

She pours the last kernels from the bottom of a bag of popcorn into her mouth. "I say it's like ten percent halftime vigil, ninety percent Ryan's ass."

"Alysia!"

"Don't be a saint. What do you think?"

I pause, considering her wildly inappropriate question. "At least sixty-forty."

Alysia scoffs. "Aww, you're so naive, GBG. You have no idea the depth of how vain this school is yet."

My eyes sweep over the crowd and settle on Nico, sitting awkwardly in the far corner of the bleachers while Lily chats with some girls by their side. He looks miserable.

"Why'd he even come tonight?" I ask.

"Imagine what people would say if he didn't come," Alysia says. "Everyone thinks his sibling killed Harper. Showing up here for the vigil shows everyone that he believes in Austin's innocence. It also makes sure that the New Right fools don't keep spewing their manifesto about how Austin and Nico don't belong at our school."

A quick flare of indignation burns in my chest. "They're seriously still on that?"

"Ooh, yeah. Big-time. I heard a couple parents even wrote to the school saying that Nico should be expelled."

"That's ridiculous. He didn't even do anything."

"I know, but some of these legacy families have been waiting to cut the scholarship program for years now. They say bringing in kids from different types of families is 'draining school resources.' Failing to mention that they have nearly limitless resources, of course. They're trying to spin the situation with Austin and Nico to fit their own psycho agenda."

A girl *died*. Are they forgetting that part?

A bitter taste fills my mouth. I believe Austin is

innocent. I have to prove it to everyone else.

"Anyway, it's a smart, strategic move for Nico to show up tonight, if you think about it." Alysia crosses her legs. "Very Model UN of him."

"Nico does Model UN?"

"He did in ninth grade, before he became all emo."

I try to imagine him participating in such a serious extracurricular, and chuckle.

"Are you still pretending that he's not hot?" Alysia asks.

"I'm not—I was never pretending."

"Ahh! So you admit he's hot?"

"What? No? I didn't say that." She wiggles an eyebrow at me. I roll my eyes. "Leave me alone."

She snuggles against my arm. "Never."

Behind me, I hear a throat clear. I recognize the familiar shape in the corner of my eye and tense up. Alysia notices and turns, eager to see who's got me stressed out.

"Well, well, well. Dick Grayson. Nice of you to grace us with your presence," Alysia teases, laying on her most obnoxious flirting voice.

"Hey, Alysia." Dick smiles back, polite as ever. "Haven't seen you in the APC for a while, Babs."

The APC stands for the Advanced Prototyping Center. A few years ago, some major rich alumni donated funds to add a 3D-printing studio on campus.

Apparently, having the best computer science program in the region wasn't enough for the school—they had to go even harder. In reality, though, the space is terribly underused because, again, how many teenagers want to spend their free period playing with laser cutters?

Usually, Dick and I keep a safe distance on campus. Since we're in different grades, we don't have classes together, which helps. But for the first month of the semester, whenever the overwhelming stress of being at a new school would become too much, I'd retreat to the APC for a moment of calm, only to find Dick there as well, working on his own prototypes. The APC is the only place where we ever let ourselves hang out at school. Or, it *was*, at least, until I started avoiding that place like the plague.

"Haven't been in the mood," I say simply.

"Right. That makes sense." He taps his foot anxiously. I've never seen him do that before. He's not one for nervous tics. "I . . . IjustwantedtosayI'msorry." The words tumble out of his mouth like an avalanche.

"For what?" Alysia asks, narrowing her eyes at him. "What'd you do?"

Dick's blue eyes bounce nervously between Alysia and me. "Uh . . ."

"Nothing," I mumble to Alysia, keeping my glare still on Dick. "He didn't do anything."

These past few days of me ignoring his texts is the longest we've gone without talking ever since we first started officially working together. Clearly, he's not taking it well.

"Sooo, what have you been up to?" he mumbles, rubbing the back of his neck. I've never seen him so visibly uncomfortable before. "Anything, uh, exciting?"

I stifle a groan. Everything about this is so awkward. It's like we've never held a conversation before. I want to yank my hair out, but instead I stand abruptly. "I have to go to the bathroom."

I ignore the way Dick's face falls at my blatant attempt to literally run away from him. I don't have time to deal with him. I don't *want* to deal with him.

My Doc Martens clang loudly against the bleachers with each step as I head back to the main school building. In the bathroom, I splash water onto my face. Is there anything more embarrassing than a crush?

At first, I thought I needed some space from Dick because I was mad at what he said and needed some time to cool off and think about things. But after seeing him tonight, my goal has shifted. I don't want to have *any* of these confusing feelings about him anymore. I don't want my heart to go rogue whenever he smiles at me. I don't want to stay up at night thinking about what might happen if we spent more time together outside of the Batcave or school. I don't want to prove the internet trolls right and fulfill my so-called destiny of becoming "Robin's girlfriend."

I glare at my reflection in the mirror. Brown eyes, soft curls, and dry skin because it's windy tonight and I forgot to put on face lotion. I point a finger at the girl in the mirror and scowl. "You will *not* engage with any emotional feelings on this topic any longer, got it?"

Right on cue, the universe responds with a thumbs-up in the form of a perfectly timed distraction: the sickening high-pitched roar of students screaming.

My eyes dart toward the window facing the football field. There had been a sea of lights a minute earlier, but now there's nothing but darkness. Is it a blackout? Probably not, because the lights are still on here in the main building. So only the field lights are down?

I unzip my backpack, pulling out my suit as I dash into a stall to change. I usually bring it with me just in case, but I wasn't planning on doing Batgirl stuff tonight. By the time I'm suited up and back outside, dozens of classmates are running straight at me, yelling.

"What's going on?" I ask one girl, but she only gawks at me with wide eyes and keeps running. Everyone around us is hauling ass away from the field. Except for me. And one guy up ahead.

A faded red jacket flaps behind him in the wind as he sprints, nearly tripping twice as he pulls out his phone. Unfortunately, I recognize him immediately.

"Andrew!" I yell, not bothering to hide the irritation in my voice.

I know he hears me, but he keeps running toward the action anyway. I speed up until I'm matching his stride. "Ignoring me?"

When he finally looks at me, there's a momentary flash of anxiety before a smug smile settles onto his face. "I must've made quite an impression to have Batgirl following me around now."

I roll my eyes. "Why are you here?"

"Same reason as you." He points ahead toward the chaos we're approaching. "Demon stuff."

Demon stuff. It sounds stupid, but that doesn't stop a chill from sneaking down my back.

I stop running abruptly and tug his elbow, forcing him to a stop. "You're not getting anywhere near whatever's going on over there."

"This is public property. You can't stop me."

"This is not public property. It's a private high school."

"Well, it's a free country."

"No, it's not. It's never been."

"Well—"

"Andrew, I don't have time for this, but I swear to god, if you take one step closer and if I see any videos of this online later, I hope you're ready for more bungee jumping. Though next time, I'll leave you hanging in the middle of campus like a piñata."

His eyes narrow. "Is that a threat?"

"Yes." Obviously, it's a threat.

He points at me and wails at the top of his lungs, "Batgirl threatened me!"

Men. Always complaining.

I've reached my capacity for annoying interactions today. I unzip my Utility Belt and throw a Batrope at his ankles. He fumbles for a moment before falling sideways onto the grass. When he drops his phone, I kick it out of reach, then keep running.

By the time I get to the football field, the bleachers for the home team are empty except for Lily and Nico holding the limp shoulders of a terrified sophomore with glasses. The visiting team watches from the other side of the field, clearly confused and wondering if this is some elaborate prank. But the sense of terror is starting to catch. Alysia's nowhere to be found, but I'll look for her later.

"What happened?" I ask when I reach Lily and Nico.

Relief washes over Lily's face when she sees me. "You're here."

I kneel beside the frazzled boy and check him for injuries. Nico hovers beside me, shifting his weight from one foot to the other. "It happened again," he says, voice hoarse.

"His name is Liam. One second, he's standing in line for snacks with his friends. The next, he grabs a knife from behind the concession stand and tries to stab Mr. Henry," Lily explains.

My heart pounds. "How'd you stop him?" I ask.

"I didn't," Nico says. "Liam took off chasing someone else with the knife. They ran across the field and I followed them. Once he turned behind the building, he snapped back to reality. First a murderous rampage, and then standing still, completely disoriented."

"It's crazy to run straight into danger like that when we don't even know what you're dealing with," I tell Nico. "Take someone with you and don't be a hero next time, okay?"

A glint of a smirk escapes from the corner of his mouth. "A little ironic coming from you, of all people."

Beneath my hands, Liam winces.

"There's also, uh . . ." Nico spins the ring on his finger around several times, then points at the wall behind the bleachers. Another bat-symbol. In *purple* spray paint.

Batman doesn't wear purple. But I do. Was that an intentional color choice by whoever left it?

"Two bat-symbols and Batman still hasn't shown up," Lily huffs. "Nico, can you call an ambulance? My phone—"

"Right, yeah," he says hurriedly, fumbling his own phone from his pocket. "Nobody's seen Batman in a while. You sure the guy isn't retired?" Nico asks me while he dials for help.

"Yes, I am sure that he is not retired." I can't let them know that he's undercover. "I'm here, though." I meant for it to sound brave, but it comes out sounding sort of pathetic.

"I know. And I'm grateful." Nico gives me a nod, sealing his vote of confidence. It feels . . . nice. Nice to know that at least he believes in me.

When I hear the faculty coming, I bolt. It's bad enough that I'm regularly interacting with Lily and Nico—I don't need to talk to anyone else while wearing the mask. The fewer people who see me here, the better.

When I check my phone, I have ten texts from Alysia and fourteen missed calls from Dad. He must've heard the emergency call come in and realized that I was probably here at the school too. I tell him that I'm fine before hiding between the tall bushes on the edge of the campus, scanning the crowd for any sign of Alysia. I can't approach her like this in my Batgirl suit, but I can at least make sure she's okay before I go change.

Half the school has already run off, but the faculty are making the stragglers wait behind until our principal can decide on the appropriate protocol for a highly public attempted stabbing at a school event. I spot Alysia, nice and safe, right at the school gate. A wave of relief rolls over me. I'm about to text her some excuse about getting lost in the crowd and that I'll meet her at her house, but I don't get the chance because the lights cut out again.

Everyone screams, but this time, it sounds different. Darker.

This time, everyone knows that when the lights come back on, something terrible will happen.

I spring from my hiding spot, pushing my way into the crowd. If there's another emergency, I'll be here to stop it. This time I'll be ready. This time—

The lights come back on. Everyone spins around wildly, trying to see what—if anything—is about to happen. A familiar school sweatshirt is in front of me.

Alysia.

I touch her shoulder, but when she turns around, I freeze. Alysia's eyes roll back into her head. The whites dissolve into a film of inky black. She leers at me, her breath growing ragged with each inhale. A crooked smile hangs off her face.

CHAPTER 12

My smoke bomb leaves all the bystanders coughing, but it gives me enough time to tackle Alysia before she can wrap her hands around the throat of the girl next to us.

Black shadows swirl around my friend, blending with the gray smoke around us. Amid the marbled mix of foggy air between us, Alysia lunges at me. Her knuckles collide with my jaw with staggering strength. I'm so caught off guard that I nearly fall back onto my ass. I knew she had been taking self-defense classes, but damn. That hurt. She swings again. This time, though, I'm ready. I duck out of the way, sliding to the side.

Her jaw unhinges so she can speak, but the voice that comes out is not her own. There's no trace of the warm trill of Alysia's usual speech. Instead, a low grumble of sounds comes out. A voice like a metal hook dragging along concrete. Nails on a chalkboard. "You got my message."

I falter for a moment. "What?"

But she doesn't respond. She can't, because she's too busy grabbing a fallen tree branch from the ground and trying to stab me in the eye.

My possession theory rapidly solidifies into fact: This is *not* Alysia.

The smoke around us is clearing. I catch glimpses of our classmates' faces through the fading fog, see tiny flashes of cellphone cameras. I can't do this here with her. Whether or not I'm trying to save her, I can't have any videos surfacing of Batgirl fighting a student at Gotham Academy on school grounds. I need to get Alysia and myself out of here—*fast*.

Surprised yelps sound out from the crowd around us. The smell of burnt rubber fills the air as a red motorcycle skids right up to my side.

"Not you," I mumble, but there's no time to complain about the driver. I'm handed a black helmet and put it on quickly. I drag a thrashing Alysia onto the back of Robin's bike, squeezing her in between the two of us. With a

jolt, we tear down the entry steps of Gotham Academy and spill onto the street, escaping the crowd and the sound of cheers punctuated with loud marriage proposals directed at Robin.

Great.

Just *great.*

Alysia snarls and thrashes between us. She goes for my neck, breaking skin with her sharp nails. But by the time we reach the street corner, she calms down. Thank god. Who knew this girl had so much fight in her?

Alysia takes a long, slow blink. When she opens her eyes, they're back to normal—crisp, clear, human. She takes in her surroundings on the bike, still moving nearly fifty miles per hour, and reflexively reaches behind to tighten her arms around me. "Where am I?"

There have been very few situations where I've had to interact with someone I know well in my regular life while in disguise. Bruce has this whole other super-deep voice he uses with the mask on, which sounds intimidating as hell. Dick does this thing where he barely speaks at all, and if he does, he keeps his voice completely emotionless and free of any of his usual speech patterns. I'm still working on my own Batgirl voice. But given that I talk to Alysia literally every single day, it's important that I don't mess this up. I clear my throat.

"You're okay. You were—" I struggle to actually say

the word *possessed* out loud. It still feels too new, too crazy. "You were attacked, but you're safe now. We'll drop you off in a minute."

Alysia narrows her eyes, examining me. I can tell she's trying to make out my face. Luckily, my helmet is tinted.

"She okay?" Robin asks. His voice comes in loud and clear through the built-in microphone communication system linking our helmets together. It's useful to drown out the roar of the motorcycle and dense traffic around us.

"Looks like it," I reply.

"Glad your smoke bombs work," Robin says. I can hear the hint of a smile in his voice. I hold back a laugh. He's still mad about last month, when I replaced one of his smoke bombs with a glitter bomb. The prank war started after he felt like I'd wrongly called shotgun in the Batmobile during a mission with Bruce and ended with Alfred lecturing us both about how harpoons are tools, not toys. Just thinking about it makes the laughter dry up in my throat. A few days ago, everything was normal between us. I miss it. I miss it so much that I get mad all over again at our stupid hug and the stupid internet and our stupid feelings for ruining everything.

"Drop her off at the next corner," I tell Robin. We're close enough to Alysia's home now without looking too suspicious that I know more about her than I should. She half stumbles off the bike. I readjust my position, seating myself more comfortably behind Robin. I glance back at Alysia to make sure she's okay, but she's just standing there. Staring.

"Everything okay?" I ask.

"Aren't you going to explain to me what happened? I have no memories of the past . . . well, I don't even know how long. But the last thing I remember was standing in front of the school and now I'm looking at two of Gotham's most elusive vigilantes sharing a motorcycle."

I do want to hear Alysia's account of what happened, but not like this. It will be easier to talk to her normally, outside of the mask.

"You're safe now. There were no injuries. We don't know much else," Dick says authoritatively.

"But we are working on it," I add.

"Okay. Well. Thanks, then." Alysia's eyes skate over Robin, then me. Her worried expression slips into amusement. A tiny smirk spreads across her face. She doesn't say anything, but I know what she's thinking. The rumors. I reflexively shift backward in my seat, adding a couple extra inches between myself and Robin, who is still crouched over the handles of the motorcycle. It takes all my strength to not scream at her, *We are not dating!*

My best friend, Alysia: always a gossip, even in the wake of a possession. Unreal.

Robin guns the engine and we take off.

The demon is back and I need more information. I need the big computer. "Can you give me a ride to the Batcave?"

CHAPTER 13

Gotham City passes by in a blur. Taxicabs honk over the rumble of the subway beneath us. Neon billboards slash light through dark gray clouds that hang low in the sky, threatening rain. Without Alysia, we drive faster. Robin weaves between traffic, lane splitting and hugging the turns tightly. The bustle of the city center fades behind us, and soon we pull into the secret tunnel of the Batcave.

Once we're inside, Dick takes off his helmet. His dark hair is messy, sticking out in all directions. It's cute like this. I hate that I think it's cute like this. I look away and head into the main chamber.

An armor rack holds a spare suit for Dick, red-breasted, with a proud *R* beside the space where Bruce's battle gear would be if he were in town. The cave has several areas—smaller offshoots of the main den. There's a well-equipped med bay, a target range, a gym, a sparring dojo, and Bruce's favorite room: the garage. The main walkway winds its way throughout the rooms, ending in an elevator leading to the mansion above.

Prototypes of new Wayne Tech gadgets hang from the walls above shelves filled with Bruce's mismatched collection of trophies and mementos. A glass case memorializing Dick's very first set of armor from when he was a kid stands proudly in the darkness. I know it embarrasses him to see it on display, but turns out Batman is a little sentimental.

I tap the keyboard on the massive computer. Three huge screens in front of me hum to life, bathing me in artificial light. I blink as my eyes adjust to the brightness. Around me, the deep expanse of the cave looms. I use a backdoor password I configured a while back to log in, so that Bruce won't be able to see my search history. Hopefully, I'll have solved the case by the time he returns home, but while I'm still working behind his back, every detail counts. Information spills across the monitors: news briefings, police calls, weather reports. An even larger screen to my right blinks to life, displaying pending case files. I try not to work here often; I don't want to rely on Bruce too much, but every now and then, I take advantage of the resources that he's offered to share with me.

After seeing Alysia's eyes morph into dark orbs tonight, I know that this case is far from normal. I need to think outside the box. I need to consider the improbable.

I skim everything on possession in the online archives from the Museum of the Occult in London. A demon enters the human realm if you open a "door." The door acts as a portal between the demon world and ours. According to several accounts, doors can be demonic objects, occult books, rituals, oaths, conversations with the dead, Ouija boards, mirrors, and water.

At Austin's show, there was no sign of water, mirrors, or a Ouija board, so it's safe to rule those out. The wand they were using could potentially be a demonic object. Austin's performance in itself could theoretically be considered a ritual—it was an art project, but they were leaning into the whole horror thing, so maybe they could've opened a door accidentally? Is that even possible?

Working a case is all about looking for patterns. It's my favorite part of both computer programming and detective work. If you take your time to review all the details, patterns emerge. And patterns tell stories. I try to connect the dots to find the story hiding in what I know so far:

Nobody has been possessed twice.

The possessions so far have lasted only a few minutes.

The possessions cause the victims to become violent.

The victims were always in a group setting in the moments leading up to the possession.

It tends to coincide with a blackout of some sort.

The blackout element is especially interesting. Is the demon only able to move in the dark, or are the blackouts merely a way to hide the origin of where the demon is emerging from?

There's still so much I don't know. Harper was killed, but the possessions tonight were much more restrained than hers. Nobody died, which is great, but also weird, given that the demon is clearly capable of killing people if it wants to. If the demon only wants to murder, then it could do so easily. But it didn't tonight. So then what's the motive?

This isn't a typical situation where a single demonic entity is preying on one single host or a poltergeist is haunting a specific location. There have been three victims in three places so far—Austin, Liam, and Alysia— each one driven to attack others once possessed. All my research says that a demonic entity must be tied to one host at a time. And the process of binding a demon to a host is complicated—it usually involves some form of ceremony or ritual. But all three of these hauntings occurred quickly out of nowhere. The bond was broken quickly as well, without any lingering side effects, to my knowledge. Whatever we're dealing with may have one host that it's bound to permanently, but it's clearly attacking other people as well in the form of temporary possession. So we're not dealing with a static entity that stays with one host all the time; we're dealing with . . .

"A body jumper." The words tumble out of my mouth on their own.

"What'd you say?" Dick asks. He's at his own workbench on the opposite wall, tinkering with the tech on a glider prototype he's been building.

I may not want to hang out with Dick at the moment, but we still work together, and as much as I'd like to pretend that he's useless, Dick is smart. And more experienced than me. I could use his input. "Maybe I've done a little *too* much research, but I think that whatever has been happening at Gotham Academy is the result of a body jumper—a demon," I say, not quite believing those words are coming out of my mouth.

"A body jumper. Hmm." Dick hums vaguely as he

connects a cord between his prototype and his laptop. "Unusual, but not unheard of."

"Have you ever dealt with something like this before?" I ask.

"Bruce deals with supernatural stuff every now and then. He's definitely gotten an occult consultation from this guy named Constantine before. Pretty sure he had to fight a vampire once when I was in middle school. And I think he almost dated a magician—like, *real* magic—before he adopted me. He won't tell me about her, but I've overheard Alfred making fun of him for it." He pauses. "I think she was hot."

"*Thank you,* Dick. Very helpful detail."

"So the answer is yes—there has been weird stuff like this in Gotham City before. No, I personally have no experience with it."

I wish I could ask Bruce for advice, but since he can't know I'm working against his orders, I do the next best thing: open up his old case log. For security reasons, I don't have remote access to the entirety of Bruce's case files except at the Batcave, so I take the opportunity of working here to comb through hundreds of documents. I'm looking for any clues, any hints, literally *anything* that might provide a blueprint for how the hell to deal with demonic entities.

Dick and I settle back into silence as we work on opposite ends of the room. After a while, Dick stands from the stool at his workbench and vanishes down the hall-way that leads to the storage room. My eyes itch to follow his movement, but I resist. Even when he returns, I commit myself to not looking at him. I'm so focused on *not* visibly focusing on Dick that I'm caught off guard when my view of the computer screen is suddenly blocked. Dick drapes a knit blanket around my shoulders, his touch impersonal but gentle as he makes sure it's in place before returning to his side of the room without a word. I take a moment too long to react but eventually manage to murmur a soft "Thanks." I actually was cold—it's always a refrigerator in the cave—though I hadn't noticed I was shivering until the blanket was around me. Dick gives a short hum of acknowledgment, his attention already back on his project.

My frustration with Dick softens slightly at the gesture, which is ridiculous because is a blanket really all it takes to confuse me again? Pathetic. I can't believe I'm down this bad. Maybe it wasn't a good idea to work here with him tonight.

It takes way more focus than it should, but I force myself to keep skimming through Bruce's previous cases and the corresponding local news coverage for each crisis. I don't find anything specifically about possession, but I flag a few reports of strange murders and accusations of people suddenly not acting like themselves. Who's to say if these were due to possession or just a symptom of how life in Gotham City can eventually break someone?

There's nothing in here about a demon either, but there is something about a fight a few years ago with someone named Doctor Thirteen? Who, according to the file, is a professional skeptic and debunker of magic? Honestly, anyone with experience as an occult investigator could come in handy.

"Hey, Bird Boy," I call out.

Dick spins around on his stool. "Yeah?"

"What do you know about Doctor Thirteen?"

Dick scoffs. "That he's crazy. Why?"

Well, there goes that idea. "Never mind."

"His daughter is cool, though. Her name's Traci 13."

"Is she a professional skeptic too?"

"No. Actually, she's a mage herself. That's why her relationship with her dad is so messed up. He's this anti-magic extremist, even though his own daughter was literally born with a powerful connection to magic. They don't talk very much these days, obviously."

Growing up with a professional skeptic parent as a mage herself must've been horrible. But that also means she's probably seen a lot—both real magic and seemingly supernatural stuff that's turned out to be fake.

"Do you think she'd mind if I hit her up?" I ask. A consult would be amazing.

"I'm sure she'd be happy to help. I'll text you her number."

"Thanks."

Dick shares her contact, then taps his phone against his forehead. "Also, earlier tonight . . . right before I drove up, Alysia said something to you, didn't she?" His voice is cautious. "Or I guess it wasn't Alysia. But Evil Alysia. What'd she say?"

"She said 'You got my message.' "

"Weird."

"For a second, I thought maybe she meant, like . . ." I remember the purple bat-symbol at the scene. "Like, maybe this thing has been trying to reach out to *me*, literally." I try to say it breezily, even though a sudden wave of self-consciousness makes the words stick in my throat.

Dick hums in thought. "Potentially. Whatever's behind these attacks could be trying to use you as bait to get to Bruce."

Every muscle in my body goes completely still. *"Bait?"*

"Yeah, you know. Target teenagers, leave bat-symbols to get you to investigate, then when you get close, *boom*. They use you to get to Batman." He says it so casually. Too casually. "Happens all the time. Villains sometimes use people's girlfriends or daughters or . . ."

"Or any girl with ties to a hero?" I cross my arms. My voice is shaking with anger, but Dick doesn't seem to notice.

"Don't worry," he says. "That's just one theory. It's unlikely. You'll be fine."

I'll be *fine*? How can he talk about my role in this space so dismissively? We've come a long way since our early aversion to each other, but deep down does he still think of me like this? As disposable?

Well, screw that. I gather my bag and leave without saying goodbye. Robin is an idiot. I'm not *bait*. I'm not a stepping stone. And if whoever—whatever—is behind these attacks thinks that I am, then I'll show them how wrong they are too.

CHAPTER 14

The phone rings twice before someone picks up on the other end. "Hello— *OHMYGOD.*"

A girl with waist-length black hair floats out of my phone and into my room. Like, *literally* into my room. Life-sized. And translucent.

"Nice room," she says, looking at my posters on the wall like it's no big deal.

I drop the phone immediately.

Traci 13 is wearing a cropped tee, baggy green lounge pants, and a mischievous smile. I should respond, but I'm too busy trying to pick up my jaw from the floor. I didn't expect her to be around Robin's and my ages—but she looks no older than seventeen. I also obviously did not expect her to appear out of thin air like a freaking ghost. I lean forward to experimentally swipe my hand through her shimmering form, but I stop myself. Would touching a magic-ghost-hologram be rude? I think it'd be rude. "How . . . how are you doing this?"

She laughs, her voice high-pitched and bright. "Astral projection."

Okay. Wow. Didn't even know that was possible. I try to play it cool, though. "Right."

"Everyone's been curious about Batgirl," Traci says, her wide smile beaming. "The others are going to be *so* jealous that I'm the first one you reached out to."

My eyebrows shoot up my face. Who are "the others"?

Traci 13—or her astral projection, I guess—paces around my room. "I can't wait to tell M'gann we met. Jaime's probably eavesdropping on the other side of my door back in Metropolis, but I promise I won't tell him anything. Oh, and Donna will—"

I shrink a little at the information overload. "Um."

"Right. Sorry! I'm talking too much." She stops pacing and whirls around to face me. "So, what's up?"

I clear my throat. "I, uh, am having trouble with a case. There was an incident at a student art show in Gotham City. Someone was killed in the middle of a performance. There were all these shadows and noises. At first, I thought it was fake, but now I'm not so sure." I pull out my phone. "Do you mind if I show you the footage? Though I should warn you—it's . . . graphic."

Traci's face slips into stern focus. She nods and I play the video. She watches the screen intently, covering her mouth when she gasps. "Were you there when this happened?"

"Yeah. I thought it had to be a hoax at first. But then it happened again last night, twice, and I think that maybe it's not a normal situation."

Traci smirks. "You mean magic?"

"Potentially. I think that these students are being . . . possessed. Maybe by a body-jumping entity?" I wait for Traci to laugh or tell me that I'm way off, but she just keeps watching me intently. I go on. "I don't have any experience with the supernatural, though, so I wanted a professional opinion."

Traci tilts her head to the side, swift and birdlike. "How did the air feel?"

"It felt . . . like air?"

"Did it feel any different than usual, though? When the girl was floating, did it feel kind of heavy and claustrophobic? Or did it feel thin, like you were on top of a mountain?"

I try to remember the way my body felt in that moment. "I guess the first time it happened, it was difficult to catch my breath, but I figured that was because of the fear gas." Traci raises an eyebrow. "There's this villain in Gotham City who sells the stuff illegally," I explain. "A nightmare-inducing toxin. It sucks. The performer leaked a small dose into the crowd to freak us out as part of the act."

Traci looks thoroughly disturbed. "Wow. Gotham City is, uh, really . . ."

"Yeah, I know. It's home, though," I say firmly, shutting down any potential *Why would anyone in their right mind choose to live there?* jokes.

Traci takes the hint. "Right. Of course." She shakes her shoulders. "Well, based on the videos, I think you're right. Whatever magic was at play led to some sort of disassociation or loss of control, or, as you said, demonic possession."

"I read that demons can only enter our realm if someone opens a door. Could someone do that by accident?"

"Of course. Happens all the time. I can't tell you how many stories I've heard about people who mess with cursed objects and then are shocked to realize that dark magic is real and now there's a demon living in their basement."

"But if the first victim, Austin, potentially opened a door—accidentally or not—then why didn't the demon stick with them? There were two more possessions, but Austin was in the hospital over a mile away. How could this thing be traveling between people so easily? And if it could theoretically haunt anyone, why would it haunt two more students at the same school?"

"Well, first off, I don't believe that this thing can haunt *anyone* at any time. Even in the world of the supernatural, there are limits to dark magic." She taps her chin. "A door can be opened accidentally, but typically, there's no way for a demon to fully take over someone's will unless they surrender to it. Temporary possession can happen unexpectedly, but a permanent connection? That requires a contract between the host and the demon. Then the demon has to physically enter the body of its host. In my experience, it's a messy, painful process. Doesn't usually happen in the blink of an eye."

"So to find the demon, I need to find the host, right?" I ask.

"Seems like a good place to start."

It's awesome that Traci knows so much about this, but I kind of want to ask . . . *how* she knows. About possession, specifically. I don't understand the scope of her magical powers, and I don't want to be rude, but if she has firsthand experience . . .

"You can ask me, you know," Traci says.

My eyes widen. "Please don't tell me you can read minds too."

She laughs. "No. Can't read minds. But I can read body language—just like you. You have more questions for me. I can tell."

"Right. Okay." I swallow. "Please stop me if this is, like, intrusive or anything, but . . . are you able to possess people?"

Traci grimaces. "I can cast a very limited possession spell, giving me limited control over someone's body." She bites her lip, casting her gaze down to the floor. "I hate doing it, though. I've only ever done it once. I never want to do it again."

"Can I ask why?"

"It feels . . . invasive. As vigilantes, we enter gray areas all the time. It's part of the job. But there's something about possession that feels wrong to me. I don't think it's fair to put moral judgments on powers—if we did, a lot of us would be stuck carrying a lot of shame. And with any ability, it's never the skill itself that makes a person a hero or a villain, but *how* the person uses it. But I don't know. I guess it makes sense to me why demons love possession so much. It's a dark thing to want to take over someone else's body, their mind."

I shudder. I feel bad for the host of whatever demon is terrorizing Gotham Academy. The host may have formed a contract with the demon, but who's to say they did it willingly? Maybe they were coerced into saying yes? Wouldn't be the first time that someone's been pressured into doing something they don't want to do.

"You're not able to get rid of demons, are you?" I ask.

"Not any easier than you or anyone else. They're tricky. I heard a mage got possessed by a demon once and it killed him. It's a dangerous mix."

Fantastic. Apparently even a literal mage can't fight a demon. Meanwhile, I'm a powerless human with zero supernatural experience. I let my hand fall onto the table and groan. Traci's soft laugh rings in the air above me. My phone vibrates against my desk. I want to ignore it, but Traci motions at the shaking device. "If someone's calling, it's probably important."

She's right. I text practically everyone I know. If I'm getting a call, it's either Alfred, Bruce, or Dad.

"Blocked caller ID," I say aloud.

"Interesting," Traci says. "Answer it."

I click the green button and wait for the caller to speak first. After a moment of silence, a hoarse voice comes through. "Babs?"

I groan. Again.

"Please don't hang up," Dick says on the other line.

"Why are you calling me from a blocked number?"

"Because you wouldn't have picked up if you knew it was me."

"That is correct." I've been extra ignoring him ever since he shared his stupid Batgirl Bait theory. And that was on top of our whole other . . . situation. Argument.

Whatever you call it. The boy's been on a streak pissing me off lately.

"Can we talk?" Dick asks.

"I'm busy."

"But—"

"I said I'm *busy.*"

I can hear him swallow. "Okay. Sorry. I'll try you another time, then."

I click End before he can say anything else. Doesn't he believe that *I* have better things to do than talk to him? More important things?

"Sooo, that sounded like a totally fine, not-at-all-hostile conversation between friends," Traci says. "Who was that?"

"Robin."

"Oh, right. *Riiight!*" Traci grins.

"It's not like that," I say, a little too loud. I rein it in. "Sorry. I just mean it's complicated."

"Of course." Traci lets the knowing smirk drop immediately. "In that case, I'm sorry."

"For what?"

"For all the rumors online."

I can respect a straight shooter. No use in playing dumb now.

"Want to talk about it? I've dated not one, but *two* other heroes, and each time has been, well, messy. There's the friendship, then the relationship, then the work partnership." She gives me a sympathetic smile. "I've been there, is what I'm saying."

Complaining about Robin wasn't on the to-do list for today, but given that I don't actually have anyone else in my life to talk to about this . . . Traci doesn't even live in Gotham City . . . so what's the harm in getting a few things off my chest?

"Part of me might . . . I don't know. I see potential. But at the same time, I don't want to be 'Robin's girlfriend.' I want to be Batgirl. But if I'm with him, nobody will care who I am. They'll only see me as the girl dating Robin."

Traci huffs. "But that isn't who you are."

"I know, but that's not what other people will think."

"You can't worry about what other people will think. No one can tell you who you are but yourself."

She's just saying whatever to be nice, but I force a smile at her anyway. "Thank you for today," I say after a beat of silence. "Please let me know if there's an opportunity for me to return the favor. For the advice about the case and the, uh . . ."

"And the never-ending cycle of shame, self-doubt, and judgment that comes from being an independent girl in the male-dominated world of heroes?" Traci supplies.

I laugh. "Exactly."

"Will do, Batgirl."

I wait for Traci's astral projection to disappear or go back into my phone or do whatever it does when it's time to end, but Traci lingers, her face serious once again.

"There are all kinds of demons," she says. "They appeal to different emotions in their victims. Narcissism, greed, anger, self-harm, lust, pride. Try to watch out for a pattern and see if you can understand what's beneath the surface. If it's repeatedly attacking students at the same school, then it's clearly trying to make a point." It sounds crazy. But also reasonable. When had the game shifted so much that crazy is now reasonable?

And with that, she vanishes, though I have no idea how. An unsettling reminder of how much there is in this world that I do not understand.

CHAPTER 15

When Alysia walks into the auditorium the Monday
after the football game possession, all eyes fall
on her. Miraculously, she holds her composure, squaring
her shoulders and smoothing her hands down the neatly
ironed pleating of her skirt as she sits next to me. Even
the headmaster stops to stare at her warily. Whispers
buzz around us in all directions.

I discreetly pull out my noise-canceling earbuds and
pass them to her. Wordlessly, she places them in her ears,
which are adorned with several gold hoop piercings.
From the corner of my eye, I detect that Alysia is clenching her jaw, steeling her gaze straight ahead in a valiant
attempt to ignore the intrusive glares of our classmates.

I grab the hand resting on her knee and squeeze. She squeezes back. This is friendship.

School starts with a very heavily rehearsed speech from the administration. I can practically feel the PTA breathing down the headmaster's neck as he recites in diplomatic terms how the school is doing everything in their power to get to the bottom of the "recent *events*" that have afflicted the school community. I'm not sure exactly what the school is doing to proactively solve the situation, but I'm guessing their strategy involves a lot of media damage control, press releases, and careful emails to donors. The first incident with Austin and Harper was a tragedy. The twin hauntings at the football game are officially a full-blown PR disaster.

Nico and Lily are among those leaning along the back wall of the auditorium. I glance their way, but they don't even look twice at me. Not like they have any reason to. They like Batgirl. They don't care about Barbara Gordon.

The stares and whispers continue throughout the assembly. Some people think Alysia was faking it. Some people think that she must be sick and that whatever affected her must be contagious. But for the most part, the energy in the room is somber, quiet fear.

Gotham Academy is under attack.

Anyone is a target.

Nobody knows who's next.

I walk Alysia to her next class after assembly. "How are you doing?" I ask.

She tightens the straps of her backpack, hurries her pace. "I don't want to talk about it."

I don't think that's healthy. "Well, I know nobody was hurt, but it still looked scary and was probably—"

"I *said* I don't want to talk about it."

I recoil a little in shock. Alysia never raises her voice at me. "Sorry. Understood."

"Thank you." She chews her lip. "So, did you have a long night after the game?" Her voice is tight. Annoyed.

"What do you mean?" I ask cautiously.

"Where'd you disappear to? Must've been pretty damn important, since you didn't bother to call to make sure I made it home safe."

Damn. I *did* make sure, obviously. I literally drove her home. Just not as . . . me.

"I'm so sorry."

"Whatever."

"Alysia, really, I'm—"

"*It's fine.*" Her words are curt. "My phone's dead, but I need to call my dad. Can I use yours?"

"Uh, sure," I say. She snatches my phone as soon as I hold it out, then sulks a few feet away to take her call. I look away to give her some privacy, but I'm trying not to panic here. She's mad. Big mad. How can I make this right while still keeping my secrets?

Before I can dissolve into a full-blown friendship-crisis spiral, Alysia's beside me again, shoving my phone back into my hand. "I'll see you after school," she says, then stomps away before I can make things right.

Classes drag by in an oppressive haze. Physically, I am at school. Mentally, I am yearning for the first moment possible to sneak off into the shadows and disappear. I hate that Alysia's mad at me. I hate that she got possessed because I haven't made any progress in the case yet. I hate that I have to suffer through the motions of school when all I want to do is investigate.

During lunch, I can't find Alysia. She's probably hiding in the art room, taking her anger at her allegedly careless best friend out on a canvas. I almost walk to the APC, but then the thought of Dick potentially being there makes me stop short. Guess I'm eating alone today.

I sulk over to the bleachers overlooking the staff parking lot. Right before I sit, a piece of paper taped to a light pole catches my eye. I squint to get a better look and immediately groan. "You've got to be kidding me."

The flier reads:

Have you seen this demonic host?

Have any tips on who the host might be?

Scan the QR code below for reward!

Of course Andrew would put up signs hunting down a demonic host as if he's looking for a lost cat. I snatch the flyer down and scan the QR code. It takes me to a website featuring a video of demonic conspiracy theories, a sketchy contact form, and an invitation to their next group meeting. I'm tempted to close the page and forget about it, but I notice that the video has a lot of views. Like, *a lot*. Two thousand one hundred and forty-seven, to be exact. Is this site actually making its way around campus?

"Uuugh." I crumple up the paper and hurl it into the nearby bin. I'm already under enough pressure to solve this case. The last thing I need is some internet troll competing with me to find the host first. Why is he even so obsessed with this in the first place? Doesn't anyone have normal hobbies anymore?

The new group meeting is in a few days. There's no location listed on the invitation. Instead, it says: *Those who wish to join us, please complete the contact form. Serious occult enthusiasts + Gotham Academy students only.*

So Andrew has also figured out that the host is most likely a student here. Great.

I allow myself a tiny sigh of frustration before anonymously filling out the contact form. I pretend to be the kind of person Andrew would trust to share the meeting location with, which means that I send the most unhinged message possible. If there's even a small chance that any of my classmates are actually going to this thing, I have to be there. Who knows what Andrew's planning, what he's trying to loop people into. Plus, there's also a very tiny part of me that wonders what Andrew might know that I don't. He did accurately anticipate the possession at the game, after all, so . . . I don't know.

Maybe the creep is on to something.

I wanted to visit Austin again after school, but Alysia insists on hanging out. I'm on thin ice with her, so I agree to her plans enthusiastically.

"Hey, girls!" Dad welcomes us as we walk into my house. He's home early—a rare occurrence. I haven't seen him much this week. This happens occasionally, when he gets slammed with work. It doesn't help that our schedules are opposite—during the day, I'm at school; during the night, he's often at work. He always makes sure to be home with me a couple times a week, but as I've gotten older, we've grown accustomed to the rhythm of only passing each other briefly for days on end. I don't like it this way. I don't think he does either. But it is what it is.

It's almost dinnertime, and he's standing over the stove cooking eggs. It's pretty much the only thing he knows how to cook, but I still wouldn't call him a pro at it. He always overcooks them. "You hungry?" he asks us.

"Alysia's vegan now, but I'll have a bite," I say.

The corners of his eyes crinkle as he smiles at me, sliding half of the portion onto a small plate. Dad's totally different on his days off with me. He's warmer, less stressed.

He holds up a jar of fruit preserves, and Alysia nods. He smears two pieces of toast for Alysia, then puts two plates on the table for us, mine next to a small glass bottle of hot sauce. This is our comfort food. It always has been. I take a bite and let the spicy sauce soothe my brain.

Dad wipes his hands on a napkin, then gives Alysia a long hug. "I'm glad you're okay, kid."

Alysia looks at my father with a small smile. "Thanks, Mr. Gordon."

"Hey, Dad." I shove a bite of eggs in my mouth. "Isn't it funny how you wanted me to go to a better school, but now the 'better school' is haunted?"

He wipes a crumb from his bushy mustache. "Ha, ha, ha."

"You should've let me stay at Gotham High."

"And insult the generosity of Bruce Wayne? No way."

What? I nearly choke. "What about Bruce Wayne?"

"He funded the scholarship that you won."

"I thought you said that you pulled some strings to get me in."

"I did. One string. Bruce Wayne is the string. Is that a problem?"

"Nope." It's not a problem at all that everyone is meddling in my life and I'm the last person to find out about it. It's fantastic, really, how they were nice enough not even to tell me such an important detail about something that affects *me* directly. I chew my eggs angrily.

"Uh, how's the investigation going, by the way? About the Gotham Academy stuff?" Alysia asks out of nowhere. She's always been good at knowing exactly when to break the tension in a room.

Dad notices my frostiness but ignores it for the sake of continuing the conversation with Alysia. "The department thinks it might be a drug thing. Some new pill targeting teenagers."

I grit my teeth. How could GCPD be *so* off base?

"Do you believe that?" I ask him.

"No. Of course not," he says, firmly. He looks directly at Alysia, who's gone quiet. "I don't believe that at all. I promise."

Alysia relaxes a bit at his reassurance. At least my dad isn't clueless, like the rest of his department. He might not know everything happening at all times, but he's no fool.

"Are they going to drop the charges against Austin?" Alysia asks.

"The first kid? No, no way. A student died. We can't let the only suspect walk just because they claim they blacked out during the incident. What would we tell the victim's family? 'We're sorry that your child died, but the kid who killed her says it was an accident, so we've let them go'?"

"But if there are other victims, doesn't that give credence to Austin's story that they weren't in control?" I ask.

"Yes. But still." Dad sighs. "Look. I believe the kid. When they leave the hospital, I don't want to see them leaving in a police car. But there's a process to follow. Protocol . . ." I twist my face like I smell something foul. Dad notices. "Following protocol helps prevent abuse and mishandling of cases. This system isn't perfect, I know, but it's all we have for now. So I'm doing my best to—"

"Yeah, yeah, yeah. Bureaucracy. Incremental change. Got it."

A tense silence.

"It's strange stuff, though. GCPD might be out of our league with this one," Dad continues. "If only Batman were here. The attacker keeps leaving him bat-symbols."

I poke around my plate, trying not to scowl. "Batman's not the only vigilante in Gotham City." I take a sip of water and try to make my voice sound as casual as possible. "How do you know they're trying to get Batman's attention and not, like, Batgirl's or something?"

Dad looks at me for a moment, mid-sip of his coffee. Then he bursts out laughing.

Nice. I try not to take it too personally, but it still stings. Is it so ridiculous that someone could be looking for Batgirl specifically?

"Thanks for the snack, but Alysia and I have a lot of homework," I announce.

"Good luck," Dad says.

Dad gives me a hug, the familiar smell of his aftershave soothing away my lingering annoyance at him. He's not perfect, but he is my dad. And he is trying.

Alysia shuts my bedroom door behind us, then clears her throat. "Hey, so, earlier at school, when I snapped at you—"

"It's all right. We don't have to talk about it."

"The whole being-out-of-control-of-my-body thing kind of brought up some . . . stuff." I swear I see a tiny swell of tears, but Alysia blinks it away before I can be sure. "When I was younger, I spent a lot of time feeling disassociated from my body. Back then, the idea of jumping into someone else's body seemed amazing to me. I had no idea that it'd feel so wrong." Her voice shrinks, becoming small and quiet. "Even before I transitioned, I never wanted to be somebody else, necessarily—I just wanted to be me." She clears her throat. "I don't want to get into it now, but all of this dredged up a whole lot of body-dysmorphia horror vibes."

"Alysia . . ." I didn't consider how uniquely triggering an experience like this could be for her. I feel ignorant. "Thank you for telling me that. And I'm sorry you felt out of control of your body again. That must've been terrible."

The strained look on Alysia's face reignites my fire to solve this case. No more victims, no more possessions. Nobody should ever have to feel that way.

"Thanks, GBG." Alysia leans her head on my shoulder. "Do you have any Advil? I think I feel a headache coming on," she says, definitively shutting down the conversation. I know it's hard for her to be vulnerable about certain things, so I don't push.

"Sure, in the bathroom, right-hand drawer." I open my history homework as Alysia rummages in the bathroom. "I saw this thing online that says everyone is either a Headache Girl or a Tummyache Girl," I call to her from the bed.

"Alas, I fear I am both girls. I never know if I want to throw up or take a nap."

I keep my eyes on my screen as I type. "Yeah, well, I guess that means you're the chosen one. God gives her hardest battles to her strongest soldiers."

I hear Alysia open and close my medicine cabinet. "Hey, also, another quick question."

"Yeah, what's up?"

"When were you going to tell me that you're Batgirl?"

Time stops.

My hands freeze so abruptly that I drop my laptop. It slides from my knees onto the rug with a soft thud. When I look up, Alysia is standing in the doorway between my room and the bathroom, dangling a black faux-leather pouch from her pinky. I swallow.

"I'm not—"

"No! Don't do that." Alysia throws the pouch at my face. I'm too shocked to move, so it hits me right on the nose. "If you're not Batgirl, then what's all this?"

By "all this" she means the makeup bag she just threw at my face. It contains an ungodly amount of black eye makeup. Normally, having a makeup bag shouldn't raise any alarms, but . . .

"You never wear makeup!" Alysia shouts.

This is true. Barbara Gordon doesn't do makeup. Batgirl does. I use it to cover the skin around my eyes that my mask doesn't cover. Batgirl's ruby-red lips have also proven to be an interesting diversion from the Plain Jane face of Barbara Gordon.

"I'm saving it for a special occasion." I glance at the bedroom door nervously, making sure it's shut in case my dad can hear us.

"Liar. It's all half-used. And none of it's old. I would

know. You think this smoky eye does itself?" She points at her own makeup as if presenting evidence to a judge.

I sit on top of my hands so she can't see them shaking. "Okay, so I own makeup. That doesn't mean anything."

"Fine. Then how about this?" Alysia crosses her arm and circles me like a shark. "My supervisor at the eighty-eight eighty-eight hotline told me that they've never, *ever*, received calls from vigilantes before, but since I've started interning there, we've received three. All from Batgirl."

Oh.

That's . . . harder to explain.

Ever since the first situation with the guy at the grocery store who clearly didn't want to hurt anyone, I've called 88-88 instead of GCPD on a few occasions. Alysia's always talking about how good their resources are and I haven't seen any of the folks I've diverted there on the streets since. It makes sense to keep giving 88-88 a shot when appropriate.

"Batgirl watches the news. Completely normal activity for her, I would imagine," I say, vaguely.

"Okay, so you want to play hardball? Fine." Alysia holds out her hand. "Let me see your phone."

I shrink away. "What? No."

"If you have nothing to hide, then let me see your phone."

I am absolutely confident that there is nothing at all on my personal phone that can be traced in any way back to my work as Batgirl. That is the only reason why, after a prolonged staredown, I hand it over. Alysia smiles in mock innocence as she plops down next to me and swipes through the apps on my phone. I was expecting her to go through my photos or texts, but instead, she goes straight to social media. "What are you—?"

"Shhh. No talking." Her thumb taps the small pink icon on the screen, unleashing my feed.

"I don't post on there," I say defensively.

"I know." She chews her lip, looking determined as hell. She taps my home page and an assembly line of suggested videos emerge one by one. The first video happens to be some random fangirl post about Robin. My face burns but I don't react, even though I can feel Alysia smirking at me. Alysia grins at the video on the screen, then swipes to see the next randomly generated video. It's a fan art drawing . . . of Robin. She swipes again and it's a guy talking into the camera, debating whether Robin or Aqualad is hotter. Then there's an ad for energy drinks, a video about disarming assailants with knives, and then a particularly unhinged video about Robin's very tight pants. Grade-A humiliation burns through me.

I snatch my phone back. "I can't control what videos these apps show me."

"You *claim* that you didn't care about any of this

stupid gossip, but when I used your phone to call my dad earlier, I saw that your feed was filled with Robin content. You don't follow any pages related to him—smart, by the way, because that was absolutely the first thing I checked—but the algorithm doesn't lie, Barbara. You clearly watch the videos when they come up. And given how many slow-mo compilations of Robin videos show up on your home page, I would guess that you watch them *a lot*."

I have never hated these tech corporations more. One day I shall take down every single social media company, piece-by-intrusive-data-selling-piece.

"These apps mine your personal browsing history to deliver personalized content to you based on your interests," Alysia continues. "And you, my dear, seem to have one very muscular, agile interest."

Okay, well. Damn.

This took an unexpected turn. I swallow the lump in my throat. How can I throw her off? Maybe a drop of honesty can save me from revealing the whole truth? "All right, so maybe at some point in time I may have had a crush on Robin. Half the girls in Gotham City have a crush on him, but they're not all Batgirl."

"See, I thought the same thing at first. Until I saw you two together in person." Alysia gives me the smuggest smile in the history of the world while I blink rapidly, trying to process her words.

"You didn't check on me after the game because you *already had*. Do not tell me that that wasn't you who dropped me off on the motorcycle with your arms wrapped all around the Boy Wonder."

Yup. This is officially one of the most embarrassing moments of my life.

"You're relentless" is all that I say because I can't bring myself to say the truth out loud. It doesn't matter, though, because she's figured it out. No hiding now. Anxiety courses through me, but so does ... relief? Still, I grab a pillow and slam it onto my face. Alysia rips it away immediately, staring down at me with a wide grin.

I roll over on the bed. "Please never use the content of my algorithm against me ever again."

"If you weren't being so stubborn, I wouldn't have had to go there." Alysia lies down, cuddling up beside me. She pulls my shoulder gently, urging me to face her. "Look . . . you can keep denying it, but I am absolutely certain that I'm right. And from the way it looks like you're about to faint right now, I'm guessing that very few people know. But you can trust me. I want you to know that I'm here for you." She leans forward, pressing her forehead to mine. "And I'm proud of you."

My mind is reeling, but I allow myself to sink into her warm hug.

"So are you done denying it or do I have to produce

more evidence? Because I have at least ten other data points that I'd be happy to share."

I can't help but laugh. Alysia Yeoh: gossip-turned-amateur-detective. If I ever need to retire as Batgirl, I know exactly who to call up as my replacement.

"I am no longer denying it, so long as you promise to never talk about it." I study her face, serious this time. "It could put both of us in danger if people know."

"Yeah, yeah, of course. You know I love a good secret. So, what's the Batcave like?"

"Alysia."

"Please! A few details. A tiny morsel of information. I am starved for insider intel. My crops are dying. Please."

I chuckle. "The Batcave is big."

"Big as in like big house big, or big as in like amusement park big?"

"Big as in large enough to fit several vehicles, but small enough to be discreet."

"Are there real bats there?"

"Yes."

"How long have you been Batgirl?"

"A while."

"Objection. Vague language. Please answer the question more specifically."

I roll my eyes. "Two years."

"Did you know that scientists found that vampire

bats make out with mouthfuls of blood to deepen social bonds?"

"Um. No."

"Pretty cool, though, right?"

"Do you have any more questions, or can we please end this conversation?"

Alysia scoffs, smiling a little. "A million. But right now, all I really wanna know is . . . are the rumors true?"

"What rumors?"

"The ones about Batgirl's boyfriend, of course."

"Should I be concerned that you're asking me this after the bloody kiss question?"

"Swear to god, GBG, if I have to pull another straight answer out of you tonight, I'm going to *scream*."

It's silly, but I can't suppress a tiny smile at the fact that she chose to say "Batgirl's boyfriend" instead of "Robin's girlfriend." Still, the smile is short-lived. A frown creeps into its place. "No. The rumors are not true."

"Oh." Alysia deflates a little. "Well then, what about the other boy who's all Team Batgirl?"

"What other boy?"

"Nico."

CHAPTER 16

"**D**ude, have you ever seen soccer before?" Austin asks, crunching an ice cube.

"This is an exceptionally difficult game," Nico says defensively, biting his lip as I send a beautiful cross to my left midfielder, who makes a clean dash toward the goal, shoots, and scores.

"*Why* can't I block?!" Nico nearly throws his game controller at the wall.

"'Cause you suck." Austin laughs, picking at Nico's hair as they curl up next to each other in the narrow hospital bed.

Having Nico here to sneak Batgirl in to visit Austin makes things a hell of a lot easier. He opens the window for me so I don't have to go through the trouble of corrupting security cameras. At first, I'd wanted to visit Austin for information. I visited a second time because I promised that I would. But now by the third visit, I've realized I'm not here out of guilt or obligation. I'm here because I want to be here.

For the past few days, I've spent my mornings before school investigating historical sites of alleged demonic activity throughout Gotham City, and my evenings here at the hospital during the late-night hours, when their parents shower back at home before returning to stay overnight with Austin. Every time I see Nico, he's a little more relaxed, a little softer. Lily's growing on me too, which reminds me—

"Where's Lily tonight?" I ask. She's been here every other night.

"She said she was on her way," Austin says.

"Did you text her to see when she'll get here?" Nico asks.

"Her phone's still broken," Austin says. "She'll probably be here soon."

From what I know about Lily, I'm pretty sure she's rich, so it's surprising that she hasn't replaced her phone yet. Then again, there's a new model dropping next week that's supposed to have the best camera ever invented. She's probably holding out for that—I know I would if I had the cash. I turn my attention back to the game and score another goal from left field.

Nico nudges my shoulder. "*Why* are you so good at this? Is this what vigilantes secretly do all day? Sit around destroying each other in *FIFA*?"

"I play this a lot with a friend," I admit. My strength in sports games is one-hundred-percent fueled by spite. One time after a mission, a bad storm broke while Robin and I were out. We headed back to Wayne Manor to wait out the rain. Dick pulled out *FIFA*, all innocent, and acted like it wasn't that hard, he wasn't that good, it'd be fun, blah blah. Turns out Dick is an excellent *FIFA* player and he absolutely kicked my ass. He didn't even bother going easy on me. He was so smug when he won that I was instantly determined to avenge my honor. Thus, I have spent many, *many* hours playing *FIFA* with Dick, or watching videos learning how to improve at *FIFA*, for the sole purpose of annihilating Dick. I don't have time for video games, but I make an exception for this one.

"Let's switch to racing so Nico has a chance at not getting stomped on," Austin says. They flick Nico's forehead. Nico hisses back.

"Austin, I'd kick your ass if you weren't already in the hospital," he threatens, though there's no bite behind his words. Just love.

The less sick Austin feels, the more the siblings' personalities come out. I learned, for example, that Austin is a huge sci-fi nerd who is deeply invested in building tiny plastic mecha models. And apparently, Nico is an animal lover. They're not allowed to have pets in their apartment, so he hangs out at the shelter sometimes and is constantly, very earnestly, watching corny videos of unlikely animal friends, like the cheetah at the Gotham City Zoo who has an emotional support golden retriever.

How could I not like them both?

Nico especially. I'm trying not to start caring about him, but he's making that virtually impossible by existing. It's the little things that doom me: The way his voice gets hazy when he talks about his favorite songs. The way he always asks if I need any water or if he can buy me a snack each time we meet up. The way he fusses over Austin, tucking them in and combing their hair so that Austin doesn't have to expend even an ounce of extra energy.

I feel myself slipping. It freaks me out. But then Austin laughs, leans their cheek on my shoulder and ... keeps it there. The feeling that blooms between us feels something like friendship. Except that can't be right, because none of this is sustainable—neither of these people even knows who I am. Once this case is over, we'll have no reason to continue seeing each other. I know this. I really do.

But even though I recognize that I should put some space between us, I can't. I don't want to.

My phone pings with a message. It's from a number I don't recognize.

> **DFG: Thank you for your interest. We look forward to meeting you tomorrow evening at 11:58 pm in Gotham Harbor. The precise location will be texted to you ten minutes prior. Wear black. Come alone. Prepare to show your Gotham Academy ID at the door. Do not be early, do not be late.**

"Seriously?" I mumble. I was hoping Andrew would share the location beforehand so I could set up a hidden camera at the location, but he's being smart about precautions.

Nico and Austin glance at me. "You good?"

"Yeah, I . . ." How am I going to swing the meeting tomorrow? If I show up as myself, in regular clothes, I'll be able to get in, but if things go wrong, I can't change into Batgirl mode without blowing my cover. I guess I could ask Alysia for help—have her go into the meeting while I sneak in and wait in the wings, but I don't want her near any of this stuff. Not after she's already been possessed. I could also ask Dick. I *should* ask Dick. He's the most reasonable choice. But if I ask Dick, then he's on the case, then all of a sudden *my* case turns into *our* case and he isn't even on the same page as me in the first place, so how helpful could he be anyway?

"Hellooo?" Nico nudges my shoulder. I snap out of my daze.

"I'm fine. Sorry. Just distracted. Investigation stuff."

"Anything I can help with?" Nico asks.

I study his face. He's serious. He said before that he wants to help. And he was brave enough to run toward the danger, rather than away from it, at the game, but still . . . Would this be going too far?

"If I can help, I want to do it," Nico says.

"Maybe. I'll let you know."

Nico leaves Austin's side to join me on the love seat against the back wall. There are only a few inches between my arm and his. When he leans back, his elbow knocks against mine. I think he lets it linger there on purpose.

I shouldn't be here like this. I shouldn't let myself get involved in their personal lives. The fact that I'm having so much fun is exactly why I abruptly announce, "I should go."

I'm immediately met with twin complaints, begging me to stay a little longer. It feels nice to know that they enjoy my company as much as I enjoy theirs.

"Sorry, y'all. I'll see you next time, though?"

"I'll walk you home," Nico says, grabbing his coat from the tray table beside the bed.

I point at the mask covering the entirety of my face. "Secret identity, remember?"

"Right, right." Nico rubs the back of his neck. "Then . . . do you want to walk *me* home?"

"You're leaving too?" Austin complains.

"Lily will be here soon to keep you company and I'll be back tomorrow," he promises before glancing back at me, eyes crinkling at the corners as he smiles. "Meet you downstairs?"

CHAPTER 17

We walk to Nico's house in silence, drifting through the dark alleyways to avoid being seen together. We fall into an easy rhythm beside one another until we reach the front of his building.

"Hey." Nico sort of lingers. I sort of hoped he would. "Can we talk?"

On the other side of the street, an old man walks out of his apartment led by a small dog. I jump back into the alley, hiding in the shadow of the building.

"It's not good for me to be seen with you," I say.

"But if we're not seen?"

It's late and I should go home, but there's something about Nico tonight—something about the warmth radiating from him after our hang with Austin—that makes me want to stay up a little longer. "Can you get onto your roof?" I ask.

He grins. "Of course."

His building is typical of many others on the street. Tall, at least twenty stories high, full of hundreds of apartment units. There's a stairwell that leads right up to the top. There's a lock on the door, but Nico picks it with practiced ease. He opens it for me and we step out into the chill of the night.

He follows me down onto the hard ground of the rooftop. I pretzel my legs beneath me while he hangs his over the edge.

"Are you moving?" I noticed cardboard boxes stacked in the corner of his unit when we passed by his window.

He frowns. "Yeah."

"Because of what happened?" I ask. Nico bites his lip. "Sorry. I won't pry."

"We are moving because of what happened, but it's complicated. The newspaper coverage on Austin and Harper mentioned that there was fear gas found at the scene. Our landlord read it and decided that Austin storing it at home was a violation of our lease, since it's an illegal substance, so . . ." He takes a deep breath. "We're being evicted."

My stomach drops. "Is that legal? Can they do that?"

"Yup." He plucks a small pebble from the roof, tosses it over the edge. "It's legal. They can do it. They *are* doing it."

"But if Austin is found innocent, then maybe—"

"Nah. The damage is done. Our landlord's been trying to jack up rent forever anyway. This was perfect timing for her."

"That sucks."

"That's Gotham City."

Dark anger swirls in my stomach. Whoever is behind these attacks is ruining people's lives. Why would anyone target innocent people like this?

A dark thought, a theory, suddenly ignites in my mind. I turn to Nico. He's looking at me with a new level of openness that I haven't seen from him before. I shake that away and try to figure out the most tactful way to ask what's on my mind. "You and Austin have lived in this building for a while, right? It seems mostly working-class. But you go to Gotham Academy. How . . . Uh. How did that happen? I heard that school is expensive."

"Expensive is an understatement. We're there on a scholarship."

So is Alysia. "Is the other student who was attacked, Liam, also a scholarship student?"

"I think so. Every spring, the school makes us attend this weird donor dinner where we're forced to shake hands and pose with the people giving money for our education. It's super awkward, like they're showing us off like little prizes. Or pets. I'm grateful for the scholarship and stuff, I'm not trying to sound like an ass, but you should see these things. The way they make us all stand up and talk about how poor we are or whatever. It's disgusting."

My skin itches at the thought. I'm suddenly struck by how grateful I am that Bruce never makes me feel like that. All the Batarangs, the bike, the safe houses—in a way, that's part of my scholarship from him too.

Nico's eyes widen with shock as he pieces together my line of questioning. "Someone's targeting the scholarship students at my school?"

"Potentially. You haven't felt anything strange yourself, right? Any blackouts in your memory?"

"No, nothing."

"Let me know if that changes."

"Yeah. Okay." He pulls his knees into his chest, nervous.

"How are, uh, you doing? Dealing with all of this?" I should've asked him earlier. I can't imagine how it must feel having his sibling accused of murder and stuck in the hospital, his family dealing with a housing crisis, and still having to go to school on top of it all.

"Not great." He doesn't seem like he wants to talk about it further, so I don't push. I'm surprised, though, when he turns the question back on me. "How are you doing?"

A laugh jumps from my throat. He watches me with a wry smile.

"What? I can't ask how you're doing?"

"You can. It's just that nobody does."

"You seem off tonight, though."

"Off how?"

"I don't know. Sadder?"

I pause, wondering how he possibly could have noticed that. Maybe he's been paying closer attention to me than I've realized.

"You know, you can talk to me," Nico says softly, a little awkwardly. "If you want to. I'm a good listener."

There is absolutely no reason why I should talk to Nico right now. And yet somehow, I find the words begging to come out. I take a deep breath, hitching up my shoulders before exhaling quietly through my mouth. "This case is weighing on me." I recline back on my elbows. "I'm starting to feel that whoever's behind this is . . ." I hesitate, remembering the way my dad laughed when I told him my theory about the purple bat-symbols, how Dick totally dismissed it too. "Never mind. It's silly."

Nico leans back as well, turning toward me with interest. "Nah, c'mon. Tell me."

I sigh. "Well, I have a theory that maybe the

bat-symbols being left behind aren't for Batman. That maybe they're ... uh, for me."

It's quiet for a beat before Nico asks, "Why is that so silly?"

"Because apparently nobody cares about Batgirl. Batman and Robin both work in Gotham City. Why would someone be looking for me, specifically?"

"Because you're really good at punching people?"

I laugh. "Right. Of course."

"Or because you're different from the others." His voice shifts to a more serious tone. "Maybe whoever's behind this sees you as a threat."

"Doubt it. Robin thinks that if they're targeting me, it's to use me as bait."

Nico hisses. "Wow. Didn't know that Robin was such a jerk."

"He's not. Usually."

Nico inches closer to me. "Can I ask you a personal question?"

He's a magnet, pulling me in. I can't stop myself from drifting closer too. "Sure, but I can't guarantee I'll answer."

A smirk tugs at the corner of his mouth. "Why'd you decide to become Batgirl?"

Huh. Not what I thought he was going to ask.

"A lot of people would think twice about perpetuating violence against women if they knew that there were consequences for their actions, and that said consequences might be delivered in the form of a furious girl who could kick their teeth in."

Nico laughs. "Really?"

"Maybe. That's part of it."

"What's the other part? An obsessive drive to protect all that's good and vanquish everything evil?" He nudges my shoulder.

"If I believed that everything in the world was black or white, good or bad, then I wouldn't be a vigilante. I live in the gray area."

At this, his expression settles back into something more pensive. "The first time you put on that mask must've been pretty scary, huh?"

"The first time I ever snuck out as Batgirl, I almost got myself killed."

Unfiltered concern washes over Nico's face. Does the thought of me getting hurt disturb him that much? When did he start caring about me? And why does that make me feel so warm? I shake that thought away and try my best to answer his question: Why am I doing this work when I could do nothing at all?

Belief. That's where it begins for me. Everyone's always asking us to believe. To believe in change, in our government, in our legal system, in our police. That's what the people of Gotham City are supposed to do—especially my generation. Believe, believe, believe.

Except there's one little problem with this: the people who are asking us to believe are the same ones who've let us down time and time again. The people who encouraged us to believe in Harvey Dent are the same ones who hid evidence of his corruption from the public. The people who asked us to not encourage the vigilantes and trust the Gotham City Police Department to do the right thing are the same ones who hold vain press conferences, apologizing for the dozens of innocent lives lost in the latest scandal of crooked officers working with the mob. The people who promised that their corporations would help clean up Gotham City's streets and build new housing are the same ones who jack up rent, trying to gentrify our neighborhoods. Not make them safer, just more expensive with less interesting restaurant options.

That's my issue with belief. I want to believe, but believe in who? In what?

The first time I ever snuck out as Batgirl, I tried to save my father after he had disappeared on duty. I don't like to think about that night, but I'll never forget what happened before I found him. There was a young couple on the sidewalk being robbed at gunpoint. I stopped to help them—using all my years of martial-arts training and self-defense to try to disarm the man. I was able to get the gun away from him, but I didn't anticipate that he'd have a box cutter in his back pocket. He slashed my arm wide open. I had never felt pain like that before, but

I forced myself to keep fighting. I told the young couple to run, but they didn't want to leave me there, fighting this grown-up twice my size. They took out their phone to call the police and the guy ran. Except he didn't look both ways as he crossed the street. A semitruck came out of nowhere and hit him in the middle of the intersection. I can still remember the sound of his macabre shout. It was terrifying. But then something incredible happened.

The young couple immediately ran to the man's side.

One of the girls was a nurse and the other was an EMT. They sat over the man and performed CPR, caring for his wounds until the ambulance arrived.

This man had literally tried to rob them at gunpoint, threatened their lives. And yet there they were: crouched in his blood, administering first aid, and doing everything they could to keep him alive.

In that moment, I found something to believe in.

I believe in Gotham City. I believe in my neighbors. And because of that, I believe that I should do everything in my power to use my skills to keep this place, and its people, safe.

I ramble a bit and stumble to keep out any identifying details in the story, but I tell Nico all of this. Afterward, I feel lighter. Only three people in the world know that I'm Batgirl: Bruce Wayne, Dick Grayson, and Alfred. Or, actually, four people now, ever since Alysia ambushed me. But still. The point is that I've never had a conversation like this with them before. We don't sit around and talk about the "why" of it all; we just do our part. I didn't realize how much I wanted, needed, to say some of these things out loud. A tiny feeling wells up in my chest for Nico. It feels something like gratitude.

When I look up, Nico's face is all admiration. "I believe in Batgirl, by the way." We make the kind of prolonged eye contact that we've avoided so far. "I believe in you."

I smile at him softly, then return my gaze to the skyline.

"Earlier, you said that there's maybe something I can help with," Nico says.

"I did say that."

"Sooo?"

"So, what?"

"Have you made up your mind? Can I help?"

"I don't . . . I'm not sure if it's a good idea."

"Why not? Do you have a vendetta against sidekicks?"

I laugh. "Not at all."

"So then let me help."

"No."

"Why not?"

"Your sibling is intricately involved in the case. You're too close to it."

"This thing is leaving messages for Batgirl. Doesn't that make you too close too?"

"That's different because this is my job."

"I thought you weren't getting paid. This isn't really a *job* if you're not getting paid."

"Well, it's my responsibility."

"Is it because I don't look tough? Despite what the pink hair may suggest, I'm super tough." He tries on his best attempt at a menacing glare, which ends up being about as scary as a panda.

"Woooow. Give the demon that look and it'd give up right away—settle down, join the angels, and probably start a nonprofit."

Nico laughs, but then his face gets all serious again. "I want to help Austin. Please."

I want to say no, but it's getting harder and harder for me to say no to Nico.

"Fine. I actually do need some help at this meeting tomorrow." An extra person to navigate Andrew's meeting will come in handy.

"Do I get to wear one of those earpiece things? Like in the movies?"

"Yes, you get to wear an earpiece thing."

He shoves a fist in the air. "YES."

"All right, chill out before I change my mind."

A comfortable silence settles between us as we look out over the city below us. Several windows in the tall brick building across the street are lit up, illuminating the people and lives unfolding inside.

"I think the woman on the fourth floor is living a double life," Nico says.

I raise an eyebrow. "What makes you say that?"

"Every time I see her, she's coming home in completely different outfits. Like, full-on makeup, wigs, fake noses, different outfits. I never see her wear the same thing twice."

"What's the deal with that couple, then?" I point to another illuminated window on the sixth floor, where a woman looks like she's about to throw a spatula at some string bean–shaped man's head.

"Oh, them? They're robots, of course."

I laugh. "That's exactly what I thought. Robots programmed to stage dramatic fights to bring the estranged couple next door closer together in solidarity. It's all part of a complex social experiment on reverse psychology being run at Gotham University."

And then, all of a sudden, we're joking back and forth. We keep going like this for hours, making up ridiculous stories. And when that gets old, Nico pulls out his phone and suggests we pick a song for every scene we see through the windows, as if we're directing a film. All my choices are pretty basic compared to Nico's, which are drawn from every genre imaginable. I take mental note of the lyrics of at least three of his choices to look up the song titles later. It's the most fun I've had in a while. With Nico, I feel young and normal. Or maybe not normal, but free, and isn't that even better?

Time slips by at any easy pace until soon enough, every light in the building across the street turns off. I know it's too late to still be out here with him, but I don't want to check the time. I don't think Nico does either. Eventually, though, the sky slips into that shade of cobalt blue that only appears right before sunrise. It must be past five a.m. at least, which means it's not late—it's *early*. We've been up all night.

At some point, I'm not sure when, Nico scooted over so the sleeve of his jacket is brushing against my arm. I've been afraid to move an inch ever since, but we both have school in the morning (in a couple hours, to be exact), so I have no choice but to turn to him.

"We should go," I say, though the words feel ... wrong. In a different world, I'd be happy to stay up here, sharing soft silence with Nico for much longer.

"Guess so," he says, shifting closer to me ever so slightly. The soft gust of his breath warms the air between us. We lock eyes for a second longer than we're supposed to. He blinks and his mouth parts, the hint of a sentence on the tip of his tongue before he shakes his head and looks away. I shuffle a few feet back from the edge of the rooftop, standing and stretching out my limbs.

"I'll miss this building," Nico says quietly. Then, "Which way are you heading?"

"That way too, for a few blocks, at least." I pull my grappling gun out of my Utility Belt and launch it toward the neighboring building.

"That never stops being cool," Nico says, amazed.

I smile. "Do you . . . want a try?"

His eyes widen. "That thing can carry us both?"

"Batman once used one of these to carry himself *and* The Penguin. They can hold a lot of weight."

Nico steps forward cautiously. "How would we charm or . . . do it?"

I guess I haven't ever used it to move two people from Point A to Point B. "What if we both hold on to the gun, and you keep your free arm around me and try not to let go?"

"Promise you won't drop me?" Nico smirks. The expression does something to me. I hope the moonlight blocks out the blush creeping across my face.

"I promise."

"All right, then."

I grip the grappling gun and Nico slips his hand over mine. He steps closer and I realize the problem with my plan. Holding on together requires us to be close. Very close. My heart beats fast as Nico snakes an arm around my waist. Up close I can smell the faint hint of shampoo in his hair—amber and pine. His hand is warm, practically burning me through the heavy fabric of my Batsuit jacket. As I wind an arm around him in return, closing the gap between our chests, I feel his mouth slip into a poorly concealed smile above me. I bite my lip to contain a smile too.

"Ready?" I ask.

"Yes."

I tighten my grip on the grappling gun and we go. Nico's eyes shut, his arm around my waist flexes tightly, holding on for dear life as he presses his face into the crook of my neck when we start to fall. But then we gain some momentum, and falling turns into swinging. The drop transforms into a roller coaster, and Nico's eyes finally flicker open. He lets out a string of hushed curses plus a prayer or two before he breaks out into a wild, amazed laugh.

"You good?"

Nico nods frantically, locks of pink hair blown backward from his face with our speed. I can feel his heart beating against me as the wind blows against my ears. When we reach the lower rooftop, I help him stick the landing.

"How was that?" I ask. The grappling gun buzzes back into place.

"Terrifying," he says, wheezing.

I've done this a million times, but my heart hammers in my chest when he looks down at me, his arm hanging lazily around my waist. His brown eyes are dancing with adrenaline when they find mine. I can feel the heat of his breath against my mouth when he says, "See you tomorrow?"

"Tomorrow?" I ask. I stare at his lips.

"The mission?"

"Right! Yes." I stumble backward to untangle us from one another and restore a safe distance between us. When I do, he lets out a small, amused laugh. I miss the comfort of his body heat immediately.

"I had fun with you tonight," he says, all soft and low, like a secret. He tosses me one more sleepy grin before heading inside.

On the way home, my body is on fire. I touch the curve of my waist where his arm was. The shivers rush back. I whisper to myself, "I'm doomed."

CHAPTER 18

I suspected that Andrew's Demonic Forces of Gotham group would have cult-y *vibes,* but I didn't expect it to be, you know, a literal cult.

Everyone gathers in a warehouse near the docks. There are about fifteen people seated in chairs. The smell of seawater fills the room, mixing with the scent of powdered doughnut holes on the folding table in the corner. It's a depressing scene, but not too different from any awkward rec center–type meeting if you ignore the giant occult symbol painted in pig's blood at the center of the room.

"Act natural," I instruct Nico through the earbud he's wearing.

"I know, I know. This isn't my first rodeo," he says.

"This absolutely is your first mission and it is not a rodeo."

"I got this, okay?"

I watch Nico shake hands with one of the other attendees through the small camera he's wearing on his jacket. I'm right outside the exit, ready to intervene if needed. All Nico has to do is sit through the meeting, then ask Andrew a few covert questions on my behalf. Simple enough.

Nico grabs a seat right in the middle with the best view of the creepy symbol on the floor, where I'm sure Andrew will situate himself like the drama queen he is. A tall man with a beard immediately plops down next to Nico. I recognize him right away. He's the man from the grocery store—the one who broke my ankle. How the hell is he out free *again*? I'm relieved to see that he's here alone tonight. But then again, should I be? Seeing this guy once is typical. Twice is a coincidence. But three times? I need more info.

"Hey, Nico. The guy with the beard on your right— I need you to say that you haven't seen his brother in a while and ask where he's been."

Like a pro, Nico doesn't visibly acknowledge my instructions, which is good. I underestimated him.

"Hey, man," Nico says, putting on what I'm

assuming is his attempt at a bro voice? It's a little ridiculous. I bite my lip to contain a laugh. "Haven't seen your brother in a minute. He all right?"

The man eyes Nico warily. "How do you know Jason?"

"Um."

Shoot. Didn't think this through. "Um. Say you met him at . . . uh . . . on the subway?" If we say something too specific, we might strike out and he'll bust us. The subway is probably the one and only universal location where Gothamites could possibly meet. I can tell Nico thinks my idea is dumb by the way he clenches his jaw, but he forges ahead.

"He did me a favor once, a while back. Been meaning to hit him up ever since," Nico says instead.

Okay, that's actually a much better lie than mine. The bearded guy clearly agrees, because he says, "Sounds like Jason."

Nico and I both let out a relieved exhale.

"That sonofabitch quit," the bearded guy says bitterly.

"Quit . . . crime?" Nico asks.

"He went all reformed on us. Cut off all contact with me and my dad. Haven't seen him since the day he went to that stupid clinic."

A glimmer of pride sparkles within me.

"And your dad?" Nico asks, taking the lead on the conversation without even needing my instruction.

"Locked up. They denied him bail."

"Sorry about that," Nico says. The bearded man grunts in acknowledgment. "What brings you here tonight?"

"Satan."

"Uh?"

A second later, at midnight sharp, Andrew struts into the warehouse wearing giant chrome goggles with reflective film on the lenses. He looks like a wannabe cyberpunk NPC. Or a very shiny bug. Depends on how you look at it.

"Greetings, everyone!" Nico and the others in the room move to take their seats. "And a warm welcome to our newest member from Gotham Academy." Andrew winks at Nico, who does a solid job at looking comfortable in the space.

"I could spend all night explaining to you the demonic lore of this city. I could read to you from ancient texts that explain the beauty inherent in the damned. But it's not safe for us to gather for long, so I will cut to the chase." He lowers his voice. "A demonic entity has revealed itself to the people of Gotham City. Our goal is simple: find its host, then unlock the demon's true power. If we do, then we shall be rewarded. Beyond our wildest dreams."

"Ask him what that means," I instruct Nico.

He raises his hand. "Um . . . hail! What is this reward?"

Andrew's gaze quickly snaps to Nico. Something dark flashes across his face, and he leans in, whispers, "If you stick with us, you'll see soon enough."

"What happens to the host when we find them? Won't it attack us?" a woman asks.

"No." Andrew picks at a fingernail. "Not if we end them first."

End them? Oh no. I desperately want to find the host too, but I'm not trying to *kill* them. This changes things. Changes *everything*. Not only are there potential victims' lives at risk, but also that of the host, who might not even be able to control what's happening to them.

"We suspect that the host attends Gotham Academy. You"—Andrew points at Nico—"will be our student mole. Our eyes and ears inside the institution. If and when you hear anything, contact me. And if at any point you should think to change your mind . . ." Andrew grins, his eyes dark and wild. *"Don't.* We are finding this demon one way or another. And once we do, I can assure you that you will not want to see the terrible things we can do to you."

I shudder, preparing to assure Nico that I will *never* let Andrew and his freaks hurt him, but before

I can, several things happen in a chaotic blur.

A door is kicked open.

A shot is fired.

And Nico crumples to the floor.

"I want to take you to the hospital."

Nico hisses in pain, sweating onto the sheets of his bed. "No."

"What do you mean *no*? You were shot. *Twice.*"

"First one didn't count. The vest caught it," Nico says between gritted teeth.

The one and only good decision I made tonight was making sure that Nico wore a bulletproof vest to Andrew's meeting. I didn't expect it to be necessary, but apparently the Mafia that runs the warehouse that Andrew foolishly picked for his meeting had other plans.

Turns out these gangsters didn't like walking into their hideout to find a bunch of random occult enthusiasts. It was a disaster. Nico, seated at the center of the room, took one bullet to the vest, the other grazing his arm. I barely got him out in time without being seen in the scramble. Nobody else was injured, thank god, but I still can't believe it. Honestly, if I were a member of a cult and my supreme leader unknowingly led us right into a Mafia den, I'd probably start questioning his leadership skills right about now. But at least they all knew how to scatter quickly.

"Hospital. Now," I repeat to Nico. I was so busy freaking out about the shot to the vest, making sure it didn't go through or break any ribs, that I didn't notice the second wound on his arm. He was careful to hide it beneath his jacket until I got him back inside his apartment.

"No. For two reasons." Nico winces as he holds up two fingers. "One: My family doesn't have health insurance. We're already drowning in bills because of Austin. I'm not going to add to that." I'm about to protest, but he holds up his hand even higher. "Two: If I walk into the ER with a gunshot wound, they'll call the cops and open a full investigation. I'll have to explain how I got the injury or they won't let me go. Austin's already in trouble. I don't think GCPD needs to see anyone in my family around guns."

I chew on my lower lip, irritated. "Neither of those reasons is fair."

"Never said they were." Nico winces as he sits up straighter. "I know you know how to do this."

"What makes you so sure of that?"

"All superheroes know first aid."

"I'm not a—"

"Really unconvincing to say while wearing a cape and mask."

"I put you in danger."

"Technically it's not even a gunshot wound. The one on my arm is only a graze. The bullet didn't go in."

"Technically this situation is messed up and you should go to a hospital."

"Give me stitches, okay? Please?"

Stubborn. So stubborn, this boy.

I sigh. "Your kitchen's down the hall, right?"

I leave the room, returning a few moments later with a bowl of warm water and a washcloth. I pull the rest of my first-aid supplies out of my Utility Belt. "Want to put on some music as a distraction?"

"No, let's talk. Keep me distracted," Nico says. "Don't want to ruin any of my favorite songs by tainting it with the memory of that time I got shot."

"But you're happy to taint your memory of me? Got it." I dip the washcloth into the warm bowl of blood-foggy water and begin to wipe at the wound on his arm.

"Your company happens to be so pleasant that not even spilling blood onto my carpet could stop it."

He gives me another one of those looks. The cautious, flirty kind. It's probably the adrenaline, but the boy is weirdly chipper for someone who just had a near-death experience. I shake my head at him before focusing back on the stitches. He winces a few times, but he's mostly well-behaved as I patch him up, saying nothing but not taking his eyes off me. If I weren't so concerned with fixing him, I'd feel embarrassed by the heat of his gaze. Once I wipe most of the grime off his arm, I realize that it indeed looks worse than it is.

"If you want to talk, then talk," I say, breaking the silence.

"Do you think you could ever start a cult?" he asks.

"Probably not."

"Why not?"

"I lack the necessary charisma."

He laughs. "True. You definitely have no charisma whatsoever."

"So much attitude," I scold, instinctively shoving him in the arm, then feeling horrible when he winces in pain. "Sorry, sorry," I breathe, placing my hand firmly on his chest.

Nico shakes his head, lets out a strained chuckle.

"What about you, then? Would you start a cult?" I ask.

"I think I'm more likely to join one."

"Not exactly what I want to hear after tonight."

"This is gonna make me sound pompous, but a while ago, I released some music that got . . . kind of popular."

I slow my movements down, trying to feign some kind of general ignorance.

"There was a very small but very intense online community that rallied around it. It obviously wasn't a cult, but their fandom was intense. They kept messaging me constantly, telling me about how the music affected their lives, and wanting to tell me about all their demons. I hated it."

I remember all the things that I heard about Nico before I got to know him. How he's so strange. Aloof. Hard to talk to. How everyone feels like they have an opinion of him.

"Do you regret making that music?" I ask.

"At first, it felt like a relief to get the words out about how I was feeling. But when it went viral, suddenly everything felt like this massive trade-off: success in art, in exchange for yourself."

"You felt like you gave yourself up?"

"In some ways, yeah. When you share your art, you give yourself up to people. Expose your heart. And that's not necessarily bad on its own, but my problem was that I didn't use a pseudonym or a stage name or create some character persona to hide behind. I gave everyone myself. My real, actual, depressed self. Sometimes I worry that I didn't save any of myself for me at all."

I wonder if I'm giving myself up too as Batgirl. I may have a secret identity, but I still struggle with this aching feeling—this paranoia—that the more I do this work, the less my life is mine. Maybe that's why all the online rumors and rude nicknames get to me. I'm okay with compartmentalizing my life, but I'm terrified of losing control of the narrative about who I am—both with and without the mask. I'm not an artist, but maybe

I'm worried about saving some of myself for me.

"Anyway. You had the right idea with the whole secret identity thing," Nico says. He reaches out a finger and gently brushes the edge of my mask. I fight back the little flutter in my chest when he does.

"Maybe. Just because I wear a mask doesn't mean that people don't constantly have things to say about me, you know."

"Yeah, but when they do, they're talking about Batgirl. Not . . . whoever you are in real life. There's some separation." It's a relief that Nico never asks me any questions. He's not trying to figure out who I am. If he's curious, he barely lets it show.

But his assumption isn't necessarily true. Sometimes I feel like Barbara Gordon and Batgirl are two completely different people. Sometimes I feel like they're the same.

"I don't have a clear sense of who I am," I admit. I pull the last stitch and clean the wound once more. "All done. You should get some rest."

He sits up from the floor and plops onto his bed. "Wanna watch a movie?"

I laugh. "You serious?"

"Yeah. You got somewhere else to be?"

"It's late" is what I say, but what I do is inch a little closer. This is dangerous territory. I'm supposed to be working to stop a string of possessions from terrorizing

Gotham Academy, not doing . . . whatever it is that I'm doing here with Nico right now.

"Then we'll just watch the beginning."

I give in and sit on his twin-sized bed, keeping a safe distance between us. Within the first fifteen minutes of the movie, Nico's eyes flutter shut. I wait for him to suggest that I head home, but he doesn't. Instead, he lies down flat and scoots over. It takes me a second to realize what he's doing. He's making room for me. To lie down next to him. On his bed. Right now.

It's innocent enough—we're both on top of the covers. Nobody's touching. I feel a little stupid wearing my mask right now, but otherwise this is totally fine. I can stay for a few more minutes. The boy literally got shot today—the least I can do is keep him company until he falls asleep. Plus, being with him like this is nice. The walk home is cold, whereas the space between our bodies is warm. So, slowly, I lie beside him, face to face.

I study his features. His thick brows, the shadow of his eyelashes, flickering slightly during the early onset of sleep. "Is this okay?" he asks, eyes still shut. He's trying his best not to touch me at all, but even with him on the opposite edge of the bed, there are only a few inches between us. The realization that we're so close with the lights off has the opposite effect on his sleepiness from moments before. I can feel him buzzing. I'm buzzing too.

When he opens his eyes, I'm not ready for how

quickly the energy builds. I watch him watch his own finger trail from where our hands rest beside one another, swirling up my arm, then down to sear a path along the length of my spine. My hand is shaking, so I flatten it against his chest. His heart skips under my fingertips. I bite back a soft gasp.

There are a million feelings curling in my gut, confusing and addictive. I'm not sure what to do with them other than block them out and focus on the way Nico's muscles feel, warm beneath his thin T-shirt.

His voice is low, hazy. A quiet whisper in the dark. "Can I . . . ?"

His quiet plea singes the air between us, setting every nerve in my body on fire. I know this isn't the right time. I know we aren't the right match. The girl with the black mask and secrets; the boy with the pink hair and nervous smile. The rational part of my brain knows that I should be focusing on anything else but this right now. But maybe it's that burden to always be the rational one that leads me to nod, watching the way his soft eyes darken, simmering with heat, when I do. He swallows before leaning in until his lips crash into mine.

CHAPTER 19

I damn near fall flat on my face rushing to catch the bus. I overslept this morning. I *never* oversleep. My uniform is wrinkled and there's a coffee stain on my shirt, but I didn't have time to change. How could I have had time to change when I've spent every second of consciousness this morning replaying last night on a loop?

I kissed Nico. My first kiss. And it was perfect. Sort of. I mean, it was perfect except for the fact that now my first kiss will have forever been with a boy who's never even seen my eyes without lenses or heavy black make-up. Doesn't even know my real name.

Okay, maybe it wasn't perfect, but who cares. It felt good. It felt *great*. My bus wheezes by a billboard for a horror movie and I snap back to reality. I'm supposed to be dealing with my own horror movie at my school right now. Not daydreaming about—

"Wait! Sorry! I'm getting off here!" I jump up and wave at the driver, begging him to reopen the doors for me at the corner. I almost missed my stop.

If Andrew finds the host before me, he's going to kill them. I have to find the host first. Traci said to look for possible sources of motivation for the demon. But how the hell am I supposed to do that during a full day of classes? I guess if I use my laptop to take notes in first period, I can at least spend AP World History secretly reading about how to create vessels to trap demons. Better than doing nothing. But even then, I still won't know how to *actually* lure a demon into a trap in the first place. There's no Wikipedia article about this stuff. Trust me—I checked.

The morning bell rings, but my classroom is across the school. I turn the corner and slam right into someone. Dick Grayson.

"Babs, hey," he says, all hopeful.

What would he say if he knew I kissed Nico? Why does it matter to me? I start to sweat.

"Are you okay?" he asks.

I take one look at those mesmerizing blue eyes and freeze up. "Um."

And then I run. Away from him. Like a little kid.

I feel his eyes on me until I turn the next corner.

"GBG!"

I stifle a groan. Why is everyone I know in the same hallway this morning?

"Hey, Alysia." I wave at her, picking up my pace to make it to class. "You're late too?"

"No." She tilts her head at me. "I have free period now."

"Right. Sorry."

"You all right?" she asks, matching my stride.

"Why is everyone asking me that this morning?"

"Who is 'everyone'?"

My work phone vibrates. It's a text. From Nico.

Nico: Good morning:)

"Oh my god," I whisper.

"Who are you texting?" Alysia asks.

"Nobody."

"Liar." She dives, swiping the phone from my hand with unexpected speed.

"Hey!"

She reads my screen and sighs. "GBG . . ."

"He's been helping with the investigation to save Austin." I'll tell her about the kiss eventually. But not right now.

"Don't you already have someone to help you with this stuff? Someone better trained?" She lowers her voice. "Someone named Robin, for example?"

I frown. "Not at the moment."

"What happened?"

"It's complicated." I try to walk even faster to lose her, but she keeps up. I wish I were in class already so I could avoid this conversation. Why is this campus so huge? "Me and him aren't talking right now."

"Is he the one not talking to you or are you the one not talking to him?" Instead of a real answer, I blush. "Oh my god, of course. Are you still upset about the dating rumor thing?"

"It's not that." Or it's not only that, I should say. It's also about my reputation—my need for people to take Batgirl seriously. "I need some space from him, okay? Be on my own, work on my own for a while. Nico has been helpful."

"Nico is only concerned about saving Austin, not helping you."

"Same thing."

"No, actually. It isn't."

I let out a frustrated sigh. "Our goals are aligned. And he's . . ."

"He's what?"

"He's nice."

"You're catching feelings for him? Right now?" My

ears burn. Alysia face-palms. "Let me guess: this sudden attraction to Nico also has nothing to do with your fight with Robin, right?"

"It's a shame you don't want to be a detective because you'd make an excellent cop, the way you're questioning me to death right now." Alysia sticks close beside me as I climb the steps toward my classroom on the third floor.

"I've literally never seen you show real interest in a guy before. So I'm a little surprised that you're in a situation that feels . . . I don't know. Messy."

"It's not messy." In fact, it's way less messy than if I were to explore anything with anyone else. Letting things progress with Robin would be a liability. Letting go with Nico is an escape. My voice shakes. I take a deep breath. "At least with Nico, it doesn't feel like I'm playing into some predetermined destiny where everyone expects me to date the most convenient guy."

Alysia crosses her arms. "So this *is* about Rob— I mean, *Roger*?"

"No." It isn't. I don't think it is? I whisper. "I like Nico."

"And you don't like Roger?"

"I like him too. Of course I do. Or at least, I did. Before. I don't know." I shake my head, frustrated.

"And you want to be with Nico?"

"I don't know! Maybe I don't want to 'be with'

anyone. I want to do my job and solve this case and maybe, if everyone can get off my ass for like *five minutes*, also enjoy some normal teen experiences, like having a stupid crush on a stupidly cute boy with stupid pink hair, even if it's *stupid*."

"Hey, sorry. It's not stupid." Alysia softens a bit. "I know you're under a lot of pressure, but I'm trying to understand what's happening. None of this is like you. You're usually so together. So tough."

I didn't realize how hard this part of being Batgirl would be. If I were to date someone as Barbara, I'd either be constantly struggling to keep a giant secret from them or I'd be willingly putting them in danger. If I were to date Robin, I'd be doing exactly what everyone expects of me and making myself vulnerable to all kinds of crap and judgment from strangers. Nico has emerged as this third option that I didn't even know existed. We connected while I was working, but he's not trying to figure out who I am—he's not trying to pressure me or turn this into anything that it isn't. He's just here, reminding me that even though there's all this chaos going on, I'm still sixteen and maybe I deserve to have a little bit of fun.

We arrive at the door of my first-period class. Finally.

"I have to go," I tell Alysia, not bothering to hide the annoyance in my voice.

She crosses her arms. "Yeah. Whatever."

We don't hug or smile goodbye like usual. I slip inside the classroom. As soon as I do, all eyes dart to me.

"Ms. Gordon," my teacher Mr. Abara says, bored. "You're late."

"I know," I mumble. Mr. Abara raises an eyebrow. "Sorry." I don't talk back at school. What in the world has gotten into me?

I'm struck by a flash of pale pink hair sitting at the desk in the corner. First period is English class. Nico is in my English class. I rush to my seat beside him, holding my breath. *Act natural, act natural, act natural.*

I know it's dumb, but I cast a sideways glance at him, even though I know that he couldn't care less about Barbara Gordon. He feels me looking and meets my eyes for a moment with an expression of absolute boredom. His gaze doesn't linger at all. Instead, he leans back in his seat, sneaks his phone out of his bag, and types something. A moment later, my phone vibrates in my pocket. My work phone. An ice age passes while I wait for Mr. Abara to turn back to the whiteboard so I can check my texts.

BirdBoy: i know we're not really talking right now but are you sure you're okay? you looked off this morning. i'm worried.

I dismiss the notification and slip my phone into my jacket pocket. Not now, Dick.

The girl in front of me raises her hand. "I'm just saying, Mr. Abara, that I think it's kind of messed up to read Lovecraft for homework when our school's getting rocked by a violent rampage."

The possessions. These goddamn possessions. If Andrew and the Demonic Forces of Gotham Society find the host before I do, they're going to kill them. Then they'll unleash hell upon our city by tapping into the "full potential" of the demon. Whatever that means. He's building up his cult, preparing for chaos, and yet I'm sitting here, in class, not doing anything at all. I could've spent last night investigating, but I was too busy.... A ray of sun breaks through the heavy clouds out the window, spilling across Nico's desk and bathing his tan hands in warm light.

I need some air.

I practically sprint out of the classroom, ignoring my teacher's question about where I'm going, ignoring my classmates' stares. I keep running until I'm outside at the benches overlooking the football field. There's a PE class going on below. Even from here, I can make out Dick's relaxed figure, pretending to jog slowly at the back of the pack even though I know for a fact that he could outrun anyone at this school in a heartbeat. Another school bell rings, signaling passing period for the freshmen. I check my phone to see how much time I can waste out here before a quick break turns into full-blown ditching.

I take a deep breath, but when I do it . . . hurts?

The ground twists beneath me. The air around me is suddenly dense. Suffocating. I half fall, half crouch down, clenching my jaw to still the throbbing in my temples. A sharp dagger of cold air pierces my lungs. My knees hit the damp dirt.

Everything changes in an instant.

CHAPTER 20

I am awakened by the iron taste of blood on my tongue. There is a horn blaring inside my brain. No, not inside my brain. *Outside?* Bright white lights beat against my closed eyelids. My forehead is leaning against something hard. My neck hurts.

Get up. Get up. Get up.

My body is heavy, head lolling from side to side. A dull ache roars to life from somewhere I can't place quite yet.

With monumental strength, my eyes flicker open. A blaring noise beats at every attempt to think straight. I command my neck to lift my head. To my surprise, I am sitting. In a chair?

Broken glass crumbled like pebbled sand digs into my palms. It starts to come back to me—school, darkness, a strange dream . . .

Fear courses its way through my body as I creep into consciousness, my heart threatening to beat out of my chest. I take in the scene around me. I am in my school uniform. I am in a car that I do not recognize. The front of the vehicle is smashed into a brick wall. Smells of smoke, oil, and vehicular carnage steep the air. I am in the driver's seat.

There is a piece of paper taped to my chest. I tear it off and turn it over so I can read it. All the air in my lungs whooshes away as I see the purple bat-symbol, encircled in a yellow heart.

Sirens blare in the distance, quickly closing in. I could try to run. Escape the scene before the police arrive. But then again, there are cameras everywhere these days. And how would I explain a hit-and-run?

I try to think things through, but the problem is I'm so sleepy. My thoughts are stuck in molasses. Even if I wanted to run, I couldn't. Too dizzy.

Someone shakes my shoulder, but I don't want to be awake. My vision is too blurry. I think I fell asleep again. I'm still in the car.

I catch sight of someone's eyes. I panic for a moment, but luckily, they're regular eyes. Not pitch-black ones. Not those haunted eyes. A sigh of relief escapes me.

"You're okay, kid. You've been hurt, but it's going to be okay," the voice says.

My rib cage is throbbing. I shift a little and the pain explodes. Reality becomes even blurrier after that: bright headlights, black smoke . . . the feeling of something taking over me . . . a cracked phone screen . . .

"Hey, hey, stay awake. Keep looking at me." Then: "Call the commissioner. I think this is his daughter. *This is too much blood.*"

I whimper. How could I not? Where am I? Where's . . .

"Slow down the bleeding," I hear someone else say tensely.

Everything slips into black.

There is a steady beeping noise in my ears.

My eyes flutter open. I grimace. My body aches like it has several knives stuck in it. I look around, vision still fuzzy. I'm in a hospital room.

Dad is standing in the doorway, talking to someone in a white coat. A doctor?

I can't make out the voices. Dad notices me immediately and comes closer. I try to stay awake, but it's too hard. I slip out of consciousness all over again.

Something pinches my arm. My eyes fly open and I see an IV. I stare at the ceiling fan whirling stale air around the room. What the hell happened?

"Hi, Barbara," someone says softly.

I turn my head to see Dad and . . . "Dick?" My voice is hoarse.

"How are you feeling?" asks Dad in a low, soothing voice.

I want to say I'm fine, but when I shift my weight on the mattress, everything hurts. I wince.

"Take it easy, Babs," Dick says.

Is he really here? For a split second, I think of Nico.

"Barbara, you never told me that you were friends with Bruce Wayne's boy," Dad says.

I blink twice.

"We met at school this year," Dick says to my father with an easygoing charm, though his eyes are locked on mine. A convenient enough lie. Dad clearly buys it.

My mouth feels dry. I cough a little and it hurts. "What happened?"

"You were in a car accident," Dad tells me.

"But I don't have a car."

Dad exchanges a quiet look with Dick that makes me uncomfortable. "What happened?" I ask again, letting some of the panic coursing through my body seep into my words.

Dad is struggling to find the right words, so Dick glances at him again, asking for permission to take the lead. Dad gives him a nod and Dick clears his throat. "You walked into the school parking lot and broke the window of a car about to pull into a spot. You yanked the driver out of their seat, then drove away in the car yourself. You were only behind the wheel for a minute before you veered out of the lot and onto a sidewalk into a crowd of pedestrians."

My stomach gurgles with the threat of vomit.

Please don't let there be any casualties, please don't let there be any casualties, please—

"Nobody else was injured," Dick says, reading the panic on my face.

"Good." I sigh in relief. Every exhale hurts.

"You have some bruising from the crash, but nothing's broken. You have a concussion, and some glass cut the scalp at the top of your head, so there was a lot of bleeding—that always makes it look worse than it is. But otherwise, you're okay," Dad says, listing the details like the good cop he is.

Except I don't feel okay. I feel stupid. This is my fault that I'm here. If I had solved the case sooner, then none of this would have happened. I've been tracking this thing down just for it to get me so easily? And nearly kill me in the process?

I remember the note taped to my chest when I woke up in the car. The purple bat-symbol and the yellow heart. When Alysia was possessed, a mysterious voice asked Batgirl if she got the message. Two thoughts collide in my brain at top speed. The first: Whoever's behind this clearly doesn't know that me (Barbara) and Batgirl are the same person. If they did, then they wouldn't have left a note for her like this. This is a relief. The second: The demon *is* targeting Batgirl. I know that for sure now. But why?

"I don't remember doing any of that," I tell my dad. "You have to believe me."

"I do believe you." Dad watches my face stonily. "I don't understand, but I believe you."

"Dad, can Dick and I have a moment alone, please?"

Both Dick and my dad stare at me with undisguised surprise.

"Oh. Uh . . ." Dad looks between me and Dick, trying to ascertain the threat level of leaving us alone. "Ten minutes," he says finally.

Dick puts on perhaps the most awkward smile in the world as Dad walks out the room, muttering about checking out the cafeteria. When he's gone, Dick rubs the back of his neck, opening and closing his mouth like he's trying to find something to say. I think he's bracing for an awkward conversation or something. Or maybe he realized how much of a jerk he was the last time we spoke at the Batcave and is trying to think of an apology. There's a tiny part of me that wants to tell Dick straight up that he hurt my feelings the other day. That him not believing in me hurts because I want to be taken seriously—by him maybe even more than anyone else. But how humiliating is that? So instead, I push all that aside and say, "I need you to do me a favor."

I can tell from the slight slump in his shoulders that he probably was hoping for—as much as dreading—a chance to clear the air while we're alone, but he knows me well enough to understand that if I'm asking him for a favor, it's urgent. He stands up straighter at the seriousness in my voice, meeting my eyes with focused attention. "What's up?"

"Make sure my dad stays out the room for the next ten minutes." I push myself up into a seated position and pull the IV from my arm.

Dick winces. "Hey, whoa, Babs, stop that."

"I need to go see Austin," I explain as I swing my legs over the side of the bed. "Do you know if they are on this floor?"

"Down the hall, but *you* need to rest. You're literally in the hospital. Don't be crazy."

"Don't tell me what to do."

I give him my best unmovable stare.

He gives me his best Bat-Family glare.

Eventually, though, he sighs. "Fine. Ten minutes. But we have to hurry. Your dad will kill me if he catches us."

"Afraid of Commissioner Gordon, are we?" I tease.

"When it comes to his daughter? An entirely well-founded fear." He helps me to my feet.

The journey to Austin's room isn't easy. I lean on Dick. He holds me steady. We compartmentalize our own drama and focus solely on the mission: getting me to Austin's room. When we arrive at our destination, Dick hangs back in the hallway, standing guard, while I push open the door into the dimly lit hospital room. Outside the window, the sun is setting. The haze from the pollution scatters the light in a way that makes the city skyline glow. That's Gotham City for you: all contradiction. Smoggy air that somehow still manages to form a beautiful sunset.

Austin's bed is at the far end of the room on the other side of a heavy white curtain. I step closer, getting ready to announce myself, but when I see Austin, I hesitate. They're sitting up in bed, but crouched over like a little kid, their hair hanging in a heavy curtain in front of their face. It's not until I notice the way their shoulders are shaking that I realize Austin is crying. Hard.

A heavy stone sinks from my chest to the pit of my stomach. What will happen to Austin if I don't stop this thing? How many more people will get hurt, or worse?

The stakes are clear: Austin's freedom, my class-mates' lives, the safety of Gotham.

I need a breakthrough on this case. I need a win. For all of us.

I leave without a word.

CHAPTER 21

My first night back home, I dream that I am Robin. Then Batman. Then my father. Then Alysia. Then Nico. Then Austin. Then Lily. Then Harper. Then the Scarecrow. Then the old woman next door. Then the cashier at the bodega. Then the train conductor and the mayor and the doctor pacing the hospital and the patient in his care. Soon I had dreamt that I was everyone in Gotham City except myself.

There are tears on my pillow when I blink away the sleep. Losing myself is lonely.

I've yanked the shower curtain to the side three times so far, certain that I saw a shadowy figure standing out there, sure that I heard footsteps or smelled smoke. *It's just nerves,* I tell myself, again and again. *This paranoid feeling will pass.*

It has to.

Dad takes pity on me and lets me stay home from school the next day. I spend an hour or two wrapped up in my bedsheets like a burrito with earphones, the way Dad had taught me to do when I was younger and my brain was racing too fast to function. Dad took the morning off too, to look after me, even though I insisted that he shouldn't waste his paid time off on me. He checks on me every half hour. If he hears me get out of bed, he follows me around the house like a worried puppy. He's always close by. But then again, his presence is appreciated, no matter how much I feel like I don't want it. Every time I fall asleep, I have nightmares. Every time I look in the mirror, my skin crawls. In fact, I can't even bring myself to *actually* look in the mirror. Each time I catch even a glimpse of my reflection, I flinch.

I'm not necessarily in my best shape.

When I walk into the kitchen to grab a snack before dinner, Dad greets me with a soft kiss on my forehead. "Hey, honey. How was your nap?"

"It . . . Uh. It happened. I'll leave it at that."

"Nightmares?"

"Eh." He started asking about nightmares ever since last year, when I had my first run-in with the Scarecrow. I blamed the nightmares on a scary movie when Dad asked, but I had night terrors for weeks. I'm better now, but my usual sleep pattern isn't necessarily straightforward either. Sometimes the line between dreams and nightmares gets blurred. I'm not always sure how exactly to classify the thoughts that pass through my sleeping brain.

"So, Dick Grayson?" Dad asks, raising an eyebrow.

I pour myself a glass of water. "What about him?"

"He calls you Babs?" Dad asks with interest.

I ignore his question and stare at his badge resting on the countertop. I stiffen up. "What happens to me now? Am I in trouble? For taking the car?"

Dad runs a tired hand over his face and rubs his eyes. "I'm not sure yet. I'll explain the situation to GCPD and see what I can do."

"And for Austin? Whatever happened to me happened to them too."

"I'll see about Austin too. Whatever this is . . ." He pushes his glasses up his nose. "God, I don't even know what to make of this. I wish Batman were here."

Me too.

When I look over at him, I see that he's studying me intensely. "Barbara. Even before your accident, you've been acting . . . different. I'm worried. What's been going on with you lately?"

What's going on with me? Well, nothing. And . . . everything. All at once. My life is pretty much the same as it's always been for the past two years. I go to school, come home, eat dinner, do homework, get a few hours in as Batgirl, then get ready for bed. Not exactly the same schedule as every other kid in high school, but—minus the whole vigilante thing—close enough. Except now there are all these new factors. I'm chasing after some demonic entity without a plan and every new possession feels like a personal failure on my part. There's a crazy cult eager to usher in some demonic apocalypse, and if I can't crack the mystery before they do, then someone will die. I'm fighting with one of my closest friends and have hardly talked to him beyond work stuff in two weeks. I'm supposed to be solving this case, but I keep getting distracted by a boy with pink hair and kind eyes who'll probably never hang out with me again after this is all over. Nothing has changed, yet everything has.

But I can't tell my dad any of this. So I force a fake smile and say, "I'm okay, just tired."

I can tell he doesn't believe me by the way he looks at me, his eyebrows knitting together above his glasses. But he doesn't push.

The worst part of being a vigilante is all the lying. I've never been comfortable with the level of deception necessary to do this work safely. It's not because I think I'm a saint or anything, but because I'm quite good at it. Excuses come to me like breathing. My dad asks about my day, and I share with him half-truths or pivot the question back on him in hopes of steering us off topic. If he were working, he'd notice my evasiveness. He'd clock it right away as a sign that I was hiding something. Luckily, my dad never treats me like a suspect. He believes he raised an honest daughter. He takes my word at face value. That makes me feel even worse. I want to tell him, I don't want to tell him. Sometimes I have nightmares that I'll never get the chance to tell him. On these occasions, when I wake up with bloodshot eyes the next morning, I never know if the emotion slamming my chest is regret or relief.

Dad heads to the precinct, which is actually comforting—he can probably do more good for the case by working than staying here worrying about me. He also tends to be a workaholic, so it's really all for the best to let him go do the thing he loves doing.

Alysia stops by in the afternoon with a bag of cookies and a worried smile. She hugs me, then swears that if the demon had hurt me badly, it'd be her own villain origin story. I laugh a little and it doesn't hurt. Physically, I'm feeling almost back to normal now. Mentally, I'm still shaken. She wants to stay, but I can't face her right now. I can't face anyone. Not until I get a handle on things. So I send her home, promising to call her later, then retreat to my self-imposed isolation.

The rest of the day passes in a manic frenzy of brainstorming interspersed with brief moments of panic. How can I catch this thing off guard? So far, the demon's been calling the shots—showing up whenever it wants to terrorize us. But how can I turn the tables and make it come to me when I'm actually prepared? And once I do . . . then what? And what if I can't—

Nope. Not going there. When I feel the chilling thrum of a self-doubt spiral brewing, I finally pick up my phone to call someone for help.

In a blink, Traci 13 appears in my bedroom, though she looks different this time.

"Batgirl!" Her voice is warm and bright, matching the energy of the slicked-back high ponytail she's wearing. A stark contrast to the gloom I'm emanating.

"Hey, Traci," I say. "You look . . ." I lean forward to wave my hand through her, but I'm met with solid mass. I fall backward.

"No astral projection this time," she says with a wave of her hand. "Decided to teleport." She glances around my room carefully. "Dang. I was hoping you'd call me from the Batcave. I always wanted to see inside there."

"Sorry to disappoint," I say as she plops down on the chair in the corner of my room. "How are you?"

"I'm good. Natasha Irons and I had to fight this ninja. She almost took my head off with a sword—crazy, right? Afterward, Natasha stayed over, though, so it wasn't all bad, even though Jaime got all weird about it." Am I supposed to know who these people are? I haven't done much networking yet—sometimes I forget how many young heroes there are throughout the country. "Anyway, I'm happy to keep telling you about all the drama here in Metropolis, but I doubt that's why you called."

"Right." I take a deep breath. "I'm struggling over here. The possessions keep piling up. I don't know what to do."

"Are they still asking for Batman?"

"I actually think that they're looking for . . . Batgirl."

I'm expecting her to doubt me like the others, but she simply says, "That makes sense."

"I've read everything, consulted every source, and there's nothing out there about defeating a body-jumping demon. And all my computer skills are virtually useless, given that the demon is supernatural and doesn't seem to trigger any reactions on the multiple radiation detectors I set up around campus. I don't know what to do." I lean back and groan. "Hey, if I fail this case, can you please do me a favor and possess me, so that I don't have to face Batman alone when he comes back to Gotham City? I'll make sure to do it in the Batcave, so you can have a proper look around."

Traci's eyebrows shoot up. "Batman doesn't know you're working this case alone?"

"Nope."

"Damn, girl. Living on the edge," she says. "Well, you know my stance on possession, but for you, I'd make an exception."

"Thanks. Appreciate it." I'm going to need all the support I can get. I wonder if he'll cut off my resources for failing. That would suck.

Traci watches me wallow for a moment, then stands up straight. "Look, Batgirl. You're not going to book-report or code your way out of a problem with a demonic entity. Time to go on the offense and surprise and capture this thing."

I pull the drawstring on my hoodie tight around my face. "I know, I know. I have to lure it in somehow. But I don't want to put more people at risk. I try not to head into situations without knowing as much as possible. I still don't even fully know what I'm up against."

"Yeah, but when do we ever know what we're up against when we're fighting?"

Fair point. "How should I do it, though?"

"You tell me," Traci says. "What's the plan?"

I hang my hand over the edge of the bed and rip open the bag of cookie crisps Alysia brought over earlier. I shove two into my mouth. For morale.

"The new plan is to think of a new plan," I mumble.

"Brilliant. So innovative. Such clear vision."

I roll over, sigh. "Fine. New plan is to lure in the demon and trap it, but I still need to figure out who the host is first. The problem is that the host might not know that they're the host. When I woke up after being possessed—"

"It got you too?" Traci stares at me, horrified.

"Yup." Don't really wanna revisit that right now, though, so I keep pushing. "When I woke, I didn't have any memories, which makes me think that the host might not realize what's happening to them either."

"Good, good! Now we're getting somewhere!" Traci claps in my face like a woefully optimistic coach trying to hype up her team of underdogs. "Have you noticed any patterns with the possessions so far?"

"I have one theory." I wipe my hands on the front of my jeans. "All the possessions have happened in group settings. And they've all only lasted a few minutes or so."

Traci leans in. "Go on."

"Well, if the temporary possessions can only last a limited amount of time, then the body jumper has to go somewhere at the end of each possession, right? Return 'home' or whatever?" Traci nods. "And then there's the piece about proximity too. At the football game, the first victim dropped the knife as soon as he ran away from the crowd. The next victim came back to consciousness as soon as Robin and I drove her away from the scene. And when it got me, I stole a car, but once I drove it around the corner, I woke up. I think the host has to be physically near the victim for the temporary possession to hold."

"Interesting." Traci grabs a crisp and chews carefully. "Seems like the demon can only last in other bodies for so long, and when it's done, it has to return to its true host. So what if you—"

"—encourage the demon to make an appearance, but this time, instead of letting everyone run away after, track the demon back to its true host?"

"There it is!" Traci says, grinning. "Those famous Bat-Family detective skills."

My brain is whirling now, operating at full capacity. The mental fog of the past couple of days clears as the final pieces click into place.

The demon loves busy moments: the art showcase, the football game, campus during passing period. All I need is a big event to draw it out. An activity involving a lot of my peers in an enclosed space, or . . .

Of course.

I look up at Traci 13, let myself smile. "I know how to trap the demon."

The young mage lifts an eyebrow.

"We throw one hell of a party."

CHAPTER 22

A kid with a beanie pulled over his eyes opens the front door. When he smiles at me, his eyes are red and hazy, his voice slurring as he waves me inside. I take one step and nearly trip over a mountain of discarded shoes. Combat boots, wedge heels, and expensive sneakers litter Lily's parents' fancy marble floor. Another step and I collide with a very tall guy with a very deep voice, carrying a drink, who looks at me, says hi, then immediately excuses himself presumably to be ill somewhere. His friends bust out in laughter, breaking the tabletop where they had been watching from. Behind them, bodies upon bodies sway and jump in costumes that range from inane to ridiculous. Bass-heavy music blares at ear-splitting volume.

Welcome to Operation Party Trap.

Alysia literally squealed with excitement when I called her last night to explain my idea to lure the demon in with a party. She said we should have a costume theme, given that it's spooky season and all. I agreed, only because it gives me cover to show up as Batgirl. I called Nico next and he was down too. He didn't think twice about Alysia's sudden involvement in the case after I reminded him that she had been possessed too. We're all eager to take this demon down once and for all. Nico can't invite people to his place and Alysia's parents would kill her if she ever threw a party, so we looped in Lily. Her parents were robbed last year and installed a pretty advanced security system as a result, which will come in handy for my plan. Plus, her Sweet Sixteen was professionally photographed by this big shot artist and got over a hundred thousand likes online, so when she throws a party . . .

". . . everyone will be there," Lily promised. And she was right. The entire sophomore, junior, and senior classes of Gotham Academy are here tonight—and among them, hopefully, the host.

Lily's house is grand in a shocking way. I knew she had money, but I didn't know that her family had *money*.

We're in Bristol, the fancy, low-density residential area home to Gotham City's millionaires and CEOs. Lily's mansion isn't Wayne Manor–level grandiose, but it's giving Intergenerational Wealth nevertheless. It's the kind of home that probably has some historic landmark designation because it has that classic Art Deco style that's becoming rare in Gotham City. It's almost too bad that the party raging inside is turning the place into a debaucherous mess.

The entire first floor is rank with body heat. The marble table in the entryway is covered with bottles of liquor stolen from parents and cases of beer purchased with fake IDs. (My dad would have a heart attack.) Everyone's talking over one another, laughing loudly. It's so weird walking in here in my Batgirl suit. Everyone thinks it's only an accurate costume, but still.

A guy in socks dressed as Wonder Woman slides across the tiled floor of the entryway, crashing into a giant stack of Jenga. The mummy and the mermaid who had been playing scream at him, throwing the scattered wooden pieces at his head. He shields his face, laughing, until he catches hold of the mummy, wraps his arms around his waist, and kisses him eagerly. The mummy drops the Jenga block he had been yielding and melts into Wonder Woman, making everyone around them laugh and "boo" affectionately.

I find myself looking for a flash of pink hair in the crowd. I haven't seen Nico since the kiss—not as Batgirl, anyway. Maybe if things played out differently, I could've gotten to know him at school as my regular self. Then maybe we'd go to parties like this together all the time. Not just costume ones, where I can hide among the crowd. What if I messed up by getting to know him as Batgirl instead of as Barbara? I think he might like me, but he likes Batgirl Me. Not *Me* Me. I guess I don't blame him. Whatever, though. Where is Alysia? I check my phone.

Alysia: running late!

Barbara: *you're* the one late tonight?? Wooooow

Barbara: oh how the tables have turned

Alysia: shut up

I call Nico, but it goes straight to voicemail. Lily's still phoneless, so until I can find them in this sea of my classmates, I guess I'm stuck here alone. Wonderful. Not socially anxiety-inducing at all. And because the universe has a cruel sense of humor, the first person I actually recognize is Dick Grayson.

Even in a densely packed crowd, he stands out. He's

not the tallest guy in the room; other guys are bulkier with bigger muscles as opposed to his lean, fit frame. Still, there's an undeniable gravity in the way Dick stands with his perfect posture, one hand casually holding a cup, making everyone around him laugh.

He's dressed as . . . Robin. Of course. Though instead of his usual armored top, he's wearing a red shirt that's snug enough to hug his body nicely without being too tight. His dark hair is mussed with a few strands falling in a curtain on either side of his eyes, framing his face. He's so handsome that sometimes it seems incredible to me that everyone isn't staring at him all the time.

Suddenly, his head whips up from his conversation. Even behind his mask, I can feel his gaze zero in on me. His jaw drops open ever so slightly. I spin around on my heels. Maybe I can act like I'm in the middle of something and he'll stay away? It's no use, though. It's too loud in here to hear his footsteps, but I can still feel his presence when he stops a few inches behind my back, so close that I can feel his breath on my neck. When he speaks, his voice falters. "H-hi."

The tiny crack in his composure wills me to turn and face him.

"I'm sorry for what I said the other day," he says. "About Bruce. And the bait. I don't know why I said that."

I look around, shocked that he's bringing this up right now, with all these people nearby. Nobody could hear us over the music, but still.

"I grew up in this world surrounded by a lot of men with big egos. I guess some of that thinking rubbed off on me. Not an excuse, but I am sorry. And it won't happen again." He takes a nervous sip from his cup but forces himself to keep his gaze locked on mine. "I respect you a lot—I literally trust you with my life—and I know that you're extremely capable. Sorry for being dumb and making it seem like I didn't."

My shoulders relax, releasing weeks' worth of tension. I know his apology is sincere. Dick Grayson may sometimes say the wrong thing, but he doesn't lie. And he's a good student; he knows how to learn from a mistake.

"It's okay . . . *Dick.*"

A startled laugh bursts from both of us. "Wooow. So original."

"I haven't made a dick joke around you in months. You deserved that one."

"Fair enough." He smirks into his drink. "You're empty-handed," he observes.

"I don't drink. And neither do you."

"This is seltzer." He gives the cup a little shake. "I think we can find you a water bottle, though." He pivots toward the dense crowd separating us from the drinks table across the room. He ventures into the mass of bodies, looking back at me over his shoulder. "Coming?"

I should find Alysia and touch base with Lily and Nico, but after clearing the air with Dick, I realize I'm not ready to leave his side just yet. And I can continue to survey the crowd.

"Lead the way," I reply.

Dick navigates us through the mess of bodies. I can't stop the slow spread of comfort as I follow close behind him like a shadow. Why does being near him in a crowded room immediately put me at ease? I focus my eyes on the Utility Belt hanging loosely from his hips. It swishes slightly with each step.

Oh, yeah. That's why.

"Nice costume," I say when we reach the drinks table.

He examines my outfit with the quirk of an eyebrow. "You did the same thing."

"Yeah, but at least I have a valid reason. I'm on the clock. You, on the other hand, only wanted an excuse to wear your tight shirt and pants."

I can see the threat of a dumb joke tugging at his lips, but he bites it back with a smug grin. I laugh with him. This boy can annoy me, but when we're good, we're good. It's so easy with him. It's always easy with him.

I lean against the wall and observe the crowd as he fishes around in a cooler to find something for me that's nonalcoholic. "There are, like, five other Batgirl costumes at this party and it's so dark in here. How'd you know which one was me?"

He shakes his head, smiling. "There's something about you that I'll always recognize."

A slow, delighted ripple rolls through me at his words. The feeling is familiar. It's the one that teased me before our fight. Before Nico.

Nico. How did my personal life change so much since I last spoke to Dick? I don't regret kissing Nico. It was amazing. And if the timing is right, I wouldn't mind doing it again. Still, the thought briefly short-circuits my brain. My first kiss was with Nico. I always thought it'd be with Dick.

"Want to voyage to the kitchen next?" he asks. "We can scavenge for snacks. I'm starving."

I can feel his anxious hope radiating off him in waves. Still, I say, "You don't want to hang out with your friends?"

"Babs," Dick says, swapping out the charm for something much more sincere. His gaze finds mine and stays there. "I want to hang out with *you.* I've missed you."

The softness in his voice sends a rush of warmth

straight to the base of my spine. "I've missed you too."

The air between us shifts. After stealing glances for the past several minutes, we finally let ourselves look at one another like we've been wanting to all night. He's seen me dressed as Batgirl a million times before, but you wouldn't know that by the way he lets his eyes linger on every curve, every hem, of my outfit. The muscles in his arms are relaxed, yet firm from all his training. The stripped-down, casual version of his suit makes him look like a daydream.

This is an unexpected side effect of our fight: now that feelings have been acknowledged, we can't make them unknown again. When I look at him, and he looks at me, we both know there's something beneath it all, scratching right below the surface. Before our fight, we'd try to hide these looks. But now?

The music changes abruptly from Top Forty rap to an industrial beat. It reminds me of Nico. What am I doing? I need to find him. And the others.

"Can you do me a favor, please?" I ask Dick.

He gives me one of those heart-on-his-sleeve gazes of his. "Anything."

"Can you ... leave? This party. Please?"

His eyes widen. "Why?"

"Tonight is important to me. I can't focus if you're here. Okay?"

"I'm distracting you?" He tilts toward me, playfully. My core swirls. Whoa. "Are you doing something with your investigation? Because I can help," he adds, slipping seamlessly back into our regular professional tone. "You call the shots, I'll support."

While I appreciate the way he calls it "my" investigation, that won't be enough. Dick hasn't been possessed yet and I'd like to keep it that way.

"No. You gotta go. I lead two lives, and right now, there's a demon in both of them. I need you out of here for my plan to work."

I can tell he doesn't want to leave, but he knows that since I just forgave him, he's kind of at my will here. "Fine." He fishes for his keys in his pocket. "Call me if you need me?"

"Will do."

I watch his figure until I'm sure it's disappeared out the door. I'm not even drinking, but I'm dizzy. That was nice. That was a relief. That was ... What even was that? How am I going to move around him now that I know that if I ever change my mind about ... us ... all the feelings would tumble back so quickly? That all we'd need is a spark?

Tuning in to the plan feels like a good distraction right about now. I've wasted enough time tonight and who knows how long we have before the demon shows.

I slip up the spiral staircase in the entryway. I find Lily at the top of the stairs, looking down at the party below. "Whoa!" she says as soon as she sees me.

I look at her costume and laugh. "Neo from *The Matrix*?"

She grins, waving her arms down her all-black attire. "Yeah. It felt fitting for the vibe tonight. The black trench coat is an Austin wardrobe staple." Her smile falters at this, but she holds it together. "I saw a couple people downstairs dressed as Batgirl."

I laugh awkwardly. "Yeah. That's a first for me."

"I'm sure by next Halloween, you'll have won even more people over. Kids will love having a cool diverse hero to dress up as."

"Oh. Um. I guess?" I grimace back at Lily as she hits me with the most sincere smile imaginable. She could've left out the diverse part, but sure. I see her point.

"Anyway," she says. "Here. Let me show you the security system."

It's exactly as she had described to me earlier. There are only four cameras. They're stationary. One at the front entrance of the dining area, one in the back of the house, one in the living room, and one in the kitchen. None of them gives me much to work with, but they offer a modicum of surveillance. The most important security feature is the panic button anyway—but that's for later, in case of emergency only. And I disengage its connection to the GCPD. I don't need their interference—or my dad showing up.

My phone vibrates.

Alysia: yo just got here

          Barbara: no worries I'm upstairs

Alysia: how are you doing on tech?

          Barbara: hacking into the home security cameras now

          Barbara: put in the earpiece and we'll communicate over the comm system

Alysia: roger that

Despite the background noise, Alysia's voice comes in clear through the high-quality comms. "I'm in position."

"Great. I'm not seeing shadows or other signs of movement on the cameras yet, but I'm going to keep an eye on them as I survey downstairs again. If you hear anything, let me know."

"Copy," Alysia fires back.

I hand Lily an earpiece. "Keep this in, all right?" She places it in her ear. "It goes well with the outfit."

She smirks. "I was hoping it would."

I leave her at the top of the stairs to keep an eye on the party below while I go look for Nico. From the window, I see him walk out into the backyard. Alone. He circles around to the side of the house where it's all tall bushes and shadows, then sits on the ground with his head between his legs. Is he okay?

I jog down the stairs and head outside. The cool air in contrast to the congestion of the party inside is a gift.

"Well, aren't you looking particularly emo tonight," I say as I approach him.

When he looks up at me, I burst out laughing. I couldn't tell from far away, but he's dressed up tonight . . . as Batgirl.

"Woooooow. Trying to steal my whole fit, are you?"

"Gotta dress as my favorite hero, you know?" It's dark outside, but there's enough light from the party through the window to see the way his eyes glow, mischief dancing in them. "I hate to break it to you, but you have no shot at winning the costume contest. Mine is much more authentic," Nico says.

"Well, in that case, let me take this mask off. . . ." I make a big show of the movement, pretending to hook my fingers beneath the mask and pull it over my face. It's a joke, obviously, but as I pantomime revealing my identity, I catch a brief moment of shock in Nico's expression.

His eyes widen slightly, lips parting as he watches me. His sharp exhale clouds the cold air, leaving his mouth momentarily obscured by a tiny swirl of fog.

I freeze. Does he actually want to know who I am? The real me?

I let my hands fall from my mask and cough out an awkward laugh, shattering the moment. His eyes dart away as he shakes his head, smiling to himself. He hangs his head back, leaning against the stucco wall behind him, then pats the ground beside him. "Sit with me?"

My body moves without hesitation. I toss him an earpiece for the mission tonight, then settle down beside him. The grass beneath us is soft and slightly damp from the dewy night air, but I don't mind. I cross my legs at first, but that's not comfortable, so I shift my position, bringing my knees to my chest. Once I'm settled, I can feel the thick fabric of Nico's sweatshirt brushing against my Batsuit jacket. I didn't mean to sit so close to him. I wait for him to move, put another inch or two between us, but he doesn't. I wait for him to say something, but he doesn't do that either. All he does is turn to me. Then—like it's easy, like it's nothing, like we've done it before—he reaches for my hand.

Electricity shoots from his touch through every corner of my body. He doesn't bother to hide the way his gaze slowly drips from my eyes down to my mouth. I watch him tug his bottom lip between his teeth, letting out the smallest sigh.

A quick image of Robin flashes in my mind. Something like guilt stirs in my rib cage, even though there's no reason for it. I'm not in a relationship with either Robin or Nico. I've told both boys that I don't want to be anyone's girlfriend right now. I don't belong to anyone. I shouldn't feel bad exploring how I feel. Still, my feelings for both boys swirl together like a tornado. I think I'm getting overwhelmed. Nico releases my hand to hook a finger into the pocket of my jacket. With a light tug, a ghost of a smirk, he pulls me closer.

Yup. Definitely overwhelming.

I move with Nico in a daze. How is it that being near him feels so good too? One of my hands drifts to his side, mirroring his touch at my waist. The other settles in the place where the hard line of his jaw meets the soft curve of his neck. He hums and I feel the vibration beneath my fingertips. *Damn.*

Are we going to kiss again? Already? I never thought my first kiss would happen while wearing my mask. For some reason, it's the fast-approaching prospect of our second one that drives the reality of this home. Will every kiss be like this? Stolen between moments of chaos? Half of my face hidden behind black fabric, his eyes squinting, wondering who it is he's really kissing?

But then his grip on my waist tightens and his eyes glint with mischief and *whoosh*. All doubts are instantly vaporized. One touch is all it takes to bring me back. Pathetic.

I feel the gentlest touch of a fingertip on my throat, tracing my windpipe. A tiny thrill races through my core as strong hands pull me up onto his lap. I wrap my arms around his neck and we press closer together.

"EXCUSE ME." Alysia's voice booms through my earpiece. I practically jump out of Nico's lap.

I tap my earpiece, shaking off the embarrassment. "Alysia. All okay?"

"You need to get your ass inside, ASAP." She breathes heavily, as if she's running. *"It's here."*

CHAPTER 23

Step One is to seal the exits. Nobody in, nobody out. I understand that it's morally questionable to have thrown a party just to trap everyone once a demonic entity shows up, but... Well, dang. Okay, honestly, it is hard to justify. But we have to corner this thing.

I race upstairs to the home security system hub and slam the panic button. There's a loud lurching noise—like the sound of multiple garage doors closing all at once—then I watch as a steel plate emerges from the top of the window to slide over the glass. This is happening all around the house. Windows sliding shut, doors reinforcing themselves with emergency bolts. One thing about rich people in Gotham City is that they're plenty paranoid about some impending class war turning against them (and probably for good reason). I've heard of the local businesses that've sprung up selling lockdown systems and apocalypse bunkers for the rich, but I've never seen one in action before. Now nobody's getting in or out of here until I release the panic setting. I swat aside the twinge of guilt about what's going to happen next.

Then I run to he front door so I can show Alysia where to stand to corral everyone into the living room. I send Nico off to the back door to do the same. Meanwhile, Lily's standing guard at the top of the stairs, making sure nobody tries to hide or escape any other way.

"Do I want to know what I interrupted?" Alysia asks. She looks ragged, but it's purposeful—she's dressed up tonight as a contestant from one of those extreme survivalist reality shows, fake dirt and grime smeared over her skin, a yellow buff holding her hair back.

I meet her question with silence. She sighs. "Please tell me you didn't kiss him."

I already did! is what I want to shout, but instead I say, "I like Nico. He likes me."

"He likes Batgirl."

"Can we discuss this later, please?" I shoot her a stern look before I tap my earpiece, opening the comms with the others as I shove my way to the center of the party. "Everyone hold your positions."

I study the darkness around me, my eyes scanning and panning, trying to pick out any irregular movement.

"Bad news," Nico says through our comms.

"Did you find the host?" I ask, keeping my eyes locked on the scene.

"No, but I got a text. From Andrew." My stomach drops. "DFG heard about a Gotham Academy party in the neighborhood. They're on their way. And they're pissed I didn't tell them about it."

I take a deep breath. "Don't worry. Everything will be fine." I try to infuse the words with enough gravity to will them to be true. But that becomes impossible when I finally see it: the body jumper in action.

A kid in my math class stumbles forward. His eyes are black, gashed into his skin. He shoves through the crowd, reaching for me, fingers locked into tortured claws. He looks drunk, so a girl nearby takes out her phone to record, laughing. But then her posture changes. The first boy falls to the ground while I watch the eyes of the girl with her phone slowly roll into the back of her head, then drip into a sinister onyx. A thin trail of black smoke leaks from the corners of her eyes, worming its way from her body like a serpent. Her face freezes into a scream for a moment before she stumbles forward, pushing her boyfriend out of the way with her sharp gaze locked on mine, snarling. My mind scrambles to find something, anything, to do, but I can't seem to move my feet. The music blares around me, bass thudding in my ears, as the possessed girl hurls closer, hissing like a wild animal. She draws more attention, and more people record. She collapses. And right as her body hits the floor, the girl beside me goes rail straight, drops her drink, then lunges for my throat.

Sharp pain erupts where her nails dig into the flesh of my neck. I try to shake her off, but she only tightens her grip. Black smoke thickens the air between us. Hazy stars dance across my eyes as I gasp for breath, reaching for her hands. I don't want to hurt her, but I don't have a choice anymore. I headbutt her, hard, and she staggers backward. I sprint, pushing through the crowd, as fast as I can toward the back door.

My breathing is erratic by the time I reach Nico. He's standing his ground guarding the exit, but everyone's yelling at him. I can feel the scratches on my neck seeping blood, deep bruises forming beneath my skin. Nico takes one look at me and his eyebrows fly up his forehead. "Are you okay?"

"Something isn't right," I say through short, panting breaths.

"No shit," Nico grunts, holding strong against a guy who keeps reaching for the doorknob and threatening to break Nico's arm if we don't let him leave. It's better if nobody at the party knows the truth that even if Nico were to step aside, they still wouldn't be able to escape, now that the home's on lockdown. Less panic this way.

"The demon's been saying that it wants me, but when it finally has me in the same room right now, it hasn't possessed me," I say, my words spilling out like sand slipping between my fingers.

"Why?"

"Maybe because . . . because it can't."

Nico huffs. "Why not?"

"I don't know! I don't know." Panic courses through my veins. We hear a scream.

If the demon was able to possess me as my normal self, then there is no logical reason why it suddenly couldn't possess me now as Batgirl. Clearly it *wants* to hurt me. I have the wounds to show it. So maybe there's a problem with its method of possession.

How is it jumping? How is it jumping? How is it—?

"I'm calling the police," a scared girl cries beside me. She pulls her phone out of her back pocket, but then drops it immediately. Her eyes snap to an eerie pitch-black, just like the others.

That's it.

"Oh my god," I whisper. "That's the pattern."

The possessed girl jumps at me, but this time I'm ready. I block her easily. Everyone who was trying to escape through the back door now yells and runs away, racing for the front door instead.

"Now would be a great time to fill me in on your

brain blast before somebody dies tonight!" Nico yells.

Austin checked their phone right before they were possessed. And Alysia. The moment before I was possessed, I checked the time. That was the last thing I remembered before it took over. And as soon as the girl was getting ready to call the police . . .

"It's moving through people's phones," I mumble.

"How?" Nico asks, but there's no time to explain.

"I don't know. Just turn off your phone!" I stand on the chair in the corner. *"Everyone, turn off your phones!"* I yell. But as more chaos erupts, more cameras go off. "Don't look at your phones! Please!" I shout even louder, but the music's still blaring. The party is so rowdy that somehow, only about half of the room has even realized that there's a full-blown possession going on here and that the screams aren't part of the music.

Nico follows my lead. "Everyone! Phones off, *now.*" He rushes toward the people around us, shoving phones away from faces. "Hey, put your phones away!"

But people won't stop recording. Now that Nico's yelling, it's a spectacle. Nobody is listening.

"Keep guarding the door. Make sure nobody leaves this room," I tell Nico.

I fish a small Wayne Tech device from my Utility Belt. There's a setting on it that can break every cell phone within a thirty-foot radius. I slam the button, cut the music, and stand on a table. Another possessed guy storms at me with glassy obsidian eyes. I jump down and pull him into a judo hold. Right on cue, Alysia flicks the lights on.

Suddenly, everyone's staring at me, bleary-eyed from the sudden brightness.

"If you do not listen to my instructions right now, one of you will die," I say, my voice even despite the anxiety bubbling behind it.

Silence. Murmurs.

"Your devices are already disabled. Do NOT pull out your phone. If your phone is already out, place it on the floor, facedown." More blank stares. *"Do it."* I sound like a bank robber, not the good guy. But maybe they need to be scared for me to save them.

It's Alysia's booming voice that breaks the silence. "Do it now!"

Slowly, one by one, everyone sets their phone down. The possessed boy in my arms thrashes. I tighten my hold. "Nobody is leaving this room until I say so. Understood?"

Slow nods.

I motion Nico over. His stance is nervous as his classmates watch him approach me while I lock one of the students in a Kesa-gatame judo hold on the floor.

"What's the plan?" Nico whispers.

I nudge my head at the kid in my arms. There are thin wisps of black smoke leaking out from the corners of his eyes and from his nostrils.

"After Alysia was possessed, black smoke came out of her throat and traveled back in the direction of the school, even though we were driving against the wind."

"Black stuff was coming out of Austin's mouth too. But then the lights went off, so—"

"Nobody could see where the smoke would lead," I confirm. "The timing of the blackout felt too convenient. I think this smoke will lead us to the source. So nobody moves, nobody touches these lights, until the smoke disappears."

Alysia peeps up beside me. "How do we know he's not the host?"

I sigh. "We don't know."

"So you're going to hold him like that until . . . ?"

"Until he wakes up." I try to sound more confident than I actually am. "Either the smoke will disappear into himself, in which case that means he's likely the host. Or the smoke will trail back to its true host."

Nico looks at the boy pitifully but doesn't argue.

A girl in the front row stares at me, defiantly, though the tremble in her voice betrays the hint of fear. "You're hurting him," she accuses.

"He's perfectly safe like this," I promise, and I mean it. This is a hold meant to safely restrain, not to harm.

Several minutes pass in torturous silence. Couples huddle together while others blink back their drunkenness, probably wondering if this is all really happening or not. Gradually, the energy shifts. An eerie discomfort grips the room. The couples inch away from one another. Everyone tries to put a couple feet between themselves and others, forming their own tiny islands. A special type of fear sets in: the kind of knowing that someone in this room killed one of our classmates. And any one of us could be next.

Everyone a suspect, everyone a potential victim.

A girl is crying. I don't blame her. We are all clinging to a cliff with our fingernails. We are vulnerable. We are helpless. We are afraid.

The boy in my arms twitches. Everyone flinches. His eyes lock onto mine as his chapped lips pull back over fiercely gritted teeth. The tiny tendrils of smoke from his eyes grow thicker. The smell of decay in the air grows denser. I glance at Nico by the door and Alysia by the lights to warn them to be ready for what comes next, except—

I don't see Alysia there anymore. Where is she?

With a choke and a gasp, the boy's eyes clear. Under the harsh lights of the room, the smoke swirls out from his body and up into the air, rushing straight to . . .

No.

My heart stops.

All eyes lock on Nico, frozen by the door, surrounded by smoke.

For a moment, I am horrified. But then Nico frantically points at his feet. The smoke is moving underneath the crack below the door.

It's not him. Thank god, it's not him.

I fling the door open and sprint out into the long, empty hallway. My heart beats wildly as I chase the rapidly fading trail of black smoke.

I think I lost it, but then I notice a discreet door to my left. I kick it open. It's a bathroom. For a moment, I don't see anyone. But then I glimpse a familiar pair of shoes. Someone's hanging halfway out the window above the sink.

My voice dries in my throat. "It's you."

CHAPTER 24

Her eyes are wide, unblinking.

"Where are you going, Lily?" I inch closer with my hands outstretched, approaching her as if trying to coax a terrified animal caught in a snare. I don't want her jumping out that window. Not before I know what the hell is happening.

"I was just—I only was—"

Her bottom lip trembles.

"I'msorryI'msorrypleasehelpmeI'msosorry."

She wilts away from the window and crumples into a tiny mess of tears, leaning her head against the expensive tile of the bathroom sink. I don't know what to do.

She looks terrified. And she's crying. But she was trying to escape. . . .

"I know how it looks," she says, voice shaking. "I got scared. You have no idea how terrifying this has been for me with this . . . this *thing* living inside me."

Hearing her say it out loud sends a chill down my spine. I take another cautious step forward and she flinches. "Please don't hurt me," she begs.

Something tightens in my throat. "I'm not going to hurt you, Lily." I join her on the checkered tile floor. She watches me warily. I take a deep breath in, then let it out. I encourage her to do the same. "How did this all start?"

She draws her knees to her chest and keeps her gaze fixed on the floor. "It was an accident. Promise me you'll believe me?"

"Tell me what happened, okay? Then we'll go from there?" It's not exactly what she wants to hear, but it's all I can offer her. So she takes another deep breath, then begins.

"It started a few weeks ago. I was staring at my phone, waiting for it to buzz with a notification, when I saw my reflection in the screen. It was me, but it wasn't me. The differences between me and my reflection were subtle. Her features were a bit more symmetrical, her skin clearer. It was like looking at a prettier version of myself. Except for the eyes. Her eyes were pitch-black. It was scary at first, to see her move on her own, but then she started talking."

That explains why Lily's been willingly phoneless for weeks now. That must've scared the living hell out of her. I fight back the creeping discomfort tickling my spine. "Did it attack you that same night?"

"No. Once I saw her that first time, I started seeing her everywhere. In mirrors, in windows. All over. She comforted me about my day, my family. For a few days, it was nice. I know it sounds crazy, but having her there was . . . comforting. My life is boring. I'm alone all the time. My parents are always gone, spending their new money. I used to hang out with my uncle and cousins, but my uncle's in jail now and my cousins are a mess. One's doing god knows what around Gotham City while the other's ghosted us all on some spiritual journey. It's pathetic to admit, but I'm lonely. So I didn't mind having someone to talk to. Until one day, she told me that she'd seen how sad my life is, and . . . she asked me if I ever felt like I wanted to be someone else." Lily grimaces. "I had been scrolling through the beauty tips on the internet for an hour. *Of course* I had thought about being someone else. So when she told me that she could give me the ability to become different people . . . I let her in."

I know what it's like to not always want to be yourself. An hour ago, I was low-key jealous of myself—of Batgirl—because Nico likes Batgirl, not me. If I truly felt confident as Barbara, then I probably wouldn't have hidden behind a mask for my first kiss. Would I have made the same choice as Lily? Absolutely not. But do I understand the headspace that brought her to that moment? Sure.

"So you blinked and then, *boom,* you were possessed?"

"No. I said the words into the reflection, then she—it—came at me."

So the demon isn't literally moving through our phones, it's moving through our reflections. It uses the phone screen as a mirror. A modern trick for an ancient evil. Damn.

"The first time was nothing like the temporary possessions you've seen. When I became the host, it was . . . different. More thorough, like a physical thing—not just shadows. I don't remember the details, though."

"Why not?"

"I passed out."

"From fear?"

"From pain."

Quiet.

"I didn't know that it was going to make me do these horrible things. I didn't know, I swear." Lily's crying again now, leaving distorted streaks of ruined makeup down her face. "I thought that maybe I'd spend time with a family that actually gives a damn about their kid. Peek into other people's lives. I thought it'd be harmless. I never wanted to hurt anyone. I tried to send the demon away, but it just laughed at me. It said now that it's out in our world, there's no way to destroy it. The only way that I can get it out of me is to transfer it to a new host. But . . . but I don't want to make someone else suffer like this." Her voice cracks as she wipes tears from her face.

"I'm so sorry, Lily." I wrap her into a hug. "We'll figure out how to get this thing out of you." She's shaking in my arms, so I hold on to her tight. I have a dozen more questions, but—

"There you are!" A voice rings out over my shoulder. Nico rushes in, dropping to his knees on the floor beside us. "What happened? What's going on?"

"Lily is the host. The demon is inside of her," I say as calmly as I can manage. Nico recoils, nearly falling over in his rush to put as much distance between himself and Lily as possible. "It's not her fault. She can't control the attacks."

Nico eyes Lily warily. She looks up at him, the whites of her eyes bright red. "I'm so sorry, Nico. I can't control it, I swear."

Nico studies her a bit more, his brow furrowing. He doesn't try to hug her again. "So then what's the plan?" Nico asks, voice ragged.

"Well, Lily's possessed, so I guess that means . . ." I glance down at her. "We do an exorcism."

Before anyone can comment at the absurdity of what I just said, Nico's phone vibrates. He glances at the caller ID quickly, then does a double take. "Sorry. It's my mom." I motion for him to take it.

"Hi, Nanay," Nico says. His face hardens. He raises his palm to his mouth.

This isn't good.

"I'm on my way." As soon as he hangs up, he punches a wall.

I flinch. "What's going on?"

He clenches his fists again, but his voice comes out so small. "Austin."

When a dark glassy film of tears slips over his eyes, I understand.

CHAPTER 25

From my motorcycle in the parking lot in front of the hospital, I watch the shadows of Nico and Austin's family members drift past the window, preparing to do the impossible. To say goodbye.

Nico rips open the borrowed car door and sprints into the building before he can even park it in a space. I watch him frantically rush inside, and I bite my lip. Austin's health took a turn. The surgery to remove their spleen left them vulnerable to infection. The symptoms of a meningococcal disease caused by the bacteria *neisseria meningitidis* came on quickly. There was no time for the doctors to prevent it, and now that it's in an acute stage, there's nothing they can do.

And just like that, another young life is about to end.

I want to cry for Austin, for everyone they're about to leave behind. But there's no time for that. As soon as Nico's figure disappears into the gloomy hospital, I park my motorcycle, then walk toward the car, where a very exhausted-looking Lily sits in the passenger seat.

We had kicked everyone out of the party, though you could hardly call it that because as soon as we opened the doors, everyone sprinted out, confused and terrified from the events of the night. Alysia hung back to make sure everyone made it out okay, while Nico asked Lily to borrow her mom's BMW to get to the hospital. It was the least she could do, given that she kind-of-sort-of-accidentally possessed his sibling. I volunteered to drive my motorcycle ahead of Nico to clear a path and make sure he got here as quickly (and safely) as possible. We couldn't leave Lily alone, so she piled into the car with Nico. Now that he's inside, though . . .

"We have work to do," I tell Lily as I climb into the driver's seat. "I want to try something."

Time to call upon my old friend: the scientific method.

Observation: Lily's demon approached her through her reflection. Austin said that the mirrors in their hospital room made them nervous. I felt the same way for a bit after my own possession.

"What happens when you look in the mirror?" I ask Lily.

She shivers. "Can't."

Hypothesis: While the demon may move through mirrors, it doesn't like its own reflection. Time to test this with an experiment.

I adjust the rearview mirror above the dashboard, aiming it down at Lily and me, though I make sure to not look at it myself. I've already gotten got by this thing once, and that was certainly enough for me, thank you very much. Lily shuts her eyes immediately, flinching from the mirror as if I pulled back a curtain, unleashing harsh sunlight into a dark room.

"Open your eyes, Lily," I say.

She shakes her head. "You don't understand. Even if I wanted to, I just . . . I can't. Like, I physically can't look at my reflection anymore. I haven't been able to look at my reflection even once since becoming the host. It uses other people's reflections to body jump, but it won't come out if *I'm* the one looking in the mirror."

Hmm. We'll see about that. I pull out my phone and quietly position it between us. I'm about to try to trick her into looking at it, but she scoffs, her eyes still closed. "I know that there's a mirror there. Even if I can't see it, I can, like . . . feel it."

I know she's saying she can't, but what if . . .

I dig into my Utility Belt and pull out a compact mirror. With my usual cowl, I have to obscure my eyes with black makeup, so the compact comes in handy during quick changes. I hold the palm-sized mirror directly in front of Lily, then flick the side of her face. Hard.

Several things happen in quick succession: Lily's pain reflexes kick in, forcing her eyes open for a split-second. She lets out a yelp like a deer who'd just been hit by a car. Then she hisses, grabs my hand that's holding the compact, and bites into my skin like it's an apple.

Sharp pain rips through my body as her teeth sink into the soft flesh around my thumb. *"Ow!"* I try to yank away, but her eyes are shut tight and she's hissing like she won't let go. *"Lily!"*

I literally have to tear my hand away like we're in some twisted game of tug-of-war. As soon as I'm finally free, though, Lily snaps out of it.

We're both panting and out of breath from the struggle, staring at one another with wide eyes. A deep scarlet blush washes over Lily's face. "Batgirl, I am *so* sorry. I don't know—"

"Swear to god, if you're also a vampire or something, I'm absolutely going to lose it."

"Not a vampire," she says, defensiveness and embarrassment warring on her face. "The demon got angry. I warned you that I couldn't look in the mirror."

Right. Okay. My initial experiment did its job: I've

gathered relevant data, which is that the demon really, *really* hates mirrors. Lily (or her demon, I guess?) went full feral on me, instinctively doing whatever she could to get the mirror away from her. The reaction felt primal—a type of fight-or-flight survival instinct. So the most reasonable conclusion? Forcing the mirror-shy demon to face its reflection might be the key to banishing it once and for all. I just need to figure out how the hell to force her to look without getting my hand bitten off. Then if she *does* look, and the demon inevitably freaks out . . . what do I even do next?

I groan. This is so much harder than I thought it'd be. Earlier, I was so intent on finding the host that I hadn't thought through the next logical step: how to actually get rid of the demon. Turns out, not all villains and obstacles can be stopped with computers and karate kicks. I need to find a solution and backup plan ASAP.

"Wait here," I tell Lily, opening the car door to step out as nervous energy courses through me.

"Where are you going?" she asks.

"Nowhere. I just need to look up some stuff on my phone and don't want you to accidentally, uh . . ."

"Oh. Right," she says.

"Can you, uh, try to take a nap while I research?" God, what a ridiculous request. But luckily, I don't have to explain myself. She understands that she's only putting us both in danger being awake right now. I'll make sure my phone is as unreflective as possible, and I'll take all the necessary precautions to prevent a body jump, but we can't risk the demon taking over.

So while Lily rests in the back seat, I lean against the hood of the car and tap into the Batcomputer's search engine through my phone. My first search is on reflection lore. There's a Chinese myth that claims images in the mirror are actually demonic beings only pretending to be our reflections while silently plotting our deaths. Then there's Narcissus—the Greek myth about the boy who died from gazing at his reflection—and the parallel early Christian myth of Adam, who lost his divine nature by gazing at himself in a pool of water. I think back to my own childhood, the pickle of anxiety at sleepovers while chanting "Bloody Mary" three times into a dark mirror, hoping to conjure a witch, who, if you failed to pass her tests, would kill you. No matter the culture or the time period, humans have always had a strange and strained relationship with our reflections.

Phones were originally intended for connection and communication, but with the invention of the smartphone and then, of course, the selfie, something shifted. The ability to watch ourselves while our image is captured screwed up our lizard brains. The phone—originally intended as a window into others' worlds—has become a mirror.

Of course a demon today would use the black mirrors of our phones to enter our world, our bodies, our minds.

A few years ago, I never would have imagined that I'd be sitting in a parking lot one weekend in my junior year of high school, looking up "How to perform an exorcism," but alas. Here we are.

The internet offers thousands of articles about performing exorcisms, but most of them seem to follow strange religious traditions. I'd maybe get it if the demon we're working with came from a cross or a church or something, but it came out of a mirror, so to me it seems . . . I don't know. Secular? Problem is that there's way less information out there on nondenominational exorcisms. I blame Hollywood.

I find one article that promises instructions for the exorcism process: "At first, a demon will conceal itself. If prompted, it will show itself. Beware of what the demon says, as it will try to manipulate you. Next, you will engage in a spiritual battle with the demon before finally reaching the point of expulsion. Then the demon will be driven from its human host per your efforts."

"Per my efforts?" I mumble. Well, that's vague.

I have more questions than answers. The demon tricked Lily into inviting it inside her. But why did it first reveal itself to her anyway? I walk around every day in this same city and haven't once seen a literal demon speaking to me through my reflection. What made Lily vulnerable?

I steal a glance at Lily's figure, dozing off in the back seat. Maybe if I can understand Lily better, I can learn how to help her.

I pull up her social media profile. She posts a lot about her art, but the photos don't get many likes. Whenever she posts pictures of herself or her friends, though, she gets tons of attention—literally hundreds of likes. She doesn't look lonely, to be honest. In nearly every post, there are photos of her with other people. Nico or Austin or other kids from Gotham Academy. But then again, being around other people doesn't mean much. I've never felt lonelier than in a crowd of people who don't care about me.

Within a minute, this is already starting to feel like a dead end. You can't get to know someone by what they post. That's their external self. It's all fake. Or, at least, it's all so heavily curated that it doesn't really mean anything. I personally go out of my way to make my online presence as Barbara Gordon as boring as humanly possible to protect my secrets, which—

Alysia saw right through.

The memory of Alysia confronting me about Batgirl bubbles to the surface with a quick tinge of residual embarrassment. "The algorithm never lies," I mumble. An image of Robin at the party earlier flashes across my brain and I feel my face get hot. I shake aside the sudden flush of feeling. *Focus, focus, focus.*

I won't learn much by stalking Lily's social media from the outside; I need to observe from *within* her account. I hate to violate her privacy like this, but given that she's literally possessed by a demon—and she did bite me—I think I get a pass?

Within a few minutes of using a Wayne Tech encryption app that I modified to my liking, I'm logged into Lily's account. Her home page floods my screen. The first few videos on her feed are all by makeup influencers: tips to make your lips look bigger, how to find your optimal eyebrow shape, how to create the illusion of an hourglass figure. It's depressing how quickly I find myself lost in the videos, forgetting that I'm here for research, not beauty hacks. The internet is excellent at sucking you in, making you forget.

The mental fog clears and I keep swiping. There are another few videos about shapewear and at-home teeth filing, then right as I'm about to declare this an absolute waste of time, a new type of video pops up. A young, pretty white girl named Emily sits on the steps of what looks like a university campus. I'm about to swipe it away, but then I notice a familiar profile active in the comments: Kyle from the school conservative club. If that guy likes a video, I'm sure it's sus.

I click on the Emily girl's profile. A quick skim of her bio and credentials tells me that she's one of those anti-immigrant, anti-trans, anti-woke influencers. Interesting.

I return to Lily's feed. On-screen, Emily gives me a plastic smile. "Our world is gripped by cancel culture. Everyone's so afraid to say anything anymore. What happened to free speech?"

"Good lord," I mumble.

I flick the video of Emily away, only for another one to show up. This time she's talking to another woman, with a caption on the screen: *Has the Sexual Revolution Failed?*

Never did I think I'd find myself on an anti-feminism site, but again, this case has take me all sort of new places.

I've heard of these well-dressed, well-educated influencers repackaging problematic ideology into sparkling, provocative "truth-telling sessions." They're the Main Characters of this movement dedicated to making white-panic conservatism cool again with big-city people our age. Kyle's club at school eats this up. Except Lily isn't part of that club. Neither are any of Lily's friends. I check her followers list, and she doesn't interact online with any of the conservative kids from school. I don't think they hang out in person either. Clearly, though, she's been watching their overlords' videos. But why? Could this right-wing extremism be the demon in her talking?

I imagine a headline for the case as it stands now: "Local girl haunted by a demon with suspect political views." Not what I was expecting, but it checks out.

"Hey."

Nico walks through the thick fog of the parking lot, coming my way. His eyes are red, his hands buried deep in his pockets. I glance back at Lily, stirring awake in the back seat, before rushing to meet him. I don't know what to say, so I hold out my arms. Nico swoops in, allowing his tall frame to crumple slightly in my arms. I hug him how I'd want to be hugged if I were in his shoes. I hug him like if I hold him just right, then maybe all of this won't hurt as much.

Nico doesn't speak for several seconds. When he finally does, his voice is ragged. "Austin isn't going to make it through the night."

I swallow deeply. "I'm sorry."

"He's asking for you."

At this, my muscles tighten. "Me?"

Nico pulls out of the hug, takes a step back. "Yes."

"Why?"

"I don't know."

I glance back up at the hospital window, where the shadows of his family are still milling around. "But everyone's in there."

"You can manage a brief five-minute distraction. I'll keep an eye on Lily," Nico says, rubbing his eyes.

I don't want to go up there. I don't want to intrude on such a vulnerable moment. I don't want to watch someone who I've started to think of as a friend die. And I definitely don't want to leave Lily until I can run more experiments and make sure that this demon won't claim any more lives. But I can't say no to Austin. How can I refuse a dying person's wish? So even though my gut feels sick at the thought, I prep my Utility Belt to sneak into Austin's room. One last time.

Austin doesn't smile when they see me, but their brown eyes lock steadily on mine with a fierce intensity. I was expecting them to look tired, not at all like this—sharp, focused. There's a beat of silence before I speak. "I'm glad we met," I say, which sounds futile, but what else can I say? I sit on the edge of Austin's bed. "I'm not happy about the circumstances, but I'm glad I met you."

At this, Austin finally smirks a bit. "Am I the coolest non-vigilante you've ever met?"

I chuckle a bit, even though it feels wrong to laugh right now. "Yes. You absolutely are."

Austin smiles weakly in a sad way that snaps me right back to the reality of the moment. Austin is *dying*.

I think about death a lot. When I was little, I knew my dad was a police officer, but I didn't necessarily understand that his job was dangerous until the day we thought that he had been killed. There was a drive-by shooting at a press conference about Gotham City crime syndicates and he threw himself in front of an elected official. It was all over the news—"Jim Gordon: Dead in the line of duty." GCPD held a funeral and everything. I watched my father be buried. I watched his casket lower into the ground.

Forty-eight hours later, my dad appeared again at our front door. I thought he was a ghost. My mother screamed. Slapped him in the face. Dad kept apologizing over and over again. The truth was he faked his death as part of this massive plot to stop one of the insane Super-Villains who plague Gotham City. Pretty messed up and traumatizing for the rest of us, but what can you do. Duty calls. While I was relieved to have my dad back, thrilled to know that the past few days had only been a horrible nightmare, the experience had some lasting effects on me. For one, I became hyper-paranoid that one day, my father would go to work and never come home again—for real this time. The other side effect was more subtle. Somehow, his undercover stunt left me with the troubling hope that perhaps, somehow, death could be cheated. Rationally, I know that death is final and there's no way around it. But the little kid in me—the one who still remembers when my father came back from his own funeral—still holds on to a bit of magical thinking, that maybe, if we're smart enough, we can trick our way out of dying too.

Maybe this is why I'm not as afraid as I should be when I go out at night as Batgirl. I understand the risks, but I'm an optimist. With enough preparedness, maybe I can keep myself and others safe, even in the face of death.

It's this thinking that typically makes me brave. It's this thinking that currently makes me want to scream.

Austin will not cheat death. They are young, and they are going to die. The unfairness of it all makes my stomach churn. There is a demon in Gotham City who is targeting people and ruining lives. *Ending* lives.

"I'm so sorry, Austin," my voice says, wavering with emotion against my will.

"Aww, hey, hey, don't do that." They say it with so much tenderness that I feel horrible all over again that they're the one comforting me right now. "What's the update on the demon case?" Austin asks in a futile attempt to distract us both from what very well might be their final night of existence.

"Lily's the host." I don't really want to talk about this now, but if Austin's asking, I won't lie to them. "Whatever is inside her is afraid of its reflection, which feels significant—possibly the key to facilitating an exorcism. The only problem is that the demon has this intense hold on her that prohibits her from looking in the mirror."

"But if you can get the demon to look in the mirror, you think something will happen?"

"Maybe? I don't know for sure, but I think so. Except it might be impossible either way. The thing literally refuses to show itself around any reflective surfaces."

"Is there another way to get rid of it?"

"I wish. The demon said that now that it's been brought into our world, it's impossible to send it away. It can only be transferred to a new host. So we're stuck."

Austin frowns. "That's what Nico told me."

If Nico already told them, then why are they asking me now?

Austin slips their hand from under their blanket. "I want to help," they say, quietly.

They look so weak. So small under these lights with all these wires stuck to their body. "Austin..."

"No. Don't say my name like that. I want to help. Let me help." Their hand moves again, inching toward mine.

I grab it, letting our fingers interlace. Warmth gathers between our palms in a way that makes my heart squeeze. "How do you want to help, Austin?"

Their eyes lock onto mine as they raise their chin ever so slightly. "Let's trick the demon into showing itself. Getting it in its most vulnerable state."

"How?"

Austin wiggles their IV line while casting me a determined glare. It takes a second for the idea to compute. Could they mean . . . ?

I recoil. "No. No way. Absolutely not." I try to drop their hand, but Austin maintains their hold, surprisingly tight.

"Let Lily try to transfer the demon to me. You said the demon prevents her from looking at mirrors, but what if we can lure it out, then catch it off guard. Then you can see what happens when it confronts its reflection, or we can kill it, or—"

"No. It's too dangerous."

"We don't have another option."

I hate this. It's reckless. And Austin's already suffered enough. But I will admit . . . it's not a horrible plan, *if* I can be sure that I can somehow defeat this thing during the transfer without harming Austin or Lily. Big if. I sigh. "And if it doesn't work? If the demon shows itself, but my mirror theory is a bust?"

"Then let me become the new host, and . . ." Austin hesitates, takes a deep breath. "Then let it die with me."

"Austin."

"Please," Austin begs. "If the only way to get this

thing away from my brother—from my friends—is to pass it on to another host, then worst-case scenario, I'd want Lily to pass it on to me. When I die, it dies with me."

"I could never let you do that."

"It'd be my choice."

"I don't even know if that's possible. What if—"

"Think of an infectious disease. When the host dies, the virus does too. It's like the demon and the host. I don't want this thing hurting more people. I don't want it to hurt my brother. So please, I need you to bring Lily here, as fast as you can, so we can end this."

"Even if we lure it out, I don't know how to trick it to look at a mirror. It can literally sense when reflective surfaces are nearby. This thing is cautious. It's self-preserving. It's smart."

"So are you. Figure it out. I know you can."

"Austin, I can't—"

The door whooshes open. Their parents are back.

I hurry toward the window. Before I jump, I look back at Austin one last time. They don't say anything out loud, but while their parents pull back the dividing curtain, Austin mouths at me, clear as day: "Midnight."

And then, even worse: "Please."

CHAPTER 26

Eleven-forty-seven p.m.

"I know it's difficult. But I think we should try," Alysia says. I video-called her and filled her in as soon as I left the building. She wasted no time in making her opinion known.

"It feels wrong," I say, pacing in the hospital parking lot. "The demon is what put Austin in the hospital in the first place. Austin shouldn't have to face it again in the final moments of their life."

"What they shouldn't have to endure is all these other people making choices about how they want to fight back against what's taken everything from them," Alysia says firmly.

"You're making it sound like I'm depriving Austin of something important."

"You are! They want to help kill the thing that's ultimately going to kill them. You can make that happen, and also save everyone else in Gotham City in the process. And yet here you are, doubting yourself and trying to make a value judgment about what Austin wants."

Sometimes I resent the fact that Alysia is the president of the debate club. I tell her this. She sucks her teeth. "It's a solid plan. You can do this. You can catch this thing off guard and kill it before it takes over Austin. You can save Lily. But the more time you waste with me, the less time you have to make it happen."

A heavy raindrop falls on my shoulder as I lean against the hood of the car. I tilt my head up at the blue-black sky, watching the start of a storm cut through the fog and smoke. My heart won't stop racing, my head fuzzy from the nonstop anxiety. I don't realize it at first, but I must be humming out loud, because Alysia leans in to the screen. "Hey. Take a deep breath," she murmurs gently. The softness of her voice helps a little. I inhale, I exhale. Why is this so hard?

"What's stopping you from doing this? For real?" Alysia asks.

"This demon has been looking for *me*—Batgirl. Austin's already in so much pain; they shouldn't be put in more danger for something that's targeting me. Austin might already be dying, but . . . if I mess this up, then it will have been my decision that caused their death. A violent, painful one, at that. And what if I mess up so badly that Lily gets hurt too? Or worse?"

"Lily and Austin have both already been hurt by this thing. You're not helping either of them—or the rest of Gotham City that's still in danger—by doing nothing. And unfortunately, girl, you don't have another plan," Alysia says gently. "It's time to stop this thing, once and for all. And Austin is bravely volunteering a solution to potentially do just that."

I curl my hand into a fist, then press it to my fore-head. "I'm supposed to protect people, Alysia. I'm sup-posed to prevent harm. What type of hero am I if I willingly endanger another innocent person?"

"You can't think like that. You're never 'one type' of hero or another. You're dealing with real life in real time. There's always nuance."

I believe in exploring the gray areas of life. But this? This feels *too* gray.

"It's eleven-fifty-two," Alysia says. "Choose. Now."

I close my eyes and count down from ten, hoping that when I reach one, I'll know what to do.

Austin requested a priest to deliver last rites. That was the cover they used for me to sneak them out of their room and into somewhere more private. It's impossible to shake the guilt of creeping into the hospital room of a dying person under the guise of atoning for their sins on their deathbed. Nothing about tonight sits right with me.

"I don't want to hurt you, Austin," Lily says through choked sobs.

"It's okay. Batgirl will handle the demon when it shows itself, and I won't get hurt. Not any more than I already am," Austin reassures her.

Austin is sitting, weakly, in a wheelchair. We're huddled together in a small, white, painfully bright room. It took a lot of sabotaging of security cameras, manipulating guards, and a few other things that Batman would disapprove of, but I managed to sneak the three of us into the one spot in this hospital that most people don't even know exists.

In a city constantly rocked by villains, Gotham General Hospital has seen a lot, and has adjusted its design accordingly. During my time with Batman, I've gotten to know the ins and outs of almost every critical building in the city, including this one, which is why I know exactly where the Special Holding Station is located.

Arkham Asylum is where most Gotham City villains end up, but occasionally, individuals are brought here to Gotham General Hospital for treatment prior to transfer. Like the newborn nursery in the maternity ward, the Special Holding Station features a large glass window separating the main holding room from the hallway. The often empty space is perfect for our plan. And by "plan," I mean the absolutely desperate, half-baked long shot of an idea that I scraped together and explained to the others while racing to get us down here in the first place.

I listen to Lily cry for another minute before I clear my throat. We don't have much time. "Are you ready?" If we're going to do this, we need to do it fast, before someone comes looking for Austin.

Austin wipes a stray tear from Lily's cheek with their thumb. "Yes."

"All right. So. Um." I fumble over my words. I don't know how to orchestrate this. "Lily. How exactly does the host transfer work?"

Lily swallows, her voice still shaking. "I'll sit with my back facing you, Austin. You should take out your phone, look at your reflection, then say, 'I let you in.' Then it will . . . exit me . . . so it can move to you through your phone and give Batgirl time to, uh . . ." *Defeat the demon and make sure none of us dies.* Nobody says it aloud, but we're all thinking it. The unsaid words hang heavy in the air between us.

"I've never willingly let it take control," Lily whispers. "I usually try to fight it."

Austin grabs Lily's wrist, tight. "Do not fight it."

"I'll be waiting on the other side of the window out in the hallway. Then, when the time comes, I'll try to—"

"Not *try*," Austin says firmly. "You will *do* your plan. And it will work. Just like we discussed."

At least one of us believes in my plan. I exit the white room, leaving Austin staring furiously at the phone in their lap, back-to-back with Lily, and step out into the fluorescent lights of the hallway. Then, when I give Lily the symbol through the glass, she lets her eyes fall shut.

Seconds pass. Then a minute. Then two. I watch the hallway door nervously. What if the demon has realized our plan? What if it doesn't want—

Black smoke begins to leak from Lily's nostrils. I inhale sharply when Lily's eyes fly open, though this time, they are not hers.

Pitch-black, glassy orbs glare at Austin. A distant, disturbed smile spreads across Lily's face as whatever monster is inside her leers at Austin. A strange, decaying smell fills the air. A chill ripples down my back. Without hesitation, without fear, Austin speaks loud and clear. "I let you in."

Lily's mouth falls open to release a plume of black smoke as her neck jerks backward at a painful angle. Lily sits disturbingly still, unblinking, while she makes a muffled sound, as if something is clogging her throat. The noise grows thicker, like mucous, making my stomach churn. She gargles again, and when her jaw un-hinges itself to open even wider, I see something swirling around her tonsils. Something *alive*.

"Oh my god," I gurgle.

Austin's trembling in their wheelchair but keeps their eyes locked on their reflection, leaving me alone to witness the terror of Lily's possession. The wormlike thing keeps crawling out of Lily's throat, rising slowly to the surface like a nightmare. Tears flow down Lily's cheeks, spilling into her open mouth. She gasps like she's choking, but the thing keeps slithering out. I can't tell if it's a solid substance or a dense gas coalesced into the shape of a rope. I watch in horror as the quivering, garden-hose-shaped thing seeps from Lily's spasming throat. Lily coughs and gags loudly as the vile entity makes it over the bump of her tongue and out into the open air at last, ripping one last pained groan from Lily on its way.

The demon has shown itself, marking the end of Phase One. Now it's time for Phase Two: confront it with its own reflection. My finger hovers over the hallway light switch, praying that this bit of science will save us from the supernatural. Because once I turn off these lights out here—and darkness floods the hallway where I've been waiting—the window separating us will suddenly turn into a mirror, aimed right at Lily's unsuspecting demon.

One-way mirrors are an old trick. I have my dad to

thank for knowing this one. Detectives use them all the time to investigate suspects. When both the interrogation and the observation rooms are bright, the glass is a regular see-through window on both sides, but when the observation room is darkened, the light in the interrogation room does a clever trick, turning the glass into a one-way mirror.

Luckily, certain psychiatric wards use them too.

The demon won't see it coming. Not at all.

I lock eyes with Lily, writhing in discomfort as the tapeworm-bodied demon, slick with spit, uncurls in the air between her and Austin. "It's time," I mouth to her before I lower into a racing stance and prepare to sprint inside as soon as I hit the lights. But right as my index finger brushes against the cool plastic switch—

"Batgirl?"

My head whips around so fast that I hear my own neck crack. I ignore the intruder, reaching for the light switch anyway, but it's too late. *I'm* too late. The wet, suffocating form of the demon notices Nico's entrance. It senses that it's in danger. For a split second, it freezes in the air, halfway between Lily and Austin. Then, fast and unforgiving, it snaps forward like a cobra, plunging straight into Austin's parted lips.

CHAPTER 27

Nico is screaming. Austin is unconscious. Lily is crying. I am panicking.

Doctors meet us in the hallway to carry Austin into the nearest empty room.

Yelling. Footsteps. Call for backup.

"Hold him back," a stern voice begs me.

Nico is clawing at the door that has become Austin's emergency room. He is howling. He is inconsolable. As I gently grasp his shoulder, he is looking at me like he wants me dead.

Lily is staring at her reflection in the mirror. She is shaking her head, whispering to herself, "I can't believe it's gone."

I can tell she's relieved, but there is no denying the grief beneath it all. She is free, but her friend is not. I do not think Austin has much longer to live.

Life is cruel.

I am trying to tear Nico away from the door when he whirls on his heels to shove me against the wall. "This thing has been targeting *you*. It's been asking for you. And yet you let its victim suffer. Twice." He is unrecognizable now with this twisted look of hatred in his eyes. "You're a coward," he spits. "I hope the demon kills you next."

The threat of tears stings my eyes.

A doctor is shouting on the other side of the door. *"Patient is coding!"* They yell again. "Code Blue! Code Blue!"

Cardiac arrest. Austin's heart is no longer beating.

Then the buzz of a heart rate monitor flatlining.

Austin's heart has stopped.

Nico crumples to the floor. More doctors are running down the hallway now. They are shoving past him to race inside to attempt to resuscitate Austin.

Nico is looking at me like this is all my fault. I am feeling like this is all my fault.

There is a loud gasp beside me. Lily reaches for me, but then her legs seem to give out from under her. Terror closes my throat, choking the air out of my lungs.

I hear more shouting in the hallway. Something more is happening, but I can't take my attention away from what's going on in the room.

Nico is hyperventilating. Austin is dying. Lily is fainting. And I am watching her eyes flicker, then fly open—startled and wide.

Black as night.

Everything around me goes dark. A bag is thrown over my head. Panic flares inside me. Lily screams. Something hard slams into the back of my head. It hurts like hell and rattles my consciousness around in my skull like dice in a cup. I topple over. It takes a few seconds to regain my senses and rip the bag off, my knuckles scraping against the hard floor.

A man dressed all in black is dragging Lily down the hospital hallway. Her screams are her own normal voice, but her eyes are black gashes in her pale face. Beside him, another man is pointing a gun at all the hospital staff, shouting, "Get down! Nobody move!"

The men are both wearing strange glasses, chrome and reflective. I've seen these glasses before: Andrew was wearing them the night at the warehouse.

The man has one arm over Lily's mouth, the other

hooked around her neck, as he and his partner finally turn to full-out sprint for the exit. Lily kicks like her life depends on it. Her life *does* depend on it.

I hear Nico say something, but my blood is pumping so loud in my ears that I can't hear him. When Austin's heart stopped, the demon must have reverted right back to Lily. How did I not consider that as a possibility? How could I have been so stupid? How could I have let Austin suffer? All for nothing? Then I let an ambush happen and Lily is snatched away right in front of me just for Andrew's cult to kill her too?

My throat constricts. Nope. Not going to happen.

I shoot to my feet and chase the kidnappers. I may not have been able to save Austin, but I can still save Lily.

Adrenaline pulses through me, but the kidnappers are moving so fast. Our only hope is how hard Lily is digging her heels into the floor, thrashing and fighting like hell. It's a frantic chase through the hospital. The guys make it out front, where a black van is waiting at the curb in the rain, door wide open. They yank Lily along, but I'm gaining on them. I'm almost there. Her gaze collides with mine, her eyes twitching with fear. The guys throw her into the open van and I lunge forward. My fingers are inches away from grabbing on to her ankle. I almost rip her free. Almost.

A howl of pain rises in the air. I heave as the boot of the kidnapper delivers a kick to my jaw.

I lose my balance and it all happens in a blink: Lily mewls faintly beneath the assailant's hand, I fall to the ground, and the van takes off driving at full speed, hurtling into the night.

dash toward my motorcycle and slam on my helmet. My tires slip on the wet concrete, but I keep my balance as I floor it, speeding after the van as it whips around the corner up ahead.

Rain pummels the visor of my helmet. Headlights stream by in hazy streaks. The van veers to the left up ahead, merging onto the main street. I pursue it, tires screeching.

I need backup. I tap the side of my helmet, configured for speed dial. Robin picks up on the first ring. "Hey, what's—"

"I need you. Now."

Robin doesn't hesitate. Doesn't even ask what's

going on. "I have your coordinates," he says, and I can already hear his own motorcycle humming to life in the background. I end the call without another word.

Cars honk and swerve out the way as the black van runs a red light through a busy intersection. I lean forward, trusting my bike's speed to deliver me through the same mess of traffic. I make it. Barely. A delivery truck nearly collides with my back tire in its desperate attempt to dodge me.

First car chase. Much scarier than I imagined.

The van banks right around a tight curb, crashing recklessly into a parked car. There's an explosion of glass, the crunch of steel from the sudden collision, but the van keeps careening up the road like a tornado. I don't turn in time. My bike scrapes loudly against the side of a stopped car before surging forward.

"Incoming call: Alysia Yeoh," my helmet announces.

"Not now." I dismiss the call.

The sound of honking horns becomes the soundtrack to the chase as I split the narrow distance between the two lanes of cars, maneuvering so fast that I can hardly see their drivers. The kidnappers' van almost hits a pedestrian as it screams through another red light. If any bystanders get hurt, I'm really going to make them pay.

The phone rings again. Why is she—

Wait, what if this call is an actual emergency? Is Alysia in trouble too?

"Accept call," I bark.

"Are you okay?!" Alysia's voice fills my helmet.

"What's going on? Are *you* okay?" I ask.

"The cult people came by the party after you left, demanding to know where you and Lily and Nico—"

"Yeah, I know."

I'm gaining on the kidnappers. But then the rear window of their van suddenly shatters, raining glass onto the street. A black glove shoves a gun through the now-broken window, pointing it straight at me.

My heart stammers for a split second before I swerve to the left, just in time to avoid the first bullet.

"What-was-that-where-are-you?!" Alysia shouts on the other end.

I glance at my surroundings. "Burnside Bridge. Driving to the suburbs."

"Where are you going?"

I hear sirens in the distance now. Finally. Took them long enough. "To save Lily." Another gunshot.

"Alysia, I have to go." I hang up and try not to hyperventilate.

The van keeps shooting at me while I swerve. A bullet clips my left mirror. Batman once explained that my suit is "bullet-resistant," not "bulletproof." When I asked if I'd be okay if I got shot while wearing it, he had said, "Probably."

Probably.

Another bullet breezes past me, lodging in a parking meter as we race past. I swallow. *Probably* isn't comforting right now.

The van driver floors it through a puddle, showering me and my bike with dirty water before flying through a heavily trafficked intersection. My heartbeat is in my throat, but I grit my teeth and follow, praying that this stupid decision won't be my last. The van clips the bumper of a hybrid, sending the car spinning out into the center of the road, hurtling right at me. I steer hard to the right, sending my bike careening into oncoming traffic, straight for the fast-approaching grille of an SUV. My instinct is to slam on the breaks, but the SUV is too close. The SUV driver lays on their horn. I crank left and promise every deity in the world that if I survive this moment, I'll never chase a speeding car ever again. My tires squeal, I smell the burnt rubber. I brace for pain—the inevitable slam of concrete, the weight of my bike crashing down over me. But it never comes. I made it. I *made* it. But where the hell did the van go?

There's a sudden flash of a headlight, a streak of red in the dark.

Robin.

The engine of his bike revs loudly, firing a detonator shot up ahead that collides with a dumpster. There's a small explosion as the garbage bursts into the air, then spills over, blocking the road. I hear tires screech up ahead, then another gunshot. *There it is.* I race as fast as I can to catch up.

"Your bike can fire remote detonators?!" I shout, our helmet communication line opening automatically now that we're in close proximity.

Robin fires again, aiming at the van's tire. It narrowly misses, but the blast is enough to shake the van once again. "Jealous?"

"You're insufferable," I say.

"Happy to be of service."

There are more sirens in the distance now. We're gaining on the van, but they're leading us deep into the suburbs outside Gotham City. Stand-alone houses like Lily's give way to even larger estates, each home surrounded by tall brick walls or fences. Funnily enough, we're not too far from Wayne Manor now. What the hell could Andrew's cult have to do way out here?

The van speeds down a dark road, heading toward an old, abandoned-looking home with a tall brick wall around it. There's a wrought iron gate in front like the one at Gotham Academy, though this one is unkempt and covered in rust. But the gate still works, because I'm watching it close, fast, right before my eyes. The van speeds up. We do too.

A masked face hangs out the broken window,

banging on the back of the van like a drum. They're going to make it inside before it closes. Robin and I are not far behind. We can make it too.

I catch a glimpse of Lily's forehead through the broken glass. Her hair is wet and caked to her skin, from sweat or . . . blood.

With a howl of victory, the van dashes through the rapidly closing gate. I'm less than forty feet behind. I yank my bike's throttle as far back as possible, maxing out my speed.

"You're not going to make it," Robin says, his bike not far behind me. But I don't give up. I'm too close. "Wait!"

The gate is halfway closed, but I'm almost there. Only twenty feet left.

"You won't make it." Robin's voice is panicked.

But I will. I know I will.

Ten feet left and only a sliver of open space left between the nearly closed gate. No time to slow down.

"Batgirl, brake now!"

I accelerate. Robin can brake if he wants, but I'm not afraid.

It's time for me to face my demon.

CHAPTER 29

"Told you so," I taunt Robin before dodging a punch a few minutes later, now on solid ground.

He flips, then kicks a guard in the kneecap. "You want to brag right now? Really?"

We made it past the gate, but the four men standing guard are slowing us down. The van drove right up to the entryway of the dilapidated old mansion before the kidnappers dragged Lily inside and locked the door behind them. They have a head start, but if we could just wrap up this fight out front . . .

I throw an elbow at one guard while Robin crashes his metal staff down onto the foot of the other. The last remaining guards scream in unison, then crumple to the floor.

"We can go inside," I huff, trying to catch my breath.

Robin faces me, the harsh set of his jaw radiating contentment and determination, already calculating our next move. "Lead the way."

And so we enter.

Maybe at one point this home was beautiful, but that day is long gone. The kitchen floor is carpeted with empty liquor bottles and cigarette butts. The wooden walls are scratched deep with graffiti, nearly every inch covered in unreadable words and crude drawings. In front of the sink, someone took a knife to the floorboards and drew an X, then beside it wrote *Samuelson Family Murders Happened Here*.

Ahh. A Gotham City cult history landmark. That explains why this place looks like it's been abandoned for the past decade. And why it's the venue of choice for the Demonic Forces of Gotham kidnapping ritual tonight.

The house vibrates with unease as Robin and I creep inside. We slip past the inside guards easily. They're all amateurs with no training. It's not even a fight to make it our way into the interior balcony overlooking the grand staircase and entryway, where I immediately spot Lily in the foyer.

She is lying on the floor, blindfolded and with her wrists tied, surrounded by thirty Demonic Forces of

Gotham members seated in a tight circle. The cult members are arranged with their backs to her while they each sit silently, staring at the black screen of their phones in the dark.

"Why do you think they're doing that?" Robin asks, slipping quietly next to me. He motions toward the cult members staring at their phones.

"I read that staring at your reflection in the dark for a long period of time can be a form of self-hypnosis. It can make the participant susceptible to hallucinations." Or worse, apparently.

"We need a plan, but first you have to tell me what's going on. Why do they have Lily? What happened to Austin?"

Flashes of what happened earlier swirl across my mind: the botched two-way mirror plan, Austin's scream as they became the new host, Nico's anger when it all backfired, the eerie sound of Austin's heart rate monitor flatlining as Andrew's armed henchmen hauled Lily away.

"Austin is . . ." My voice breaks.

Robin's shoulders tighten. "Oh."

Reality sinks in like fangs in my neck.

It didn't work. It didn't work.

It. Did. Not. Work.

I was supposed to trap this thing and make sure that both Lily *and* Austin made it out alive. But in the end, Austin made the ultimate sacrifice only for the plan to not even work.

Something inside me snaps. I slam my head into the nook of my elbow and bite back an exhausted groan. This demon has been looking for me, but I've still let it hurt all these innocent people. I press the sides of my fists into my temples, but it does nothing to calm the swell of guilt threatening to pull me under. Robin places a hand on my back, rubbing in slow, soothing circles as I clench my knuckles so hard they crack. I wait for him to tell me it's okay or offer some other platitude, but instead he whispers, "You can do this."

I open my eyes to stare up at him for a moment. He meets my gaze, unflinching.

Harper is gone. Austin is gone. I won't let the demon and these creeps kill Lily too.

I grit my teeth. "This ends now."

Robin moves his hand from my back down to my hand. He grips it tight and says, "Let's end it, then." I wince. The demon bite is still tender. Seems like nothing will ever just be right for me and him.

Down in the foyer, Andrew and his unmistakably greasy aura stalks around, gesticulating at his followers in the circle. I can't wait to punch him in the face. I almost lean forward, springing from our hiding space to get it over with already, but Robin grips my shoulder. "Assess the situation, then strike," he whispers.

He's right. I force my urge to kick Andrew's ass down as I tune in to his speech.

"People of the past used mirrorlike surfaces to keep demonic forces away," Andrew says, his voice stuffed with pseudo-grandiosity. "A bowl of water with a knife in it was placed at the entrances of homes. A demon looking into it would see her soul pierced by the knife and flee." Andrew reaches for the broken table behind him and reveals his own water bowl with a large gold dagger in it. He places it on the floor beside Lily. Behind her blindfold, she flinches as the vessel hits the floor, sloshing drops of water onto her knee.

"But tonight," Andrew says, his voice a frantic growl, edged with anticipation, "we are here to welcome the demon in. Invite it to join with all of us."

A quiet murmur of excitement rolls through the cult. Lily squirms.

"If we help the entity achieve its full power, it will grant us what we've hoped for. You will leave here changed. You will leave here whole."

Among the cult members, I recognize Jason's brother—the one who broke my ankle. It's sad to see him here, stooped this low. Andrew's preying on lonely, desperate people. It's a disgusting, cruel thing to do.

"You are all part of something special tonight. Because of you, the entity will reach its full power. Instead of being limited to one permanent host and a temporary bond with a secondary, the demon will be able to move through all of us together at once."

My heart drops into my stomach.

Multiple simultaneous possessions—*that's* his goal.

Andrew's not trying to just make the body jumper stronger. He's offering up his entire cult of misfits to become an army of possessed beings.

"Once we have faced our own reflections for long enough that we shed our sense of individuality, I shall remove the dagger from the water, symbolizing our invitation. But first, a sacrifice is needed." Andrew pulls a small switchblade from his back pocket. He holds the blade up to his arm, pressing the tip into the skin of his arm over the water bowl.

Robin tenses. "Is he going to—?"

"Enough."

I jump from the balcony down to the cult circle below. Their heads turn slowly to me, but Andrew reacts faster than I anticipated. He takes one look at me and Robin charging him, then quickly moves the switchblade from his own arm to Lily's throat. "One more step and I kill her."

Lily whimpers and Andrew nudges the knife harder, threatening to break the skin. The cult members stare at us, but Andrew shouts at them, *"Do not break focus! Keep your eyes on your reflection."*

Dutifully, the members return to their phones and remain frozen. They move like zombies, as if they've already been possessed. As if someone isn't holding a blade to a girl's throat a few feet away.

"Andrew," I say, trying to keep my voice diplomatic. "Why are you doing this? Why would any of you want to give up your free will?"

"Sometimes when you give up something, you gain something too."

"What are you gaining?" Robin asks, his voice crackling with disdain.

Andrew sneers. "More than you could ever understand."

"I don't think you get it, Andrew. When this thing gets you . . ." I hesitate. Possession is hard to explain. So instead, I say neutrally, "You won't be able to control it."

"We've been training. We'll be able to control it better than her." He scoffs as he presses the knife against Lily's neck, nicking the skin this time to draw a small drop of ruby-red blood.

That's it. I'm done talking.

I close the distance between us and punch Andrew in the nose. It bursts immediately, gushing like a fire hydrant. He holds his arms out wide and lets the blood drop into the water bowl. "That works too," he says with a laugh.

The sacrifice. Crap. Not what I intended.

He aims a kick at me, but I catch his foot and twist, hard. He crumples to the floor. Robin's almost close enough to pin him down, but Andrew—the slippery worm that he is—oozes away. He lunges for Lily and rips off her blindfold. He yanks the golden dagger from the bloodied water bowl, grips the back of her head, then shoves her face into the bowl, shouting, *"Now!"*

All around us, the cult members stare at their reflections and chant, "I let you in."

"We let you in."

"We let you in."

The chorus of thirty voices becomes a deafening roar. Lily gargles as Andrew holds her face in the water, drowning her. I break past the bodies to tackle Andrew and free Lily from his deathly hold. Robin helps her to her feet as she gasps, sputtering water. I try to catch her eyes, see if she's okay, but she flings away from Robin like his touch burns. She drops to the floor, writhing and screaming. Her mouth splits open so wide that the skin of her lips cracks, and her wails are so loud that even Andrew falters, afraid of the noises tearing from her throat. She screams for longer than her lungs should have air for. Then, one by one, the cult members' eyes slip to black, the veins in their faces staining with dark ink.

Andrew's ritual worked. Within seconds, his cult is a mass of possessed bodies, no longer human. And Lily is no longer Lily. Her empty black eyes stare at the ceiling as she lies still, sweating on the dirty floor.

Robin tenses at my side, his breathing becoming more focused. We eye the mass of demonites—men and women of different ages and backgrounds—slowly lurching toward us. They surround us, glaring with restless black eyes. Beneath my grip, Andrew's lips twitch into a sick smile.

He snaps his fingers and the fight for my life begins.

CHAPTER 30

Possessed bodies surge at us, snarling and hungry for our blood. They shove their phones into our faces, trying to get us to see the light.

"Don't look at their phones or anything with reflective surfaces," I tell Robin. If we get possessed too, we're doomed.

We sprint up the grand staircase. At the top, I give Robin a quick hand signal and he nods, immediately leaping up onto the banister. He slides down the railing before leaping into a tight flip, knocking out the first demonite with his landing. The crunch of his bones is what sets the room off.

All hell breaks loose.

A demonite lets out a feral battle cry as she sprints up the stairs, hurling punches at my head. I block each one, then land one of my own to the center of her chest. She tumbles down the stairs, knocking out another demonite behind her.

It's a flurry of fists and elbows and knees. I whip out a concussion grenade Batarang and send it flying into the middle of the staircase. Upon detonation, it knocks four demonites out. With the smoke as my cover, I throw punches in all directions. I fight off one demonite in front of me, but then another grabs me from behind. They throw me down the steps. I roll down like a rag doll, spilling out onto the dusty marble floor. Five demonites come at me, each one shoving their phone into my face, trying to get me to look. I shut my eyes and throw my elbow back, praying that I hit someone. Anyone.

My hit lands against a demonite who falls into her fellow cult members, giving me the space I need.

I notice the moon below the line of trees surrounding the old mansion's lot, so it's darker now. Harder to see. Nobody has paid a light bill in this abandoned home for years. Lily still lies unconscious at the center of the battle, the last traces of light from the window casting a shadow on her face. Behind her, I spot Andrew. Running up the stairs.

He's going to get away.

I'll catch him first, then get Lily out of here.

"Robin!" I call. He whips toward me, leaning back to narrowly dodge a demonite swinging a metal rod from the fireplace kit at his face. "Maneuver Seven!"

Without hesitation, he interlaces his fingers and kneels. I step into the base that he created, and he launches me into the air. He tosses me high enough that I can grab onto the second-floor banister. I swing my body over the railing, seize Andrew's ankle, and pull. He stumbles, then he's up again and hobbling for the window.

Robin makes it upstairs and rushes to block his path. "You're not getting out of here," he says to Andrew, panting. Andrew cocks a smile, undoubtedly preparing to say something dumb, but we can't have this monster running around Gotham City anymore. I grab his wrist and twist, painfully. He crumples to the floor.

"You zip-tie him and I'll get Lily," I tell Robin. I knock out a few more demonites as I fight my way back down to Lily. I shake her shoulder and her eyes slowly blink open. They're her usual warm brown, no trace of the sinister black. Thank god.

She massages her temple with one hand while using the other to feel around in the dark room. I catch her hand. "Hey, Lily. It's me. Batgirl."

Her hand twitches in mine. "What's happening?"

"It's going to be okay. I'm going to save you." I position her arms around my neck, bend my knees, and lift. There's a small room at the top of the staircase. If I can get Lily there, I can finally help her end this nightmare.

Lily's heavy, but I force myself to take the stairs two at a time until I reach the top. I kick open the door. Turns out it's a wine closet—an aboveground wine "cellar." A weird place for a wine closet, but it has a secretive vibe, like maybe it was built up here during the Prohibition Era. Good enough for what I need right now.

I lower Lily onto the floor gently. As I do, she whispers, "Andrew?"

"We took care of him. He can't get you in here."

"Oh." She gets quiet again.

"I think I know how to help you. Just close your eyes." Earlier, Andrew made a big deal about the dagger in the water bowl during his ceremony. He removed the blade to make the demon stronger, so I think we need to do the opposite: stab her reflection. Trap the demon, then scare it back to where it belongs. Lily will probably put up a fight like last time, but she's already dazed and exhausted. I can overpower her now. Andrew got her to look at her reflection when he tried to drown her, but I don't need to do all that—I can hold her eyes open, or even a splash of water might be enough to trigger her. Man, she's going to need some serious therapy after all this. Poor girl. But right now, I have to do this to save her. I turn around to fish out my compact and Andrew's switchblade, but I get distracted by the flicker of something nearby.

A wine bottle hits me in the back of my head.

My eyeballs see a flash of white; then my vision goes black. I drop the switchblade. When my vision returns, my head is against the floor. My neck feels like it's been wrung out like an old towel. I want to lift my head to look back, but a large shard of broken glass tumbles on me, nearly hitting my left eye. The back of my cape is soaking wet with red wine. Lily crawls over my body and knees me in the spine. I try to move my arms, but they're numb. She yanks the closet door handle and swings the door open, dumping me out onto the floor.

In my peripheral vision, I see Robin running up the stairs. I want to warn him, but I'm having trouble forming words. It doesn't matter anyway, because the demonite he was fighting suddenly picks up speed, tackling him.

Lily looks down at me as she guides her hair out of her face with the edge of the switchblade. Her eyes are . . . different. Not all black, but not her regular brown either. It's a swirled mix of darkness, half human, half something I can't explain. The thin skin around her eyelids looks swollen. A poisonous shade of gray pumps through her veins, turning her complexion sickly, half dead.

"I think we all expected a bit more from Batman's diversity casting," Lily says, squatting down beside me.

Is this the demon talking? Is it Lily? Both?

Lily laughs, soft and melodic. It's dark, so I can't see well, but I can feel her leaning in close, her humid breath tickling my cheek.

"Using Austin to try to trap the demon was controversial, but a decent enough plan. This, though? A half-baked rescue mission with no endgame? Not your best work." Her face is fixed into a tight snarl. A snake hissing at its prey.

Lily traces the blade along the back of my head, which is still throbbing with pain. "There's a Black girl running around Gotham City in a mask and now everyone's gushing about representation," Lily says. "Everyone's sooo obsessed with representation. Online. In art. At my school."

This *is* Lily speaking. Andrew's earlier words rush back to me with a jolt. He had said, "We'll be able to control it *better* than her." Better as in . . . Lily's been in control all along.

"What's so interesting about being poor, anyway? Being a person of color? Being queer? I always wondered if your lives are really that hard or are you just whining all the time. And after a few weeks of slipping into my classmates' lives, I've gotta say—I'm not impressed."

I've been played. All that stuff she posted online—I assumed it was a symptom of her possession, but I was wrong. The demon did not cause her problematic views;

the demon picked her *because* of them. She isn't a victim, she's a co-conspirator. And now she's finally got me cornered. Just like the demon wanted.

I try to sit up straight, but the blow to my head has turned my body to pudding. When I force myself onto my hands and knees, the room is spinning. Over Lily's shoulder, Robin is throwing off one demonite, only for another to come out of the woodwork and throw a fist straight at his head. We're outnumbered. Overpowered. Vomit threatens in the back of my throat. Still, I crawl forward. I have to get out of here. I will not die tonight.

"Oh, you're not leaving." Lily moves to block my path. "Not until you let the Reflection in."

The Reflection. So that's what she calls it. I force my chin up and stare into Lily's nightmare of a face. "If you welcomed this thing inside you, why let it go now?"

"Did you not see how Andrew's cult tried to murder me? I can't stay like this, now that people know. And like I said, body jumping was fun at first, but I'm not impressed with what I saw. Plus, the Reflection and I made a deal."

"A deal?"

"If I bring you to it, then it won't kill me." She says it like it's easy, obvious. I'm not sure what to make of this.

"We can find a way to help you. Help us both. Get rid of the demon another way."

"Impossible. The only way to get rid of the

Reflection is to pass it on. Someone gave it to me; now I'm going to give it to you."

I hesitate. "But . . . earlier, you said that you got it from your phone?"

For the first time since this conversation began, she looks away. "It moves through reflections. You've seen it. That's what I meant."

But I don't believe her anymore. Is she lying about this too?

"Lily—" But she cuts me off with a sharp kick to my side.

I swallow and raise my eyes to meet hers. "I won't let you do this to me."

"This isn't even about you. Don't think you're special. The Reflection doesn't care about Batgirl. It wants to use you to get to Batman."

Not this again. Dick's theory slams back with full force. I wince.

"If you resist, it will kill you. Just like Harper. And when you die, the Reflection will use your corpse to lure in Batman when it's time for him to avenge his poor little protégée. And when he comes, we'll be there waiting." She smiles, but her eyes remain predatory. "Don't look so shocked. You're a means to an end, Batgirl. That's all you'll ever be. You're the girl who takes the hit so the villain can face off against the real hero. Robin's girlfriend.

Batman's pet. You didn't really believe this was actually about you, did you?"

My body betrays me as I look away. Robin may have apologized, but maybe he was right all along. Even if he was, it doesn't matter. I have to keep fighting.

Trying to hold back nausea, I force myself to stand. I barf immediately. Hot liquid spills out of me onto Lily's shoes. It's disgusting, but wow, I do feel a bit better.

Lily gags. "Eww."

A few feet away, Robin grunts as he slams his metal staff down on a demonite's leg. There's a sudden stillness after he lands the last blow. That was the last of the demonites, which means . . . we're no longer outnumbered.

Lily's face falls.

Robin looks at me crouched over a pool of vomit on the floor, then at Lily, then back at me, debating which way to go. There's something in the set of his jaw that makes me think that he's going to run to me instead of taking down Lily, which is why I take a deep breath, block out the spinning sensation in my head, then lunge at Lily myself.

We tumble into the hall. The switchblade flies from Lily's hand and skids across the floor. We roll until we hit the banister of the interior balcony overlooking the grand entrance. Robin drags Lily off me and twists her elbow behind her back, pressing her against the wall.

"Well done, Boy Wonder," Lily purrs. "Ten points for the legacy hero." She leans back into Robin as if she were his girlfriend and this was all a game. He promptly steps back, putting an extra inch between them.

Robin's about to say something, but before his words can even form, Lily throws herself backward, crashing into his chest. Neither of us could've anticipated the speed with which she'd strike. Neither of us could've anticipated that her attack would knock him off-balance, pushing him over the railing.

Robin almost catches himself. He almost hooks his foot in the railing, but it's all happening too fast. I lunge for him, but he's already falling. I really can't tell which is louder: my own scream as he falls, or his when his body slams against the floor.

"ROBIN!"

I wait for him to get up.

He doesn't.

The prospect of losing him uncurls in me, wipes away every thought, every pain, every feeling except for a blistering panic that's more relentless than the sun. I can't blink. Can't get my lungs to suck air in the right way anymore. I reach for the banister to go and check his vitals, but Lily yanks at my cape. I crash back down at her feet.

"Let's see if Batgirl can stand alone," Lily snarls.

I remember Alysia's rant at the art show that day, about the protests and tension on campus. She said that the people who hate us are trying to distract us. And she's right. I look up at Lily, serene in her smugness, and all I can see is someone who wants to watch me struggle. Lily can talk as much crap as she wants. Make me doubt myself. I can waste my energy trying to prove her wrong. But what's the point?

Lily is just a distraction. I need to face the demon itself.

"*Show yourself!*" I yell at the demon hiding inside her. "You wanted me? Now I'm here. So face me."

Lily looks amused for a moment, but I slap her right across the face, so hard that her head spins backward. When her head bounces back, she blinks and a black film is pulled over each eye.

Lily is fully gone. The eyes of something evil stare back at me. The Reflection cocks its head to the side, curiosity and condescension dripping from its expression.

"Batgirl," it says, voice like gravel, low and harsh.

I've never hated anything more.

A drowning, suffocating fog leaks from the corners of her eyes, her nostrils. The sting of the toxic air leaves me coughing. I feel like I'm drowning, but still, I ask the Reflection what it wants. It laughs at me. God, I'm so tired of people laughing at me. Underestimating me. I'm tired of games. "What do you really want from me?"

Fear has every inch of my body on edge. I can't keep the hint of terror from slipping through my voice, but I stand my ground. I am ready to fight, to rage.

In answer, the Reflection grins at me, cracked lips curled back to reveal black teeth, and says, *"This,"* coming for me at last.

Lily's hands are like claws—or is it the Reflection now?—as they find my throat. I kick my feet out and collide with her ankle, knocking her back a step. My body is aching, but I raise my fists for Harper, for Robin, for Alysia, for Austin, for everyone who's been hurt. For *me*.

It seems darker than ever. We can no longer see the outlines of the trees out the windows, or the faint outline of the guest bedroom down the hall. Everything is pitch-black except for the one stray ray of moonlight spilling into the center of the hallway where we face off. The Reflection shifts its head, unnaturally slow, in the direction of the skylight above us. It basks in the ray for a moment, like a reptile beneath a heat lamp, before opening its mouth wide to do the most disturbing thing I've seen all night. The Reflection stretches, and black gas rises from its skin in tiny waves like water evaporating on hot pavement. Its physical form fades at the edges, blending with the darkness of the room. The most noticeable part that remains are its black eyes, glowing like obsidian pebbles, fixed on me with a devious glare.

"We don't have to do this, Batgirl. You can give up now. Become my new host. Give in," the Reflection taunts, lowering its freaky figure into a fighting stance. Always changing, like smoke, sometimes it has no visible eyes, no visible mouth, yet I hear its voice loud and clear. The tone is like the grinding of rocks. A sharp chill moves down my spine, but I grit my teeth, then lower my stance to match it.

The Reflection smirks. "Funny adolescent human."

Then, like lightning, the demon strikes.

CHAPTER 31

The first blow hits my mouth. I stagger backward into a table, knocking over an old vase. I had no idea what to expect from this thing, but its body is surprisingly dense, its fist even harder than a human's. But I can take it. High on pain, I lick my lips. A taste like copper pennies on my tongue. I spit a mouthful of blood onto the floor between us.

The Reflection throws another jab to my throat, but I shift away. I get behind it and land a brutal kick to the back of its knees. The Reflection buckles but catches itself before it hits the tattered carpet. While its back is turned, I run for cover.

Every part of my body wants to take deep breaths, but I only allow myself small sips. I can't let it hear me. The darkness of this abandoned house poses a new problem: I can hardly see the Reflection at all.

I blink rapidly, trying to force my eyes to detect any movement, but I can't see it—just the outlines of unconscious demonites scattered on the floor around us, the line of the vintage furniture in various states of disarray. The wind from an open window ripples a curtain. I flinch, but the Reflection is not there. I bite my lip, holding back the frustrated sigh begging to break loose from my throat. The Reflection could be anywhere.

A book flies toward my head and I duck. The Reflection jumps forward, throwing an elbow at my chin. It clips the corner of my jaw, but I keep my balance. I unleash a whirlwind of punches at its chest and core. Sweat soaks my collar, drips into my mouth as we fight, pushing each other back and forth across the dark room.

The next blow crashes into my ribs. Pain breaks in me like a storm. Sharp and dull and empty and full all at once. As I gasp, the Reflection closes in. It comes at me with a cocky expression, and I know what it's thinking: that fighting me is merely a means to an end. The pain in my body is intensifying. Everything hurts. Oh my god, does it hurt. But I keep my hands up. It keeps attacking, and suddenly, I'm every girl who's ever been underestimated, every girl who's ever been injured for the plot, every girl who's ever kept fighting anyway.

I scream as I force my hand into a fist, spinning to gain momentum as I swing down on the Reflection's shoulder. It winces. That hurt. I know it did. It makes a noise that sounds like a ragged inhale. It's getting tired too. I crash forward and it throws a punch. Another. On the third, I grab its arm. I straighten it out, then drive my knee into its elbow. The Reflection gasps at the sudden pain, slamming against the wall behind us. Its cry gives me enough time to pin it to the ground beneath my knees. The Reflection struggles to free itself, so I grip even tighter. When it finally stops thrashing, it looks at me with sheer hate.

My voice is harsh in my throat. "Lily says you want—"

"Lily lies," the Reflection seethes.

"Why would she lie?"

"Who knows? Habit? I am unconcerned with the personal vendettas of a jealous human girl. I allow her some freedom, but she does not speak for me."

I twist its elbow. "Then what do you want from me?"

The Reflection's gaze drops to my ankle. "That healed nicely, didn't it?"

"What?" I look at my foot that had me in a boot for weeks.

"Wait." I suck in an inhale. "Who was your last host? Before Lily?"

The Reflection says nothing.

Oh my god. Jason from the grocery store. It had to be him.

I asked him what was wrong and he pointed at his own head. His eyes were all messed up. The timeline would make sense. Jason connected with 88-88 right after the robbery. It probably took him a few weeks to regulate, but then he totally could've passed it on to Lily. How those two know each other is a mystery. But it makes sense.

"Your former host was Jason." I state it as a fact because I know I'm right.

"He and I were bonded for ten years. Then he encounters you and suddenly, he can no longer bear our union." The Reflection grunts. "He is a traitor."

"Because he got rid of you," I whisper, my mind reeling. "Is that why you want me? To punish me for saving your old host?"

"You didn't save him."

"You're right. I didn't." He accepted support, then saved himself.

The smoke rising from the Reflection's skin flares wildly, like gasoline thrown onto a fire. "You will pay for what you took from me. And the underworld of Gotham City will thank me for it. The last thing this city needs is a brat who wants to do things differently."

Down the hallway, another shadow creeps in closer

and closer. Once my eyes focus on him, I'm so relieved I could cry. *Robin.*

I tear my eyes away so the Reflection doesn't notice. I have to keep it talking. "If you just wanted my attention all along, then why'd you kill Harper? Why make everyone try to hurt people?"

"So that you'd know what I was capable of." Something hard collides with the space between my eyebrows. I blink twice but all I can see is black. I am on the floor. My palms try to steady me, but I'm dizzy. I have to get up. But which way is up? The Reflection's vile breath hisses in my ear. "So that if you refused me, you'd know what I could do."

Cold fingers wrap around my neck, pressing hard into my windpipe. It hurts so much. My stomach drops. "Let me in, Batgirl."

Over the Reflection's shoulder, Robin slowly raises his battle staff. He winces silently. Something inside him—perhaps a rib—maybe broken from his earlier fall. His stare collides with mine. He mouths to me a silent "You've got this."

I've never loved him more.

"Let . . ." The Reflection's fingers crush my windpipe harder. Robin sneaks within striking range.

"Me . . ." My vision fades in and out like waves on a shoreline.

The heavy front door swings open, startling us all.

All three of us—me, Robin, and the Reflection—whip our heads toward the entryway. Who the hell is—

No.

"RUN!" I choke, but I can hardly breathe, let alone speak. The intruder doesn't move.

Alysia.

She stands frozen, taking in the scene—the glass on the floor, Robin midstrike, the monster that is the Reflection's hands around my neck. Robin pivots, rushing straight for Alysia. The Reflection smiles. That's when I know that someone I love is about to get very hurt.

The Reflection grabs Andrew's discarded switchblade from the floor and hurls it at my best friend. Alysia screams as the blade catches the flesh of her arm. She hits the floor.

The Reflection laughs. *Again.* I lose it.

My fingers find the edge of something sharp. I wrap my hand around it, not caring when it cuts deep into my palm. I slam the shard of glass from the broken wine bottle into the top of the Reflection's foot. It howls in pain and releases my neck. I gasp, scrambling to crawl away as fast as I can, making it back to the center of the room, where this all started, where the gold dagger still waits beside the bloody water bowl, while—

The Reflection wraps the red hair of my wig around its fist, then yanks, hard. My neck curls back awkwardly as I'm tugged like a doll. The Reflection holds the bloodied shard of glass to my throat, teasing the skin. With each breath, the edges press into my skin, threatening to cut. Robin shouts my name, but it doesn't matter anymore.

"I'm going to tell you one more time," the Reflection whispers. Alysia's crying. I'm nearly crying now too, sputtering, can't catch my breath. Robin's standing between me and Alysia, his attention switching between the two of us, trying to triage. The Reflection applies more pressure to the shard. It slides against the sweat on my neck, nicking some skin right above a vein. "You *will* become my new host."

I glance at my friends. No more casualties. No more running. This ends now.

I grit my teeth. "Fine."

The Reflection may not have a mouth, but I feel its form twist into something like a sneer. "Good girl," it says, voice low.

"Batgirl." Robin takes a hurried step toward me, but I shake my head with the limited range of motion that I'm granted, my neck still in the Reflection's control.

"Go help Alysia," I say, my voice firm.

"I'm not leaving you here," Robin says.

"I'll be okay."

"She's in good hands," the Reflection says, finally releasing my wig from her grip. My neck cracks as it relaxes, lowering my head to the floor. The Reflection adjusts, but I can still feel its foot on my back.

Robin locks eyes with me. "Don't do this," he mouths.

But it's too late. What other option is there? Let more people get hurt on my behalf? The Reflection beat me to the brink of death?

Plus, more important, I have a plan.

Is it a good plan? Who knows. But it's the only one I've got.

I don't feel ready. It doesn't matter.

"When you leave, call my dad to tell him I'm okay," I tell Robin. His mouth falls open in confusion, but I cut him off. "He's called me thirteen times tonight. Let him know that I'll be home soon. Otherwise he'll send all of GCPD looking for me. I don't need them tracing thirteen missed calls to here."

Robin's livid. He doesn't want to leave. But I need him to. By some miracle, he trusts me. And he listens.

He walks over to Alysia, wraps her arm around his neck, and carries her out the front door. Alysia tries to resist, but he respects my choice and keeps hauling her away to safety. I can't see his eyes hidden behind his mask from this far away, but I can still read the boy like a book. On his face I see fear, but also care, determination, and something that looks a lot like respect. He hesitates before he leaves, looking at me one last time, then exits.

The sound of the heavy door shutting echoes through the quiet house.

The Reflection turns its full attention back to me. It's just us now.

I speak first. "I will do as you ask, but—"

My Utility Belt vibrates with an incoming call. I slip my hand inside the pocket as quickly as possible to tap my phone. The Reflection sneers at me. I use the last ounce of my strength to judo-flip the Reflection and pin its head to the ground. I can't hold the demon for long, but I'm able to keep its face down until I hear a quiet thump behind me. A chill passes through me, singeing my bones, and I gasp.

This better work.

The Reflection shoves me off. It grabs my wrist, yanks me in. I'm completely depleted. I can't fight anymore, even if I tried.

"Look into my eyes," it commands. Every cell in my body wants to rebel, but there's no going back now. I swallow the lump in my throat and meet the Reflection's gaze.

"Now say the words," the Reflection commands.

"I . . . I let you in."

This is nothing like the last time I was possessed. This is something else entirely.

The sensation of choking comes first. My eyes

water, but I can't blink. My entire body is frozen. Black wisps of smoke seep out of the wet mass that is the Reflection's face. The smoke forms an unbroken line between us, piercing through my eyes with a harsh sting. I shrink away, but there's no stopping the possession now. The demonic entity surges into my windpipe. My chest heaves. There's a pulling sensation in my gut. My fingernails claw into the floor, hard enough to draw blood. The aching in my head turns into a relentless, pounding throb.

"Why won't you just kill me?" I ask, or maybe beg, when the pain becomes unbearable. I'm speaking, but not out loud; my words echo in the dark cavity of my own mind.

"I prefer to corrupt, not kill." I can hear the Reflection's voice inside my own head. Is this what it will be like from now on? Its dark twisted thoughts in my mind? "I have chosen Gotham City as my home for hundreds of years. I stay here because it is a depraved place, full of depraved people. It is an environment in which I can thrive." The Reflection's voice in my head grows louder. "Your danger to me is your influence. All the young people you're slowly winning over. You give a different class of people a reason to stand up for themselves. You're corrupting people like Jason with resources. Spreading hope in Gotham City is a dangerous thing for me. Like little shards of glass in my meal, it cuts through the gloom that sustains me. The broken city doesn't need someone like you."

Each word magnifies the headache splitting my brain, and beneath it all: the sting of my defeat. Black tears drain from my eyes, dripping onto the floor. I tried. I really tried. But I wasn't enough.

The darkness circles my heart. Total loss of control over my soul is imminent. I'm trying to think of any last words, any final protest, but I'm quickly distracted by a flicker of light.

It is tiny, but it is there—a warm glow in the dark, overrun chasm of my mind.

My old fight mantra floats to the surface of my thoughts: *I will not lose today.* I repeat it to myself until it starts to feel real.

The Reflection's voice falters. "What are you—?"

The flurry of shadows within me pause, unsure of what to do. The fog begins to . . . clear.

I don't have much time. I will my body to follow my commands. My pinkie twitches and it's a miracle. I crawl toward the dagger.

"You shouldn't be able to move," the Reflection cries. "How are you moving?"

I free my phone from my Utility Belt, yank my cowl up above my eyebrows. When I catch my reflection in the dark screen, unrecognizable black eyes stare back at me. I fight the violent instinct to look away, to throw the phone across the room. Instead, I use the last of my strength to place the black mirror of its screen on the floor. Then I reach for the dagger and swing.

I stab my reflection. I watch, enraptured, as my face splits into dozens of distorted pieces. I drive the knife through the mirrored image again and again. Inside my mind, the Reflection screams. I scream too. I open my mouth and its darkness spills out of me. The shattered screen consumes the demon, sucking it in like a vacuum.

I destroy the glass screen of my phone until it crumbles into something resembling rock candy. Once I do, something inside me crumbles along with it. The chandelier above snaps from its chain and falls on the floor beside us, scattering debris everywhere. My eyes become heavy. I slump to the floor.

CHAPTER 32

I try to sit up but groan instead. A throbbing pain in my head brings me back to reality.

A tired voice wafts through the air. "Batgirl. You're awake."

I open my mouth to reply but nothing comes out. My throat feels like sandpaper.

When I finally open my eyes, Traci 13 is staring down at me. She smiles, then grabs my arm, helping me up to a seated position. I feel like crap and I'm still shaking from the adrenaline, but sitting upright confirms that I'm okay.

"I'm sorry, but what the hell just happened?" Alysia asks, eyes darting between me and Traci 13.

I try speaking again. This time it works. "You're okay. Thank god." I hold out my hand to Alysia. She grabs it eagerly. "How the hell did you find me?" I ask her. "*Why* did you come find me?"

She gives me a guilty look, then leans in and whispers so only I can hear. "The Find My Friends app works pretty well."

I gape at her, but she just shrugs. "What? I'm a good friend and I'm resourceful. Sue me."

Robin appears over Alysia's shoulder, gripping his rib cage. "Hey, Batgirl," he says with a proud smile.

I smile back. "Hey, Bird Boy."

Alysia squeezes my hand, hard. Her arm is bandaged where she was cut. "One second, you're unconscious on the floor, then this hot girl suddenly appears, *climbing out of your body.* Like a ghost."

"'Hot girl'?" Traci 13 repeats, raising an eyebrow. Alysia blushes.

I laugh and turn to Traci. "Are you okay?"

Traci shivers. "I told you, possession is my least favorite skill."

"I owe you one."

"How many times do I have to ask what the hell happened before someone answers me?!" Alysia screeches.

"Traci 13 is a mage. She's given me some advice on this case. When you were leaving me alone with the

Reflection, I asked Robin to call her. I knew that once he told her what was happening, she'd know what to do."

"'Tracing thirteen' was a good clue. Real subtle. It took me a second, but I got it," Robin says with a smirk.

"Right before I let the Reflection in, Traci teleported here, then possessed me. So when the demon tried to possess me as well, it didn't have sole control inside of me. Traci was able to help me maintain minimal control over my body."

"And with that control, Batgirl pulled a Hail Mary and fought off total possession until she was able to send the demon back into the mirror realm."

Alysia stares at me, eyes wide, then mutters an eloquent "Goddamn."

At the sound of approaching sirens, Robin helps me to my feet. "Shall we?"

I'm studying at my desk when I hear a tap on my window. I look up and see Dick Grayson waving from the fire escape. I open the window and let him in.

"How'd you escape curfew?" I ask. After the showdown last week, our respective guardians weren't particularly pleased with us. Dad took one look at me and freaked out. I told him that I had let my friend try to teach me how to drive a motorcycle and crashed. He gave me the longest speech on vehicle safety in the history of mankind and confined me to indoors for the rest of the semester as punishment. It was a typical standoff between us, but before he left the room, I caught him mumbling to himself, "The least that Batman can do is offer driver's ed." I asked him what he meant, but he just rubbed his mustache, though I swear I saw a hint of a smirk on his lips. He hasn't brought it up again since. I don't think he will.

"Alfred thinks I'm sleeping," Dick says, shutting the window after climbing inside my room. "Is your dad home?"

"Nope."

"Cool." He peels off his mask and plops onto the foot of my bed.

We've hung out like this every night this week. It's new territory—him being here, sitting on my childhood sheets, but it's nice. Comfortable.

The fallout after the Reflection fight has been intense. Lily has been put in the hospital's intensive care unit. Andrew was sent to Arkham. I know they both did bad things, but I still don't love hearing about how their lives will never be the same after this. There have been some bright spots, however, the biggest being Austin. When we raced out of the hospital to catch Lily and her kidnappers, Austin had flatlined. I assumed they were dead. And I guess they really were, technically, for about twenty seconds before the doctors revived them. It's unclear to me if it was the wonders of medical science or some residual effect of being possessed, but their infection cleared up. They were going to make it after all.

Austin even sent me a video message from the hospital talking about how they were proud to have put up a fight that day. It was nice to see their face, hear their voice again, even though they looked weak in the video. Their skin was pasty, and even their eyes looked a bit off. Darker than usual. Speaking of which . . .

"I saw Nico," I blurt out to Dick.

His eyes widen. "What'd he say?"

"Nothing. It was at school. He finally came back to class today." It's surreal how a trauma-bond fling could burn so bright, then evaporate into nothingness in a matter of weeks. When Nico breezes past me in the hallway now, he doesn't even know that he's ignoring the same girl he kissed during a crisis. "He doesn't know me at all. There was nothing to say."

Dick folds his hands in his lap. "Want to talk about it?"

"Not really." Saying it out loud was all I needed.

"Okay. Well. I am here for you. As a friend, you know." He smiles, all sweetness, and my pulse stutters.

I'm not afraid of these little sparks between us now. I'm over letting other people's opinions dictate my life. If anything happens between us, it'll be because it's what we both want—not because it's convenient or it's what's expected. So when Dick's hand rests dangerously close to mine on the bed, I find myself shifting a little closer. He notices with a soft inhale, but then seems to doubt himself. Instead of making big moves, he stretches his fingers out, letting them hover just above where my left hand rests at the foot of the bed between us. He's close enough for me to feel the warmth radiating off his skin, but still not touching me. Yet.

So I grab his hand and interlace our fingers. When I catch his eyes, his face is flushed. Smiling a little in that cute way he does when he doesn't quite know what to say. Ultimately, he settles for a softly spoken "I don't think I ever told you how much I like you."

I feel myself blush. A rare occurrence.

I'm inexplicably nervous. We've never done anything like this before, and I'm not even entirely sure what we are doing. All I know is that I want him to come closer.

I fold one knee in a half pretzel, then tug his hand gently so we're facing each other. Mere inches separate his face from mine. He keeps one hand intertwined with my own while the other rests on my knee. I can feel his fingers shaking. It's endearing. The ever-confident Dick Grayson, trembling before our first kiss.

He takes a deep breath, drops his gaze from mine to gather his confidence. I do the same. We smile and lean in. And then the inevitable happens.

Our comms vibrate at the same time.

We stare at each other, eyes wide with absolute awkwardness-induced horror for a split second, before we burst out laughing.

"This can't be happening," Dick mumbles. He breathes out a gentle self-deprecating laugh before pulling our joined hands to his lips to place a kiss on my knuckles. The touch is light, but it makes me feel warm all over. We smile at each other once more before I pick up the call and put it on speakerphone between us.

"Batgirl," a deep voice says in greeting.

"Hey, Bruce," Dick and I say in unison.

"Oh, you're together. Good," Bruce says. Bruce wasn't too angry when he found out I'd gone behind his back. He didn't know the full details, so he was still annoyed, but instead of kicking me out of the crew for insubordination as I'd feared, he promised to give me training on supernatural cases soon.

"There's a disturbance downtown," he says. "The locals are asking for Batgirl."

Dick's lips hitch slightly at a cunning angle with a small smile that I know is meant for me.

"We're on our way," I announce.

Dick slips his mask back on, and I slip on mine.

The Reflection chose Lily as its new host because she was sympathetic to cruelty. The Reflection chose Gotham City as its home because it sees this city in the same grim way. But while it may have been right about Lily, I think the Reflection had Gotham City wrong.

Gotham City can be a scary place. Sometimes it can be terrifying. I wish it weren't, but that's the truth.

This is a city where bad things happen. Where cops lie. Where mobsters exert way too much control. Where district attorneys fall into madness. Where terrorists burn neighborhoods simply for a laugh. Gotham City is a place where there are more guns than teachers, health-care workers, and public librarians combined. A city with demons of all kinds. But it's also a city of brave people—where strangers risk their lives to save one another.

To the rest of the country, Gothamites seem strange. They wonder, *Why would anyone live in a place like that?* Why we choose to protect it.

For my dad's birthday last year, I got him a custom coffee mug. It has a picture of the Gotham City skyline printed on it, above one of his favorite sayings: *The ones who choose to stay.* That's what Dad used to call us Go-thamites: the people who choose to love this city despite all the aggravation it throws at us. It's okay to leave. It's a valid choice to walk—no, *run*—away from this town as soon as you can. But there's something special about us:

the ones who choose to stay here as well as those who may not have the ability to choose but grow roots here and fall in love and form communities that make this city worth loving anyway.

I am sixteen years old. I can't vote. I can't run for office. I can't choose where I live. But I can be here, in this city—my home—in a real way.

I don't know if what I'm doing will help or hurt. I don't know if these new systems we're building will work. I don't know if we can save any of these institutions who've lost our trust. But I want to try. I can't imagine what this place would be like if people stopped trying, even if it's messy. Making things more complicated doesn't always mean making things worse.

Everyone's wary of Batgirl because they don't know what to make of me. I don't know what to make of me either. I don't have a tragic backstory that brought me to this moment. I don't have any superpowers. I chose this life, willingly, as soon as I was able to. To some people, my choice doesn't make sense. They think my very existence doesn't make sense. But that's not my problem. I don't have to prove to anyone that I deserve to wear this mask.

Robin approaches the scene from the south at street level while I pull out my grappling hook. I fire it into a nearby billboard, flexing my arm in preparation.

Right as I'm about to leap, I notice a cool splash of color in the corner of the billboard. It's a graffiti tag of a bat-symbol.

It's purple—*Batgirl's* purple—not black.

I smirk, take a deep breath, then leap off the edge. Cold air whips my face, adrenaline dances through my muscles. Surrounded by my city, I fly.